PURSUING THE TRAITOR

SCANDALS AND SPIES SERIES BOOK 5

LEIGHANN DOBBS
HARMONY WILLIAMS

PROLOGUE

*L*ady Belhaven's manor, London
January, 1807

THE CHATTER of the guests only seemed to add to the swell of the music, not detract from it. Couples swirled in the center of the ballroom, each garbed in a fantastical outfit and mask from a common domino to an elaborate Queen Elizabeth and everywhere in between. The dizzying whirl of color made it difficult to keep one's eye on a single figure.

Lady Lucy Graylocke, youngest sibling to the Duke of Tenwick, believed in equality even if her older brothers preferred to sequester her away from danger and intrigue. In the books she wrote, the lady was always the dashing hero able to save herself. Although she'd navigated Society long enough to learn that not all men—or, indeed, even women—shared her views, she liked to think that her family agreed with her. The three brothers currently residing in England had each married strong, capable women, after all. Therefore, Lucy didn't think it was beyond the realm of possibility that, had they been in her shoes, they would have done the exact same thing she did now.

The Graylocke family tolerated no disrespect toward a member of their household, after all. And although Rocky was their lead gardener, she was also a personal friend to the family. When Lucy cornered this masked King Henry, she was going to wring his neck for what Rocky had confessed he'd said.

No, probably not that. As much as she'd like to, violence was never the answer. But she would give him a thorough redressing and change his mind. Not only did women deserve to be in lead gardener positions, but Rocky was more capable than most. Every bit as brilliant, in fact, as Lucy's botanist brother, Gideon.

Giddy wouldn't let the man escape unscathed if he'd known, either.

Lucy followed the bobbing feather with her gaze as King Henry—or whoever he was, outside of that costume—traversed the length of the ballroom. He aimed for the orchestra, nestled in a corner of the room between potted flowers and a closed door. As he side-stepped couples and groups, she caught further glimpses of his costume; a black cloak embroidered with gold thread, his puffed pantaloons in jewel-bright colors that matched his doublet. His face was clean-shaven. Hadn't King Henry VIII sported a beard? Shaking her head, Lucy trailed him.

Unlike Henry, Lucy found herself recognized by those she passed. Women stopped her to ask after her family. Men tried to finagle a dance. Not one of them asked after the book she was writing. Not one of them truly knew her, or tried to—they cared only for the favor they could curry with her family. Using the skills Mother had taught her, Lucy left them disappointed as she expertly extracted herself from every conversation without veering from the realm of politeness.

Out of the corner of her eye, she spotted Henry slip through that shut door near the orchestra.

No. She balled her fists. She'd promised Rocky she would keep him from escaping the ballroom. If she couldn't do that, she would damn well follow him.

Pulling up the hood of her cloak to hide her telltale Graylocke ebony hair, Lucy hoped to conceal her identity as well. If one of her brothers spotted her sneaking after a man, she would never hear the end of it. Thankfully, despite the blazing hue of her cloak, she wasn't the only woman dressed as Red Riding Hood during tonight's masquerade.

The music deafened her as she reached the door. Darting a glance over her shoulder—no one appeared to be paying her any mind—she lifted the latch and snuck inside. The light from the chandelier in the ballroom illuminated a narrow staircase a moment before her body blotted it out. She shut the door behind her.

The wood muffled the music somewhat, but although she strained her ears, she couldn't hear anything beyond the strains of the orchestra. Even her pulse pounded soundlessly in the base of her throat. He might already have gotten away. Using the walls for balance, she hurried up the steps to the next floor. Once she reached the landing, she paused.

It was quiet up here, and dark. Light streamed from cracks under the doors to various rooms along this corridor. The dim illumination gave no more indication of her surroundings than the outline of furniture in sconces along the hall. One door along the hall was ajar. For a heartbeat, the light wavered as a shadow passed over it.

Triumph surged through Lucy like a heady draught of spirits. She squared her shoulders and stormed through the door, ready to confront the scoundrel who had insulted her friend.

She stopped in the doorway, meeting his gaze as he

turned from the desk in one corner of the room. All four walls were filled with stuffed bookshelves, looking down on a long sofa and matching arm chair. A branch of candles glimmered from the desk top.

The man—ten or perhaps fifteen years older than her, it was difficult to tell in the shadows crisscrossing his face—had doffed his mask and hat, revealing short-cut, brown hair. He looked...plain. Not particularly handsome, with the slight rugged cast to his chin and nose, but not abhorrent. The doublet stretched tight over a round stomach, though given the breadth of his shoulders and muscular forearms, she suspected his rounded physique was more due to padding than fat. His calves filled out his hose in a way that might have been due to padding or simply an extension of his muscular form. Despite his quick ascent to this floor, he wasn't out of breath. It was too dark to make out the color of his eyes as he narrowed them, taking her in. As he leaned his hip against the desk, he fiddled with a purple lily, rolling the thick stem between his fingers.

She brushed the red hood off her coiffure and crossed her arms. "Have you retreated here to think about what you've done?"

A bemused smile curved his lips. "And what, pray tell, might that be, innocent miss?"

Innocent? Lucy dropped her arms and fisted her hands in her skirts. He emphasized the word, like it was a bad thing. "Not miss. Lady. I'm the sister of a duke, I'll have you know."

Normally, she would throw formality out the window, but if it would help earn the apology her friend deserved, she would act every bit as ducal as her brother.

The corners of his mouth twitched. "Forgive me, my lady."

She strode closer to him, unrelenting. "I will not forgive you. That was a very bad thing to say to my friend."

He didn't budge or show cowardice, not even when she stood toe to toe with him. From the way he lounged against the desk yet still remained of a height with her, she guessed that he would be near the height of her brothers Tristan and Morgan. Six feet tall or a little over, though not as tall as Giddy.

He stopped twirling the flower. This close, she noticed that his eyes were pale—or perhaps they only appeared that way due to the tawny cast of his skin. Odd, for a man to be suntanned in the middle of winter. Had he been abroad?

Her gaze caught on a small design embroidered in white under the lapel of his collar. Four triangles, the points meeting in the center, like the blades of a windmill.

"Which friend might that be? I imagine your friends are myriad. They blend into one another."

Lucy narrowed her eyes as she focused on his face again. Was he such a callous man that he didn't realize when he insulted a woman? Or was he innocent, after all? Rocky had mentioned that she didn't know which of the Henrys in the room were the man she searched to confront, and she'd left after another as he'd departed the ballroom.

She brushed her momentary doubt aside. Despite the fact that he was plain-looking enough to blend in with any ballroom, there was something about his smug amusement and the twinkle in his eye that told her she'd found the right man. "You know of whom I speak. Joy Rockwood. The lead gardener for Lady Belhaven—" Temporarily, only until the orangery was fixed at Tenwick Abbey. "—A position she deserves, because she is every bit as capable as any man."

His smile widened. When he straightened, he confirmed her suspicions by looming over her. She held her ground.

"Ah. I let slip something I should have locked in the back of my memory."

Lucy glared. "You never should have thought it to begin with. There is nothing—*nothing*—about a woman that makes her any less intelligent than a man. Nothing."

To her astonishment, he said, "You're right. Men like me fade from the mind in comparison."

That was...all? She'd expected some debate. Perhaps even a lengthy tirade that proved him the villain Lucy had concocted in her mind. Instead, the entire encounter fell flat. Somewhat forgettable.

She couldn't put something like that in a book. Readers would never feel satisfied at such an ending.

He held out the flower to her. "Please, give this to Miss Rockwood as a token of my apology."

Reluctantly, Lucy took it. "I will."

Had Rocky misjudged him? Was he innocent of the kind of venomous thinking that she'd claimed?

As he turned away from her, striding across the room, she said, "Wait! What's your name?" When she gave the flower to Rocky, she should at least be able to name the man who'd entrusted her with it.

He reached the window nestled between two tall bookshelves, he flicked open the latch on the glass. It was freezing out there! Surely he didn't mean to open the window.

He turned, meeting her gaze a moment more as he pushed the panes. The glass swung out on its hinges, letting in a rush of cold air that raised gooseflesh on her exposed skin. She pulled her cloak tighter around her.

"I have many names, my lady. You'd forget the moment I slipped out of sight."

In a feat of athleticism that proved his paunch was a hoax, he swung himself through the open window and was gone. Lucy gaped after him. Had he just jumped from the second story of a building? She dashed to the window, afraid she'd see his broken body littering the snow beneath.

Instead, she glimpsed his figure as he hugged the wall of the manor, slipping around the corner. "That isn't an answer," she shouted in his wake, not that he made any response.

Though it would be a deliciously mysterious line for a book.

1

Fenwick Abbey
Three months later.

NEVER EVER, *ever*, would Lucy insert childbirth into one of her books. Nor would she have a child. Or put herself in such a situation that risked pregnancy. Her sister-in-law, Philomena, screamed loud enough that she was likely heard in London, two days' travel away. Given the language she used, Phil never intended to let her husband, Morgan, touch her again.

Although she didn't intend to put her heroines through quite that much agony, Lucy did scribble down an epithet or two that a ruffian or pirate might say.

Her entire family crowded in the corridor of the family's quarters, outside the Duchess's room. Tristan had his arm wrapped around his wife, Freddie, while her sister and Lucy's best friend, Charlie, bounced on the balls of her feet, anxious. Mrs. Vale, their mother, hovered in the corner, out of the way. Giddy paced anxiously while his wife, Felicia, viciously stabbed at a handkerchief with a needle and thread. Jared, Phil's lanky brother, fidgeted in the shadow next to the closed door. Catt—Giddy's best friend, Mr. Catterson —though not technically a part of the family, leaned against the wall as he comforted his anxious wife, Rocky, the lead gardener at Tenwick Abbey.

Rocky wasn't the only servant in attendance. Behind Lucy's mother, who appeared serene if one didn't notice the tight way she clasped her hands or the white rip around her pressed lips, was a barrage of servants, each stopping for a minute to speak with each other and gain an update on Phil's condition before they moved on. As the first ducal child of the new generation, this birth was an important one. Everyone hoped for a healthy delivery, whether the child was a girl or boy. Morgan's assistant, Mr. Keeling, made no attempt to pretend to be at work, but headed the swarm of servants and answered the same question over and over again.

"Has she given birth?"

"Not yet."

Everyone stared at the closed door to the room, waiting anxiously for an update from within. Although they'd tried to while away the time in one of the parlors, when Phil's contractions had quickened to within a mere minute apart, everyone had barreled into the corridor.

Except for Morgan. He was inside, with the midwife and his wife. He'd insisted, even when the midwife had protested and suggest Mother be in attendance instead. As a duke, Morgan had gotten his desire.

As Phil cursed him again, Lucy wondered if he wished to reconsider. From inside the room, a bird squawked and repeated the impolite word.

As Lucy slipped closer, cocking an ear to hear what was conspiring inside, Morgan wrenched the door open. He shoved a large, red parrot with green-and indigo-tipped feathers, into Lucy's arms.

"Take him. He's not helping."

The bird cocked his head at Lucy and squawked. "You're in a...pickle!"

Slim smiles ghosted over the faces of her family members as Morgan shut the door again. They were gone, quickly replaced by worry and anxiousness, in the blink of an eye.

"No," she corrected softly, "I think you're in the pickle."

"Pickle!" the bird exclaimed. As he kicked up a racket, Lucy retreated down the hall into the swamp of bodies.

Mr. Keeling, a thin man with a weak chin in an otherwise forgettable face, stepped up and reached for the parrot. "I'll take that, my lady."

Lucy shook her head. "It's fine, Keeling. I'll put him with Antonia in the parlor." When Phil's contractions had started coming quicker, the family had decided it was better for Lucy to leave her pet behind than have her contribute to the tension of waiting. Phil's bird, on the other hand, had been with her from the moment she went into labor.

The servants parted as Lucy slipped between them. She kept one hand on Pickle's claws, wrapped around her wrist, so that he didn't decide to fly off. Pickle was much more curious than Antonia and could spend days flying around Tenwick Abbey while the family and servants chased him. He was used to having free rein of a much smaller house.

As Lucy left the corridor behind, the amount of anxious faces she passed thinned. She breathed a sigh of relief as she gulped in the cooler air. Truthfully, she was happy for the excuse to leave. Sitting idle was not her strong point.

After she deposited Pickle into the parlor with Antonia, Lucy left both birds behind and snuck through the corridor toward the antechamber of the abbey. It was deserted. Her shoes clicked on the marble floor as she crossed the wide, dim expanse. The only light came from the high cathedral windows along the vaulting stone wall that faced the second-story balcony abutting the family wing. Lucy pressed her lips together, cocking an ear to hear whether or not Phil had given birth. The drone of conversation revealed no decipherable message or tone of congratulations.

She slipped through the wide double doors and onto the front steps. The gray sky showered her with a fine drizzle like wet powdered sugar. It clung to her skin and hair, leaving a bit of a film, but refreshing her at the same time. The steps, having endured such treatment for more than a few moments, were dark with moisture. Lucy elected to remain standing. She fished out her hand-sized notebook and shielded it with her body as she flipped through the pages, studying her shorthand notes as she mulled over whether anything written recently could be usable in her book.

Her book was missing something. Over the past year, she'd made great strides with the heroine, a swashbuckling princess who after fleeing her country to sail the high seas had become an expert in fencing and inventing her own weapons, namely guns. The story was an adventure, in which the heroine learned more about herself and her true place in the world despite her pampered upbringing. Although Lucy had written at least one hundred pages of her book, she didn't know how it would end, how her heroine would find her place. She needed to find something else, some way to make her characters grow and reveal more of themselves.

She sighed. Aside from a few epithets, nothing she'd scribbled today would help.

A rider galloped down the long drive, between the double row of trees. As he reached the stables, a hostler emerged to tend to him and his horse. The man lunged from the saddle and barely spoke for a second to the hostler before he jogged toward the abbey proper. Frowning, Lucy tucked away her book.

The man—or boy, Lucy should say, since up close he looked to be no more than fourteen years old—wore charcoal-gray clothes and a gray-green cloak to shield the weather. There was nothing about him to indicate wealth, heritage, or even allegiance. He was the kind of boy one might slip past on a London street without thinking twice about him.

As he reached the front steps and started to mount them, Lucy stepped between him and the door. She lifted her chin. "What business do you have here?"

"That's between me and the duke."

She narrowed her eyes. Was it estate business? If it had been, the boy would have been wearing the ducal colors of azure and silver, or at the very least had the family crest on his clothes. If the matter didn't pertain to Tenwick or any of the family's collective lands...

Then the boy must be a spy.

Lucy wasn't daft. She'd known for years that Morgan and Tristan hid a secret from the rest of the family. They were good at sneaking around, experts in concocting believable lies or turning the conversation, but Lucy loved a good mystery. She'd known they were involved in Britain's spy ring since before Morgan had married. Since she suspected Mr. Keeling knew or contributed, sneaking into Morgan's office at Tenwick Abbey was tricky but not impossible. And copying the ciphers she found there, a delight. She'd almost made the heroine of her book a spy, but she hadn't been able to find a way to fit that in with the plot. Besides, if one of her brothers ever read it, they would know that she'd caught on to the secret and work harder to conceal their affairs in the future.

Although, at first, she'd been relatively certain that Giddy was too swept up in his plants to take notice of the affairs blossoming beneath his nose, he'd spent too many late nights with Tristan of late. Her two oldest brothers had likely welcomed him into their spy ring.

She wondered if her brother Anthony, a captain in the Royal Navy, was in on it too. She missed Anthony terribly—he hadn't been back but for a visit in years. But even though he wasn't within the household, he could still easily be part of their spy ring, especially given his position in the Navy.

It was unfair! Lucy was every bit as capable as they were, but she couldn't even put on a pair of breeches and walk the London streets without one of her brothers nearly suffering an apoplexy. Because she was so much younger than them, they thought her a petty, pampered child and that was far from the truth.

Lucy barred the boy from entering the estate. "The Duke is otherwise occupied at the moment."

It wasn't a lie. Morgan would likely send Tristan or Keeling to attend to whatever business this boy had for him.

Lucy added, "If you've a message for him, I can take it to him."

The boy's lips pressed together. "I was told to deliver the missive directly into the duke's hands, no one else's."

Raising an eyebrow, Lucy donned an air of confidence as she bluffed, "This is Tenwick Abbey. You can trust the missive to me." She held out her hand.

She had no proof that anyone save for her brothers was involved in the spy network, but her instincts had long raised the question that it was more than that. If Morgan was involved, Phil must know—Lucy couldn't imagine Morgan withholding such a pivotal aspect of his life from her. The same with Tristan and Giddy's wives. That numbered at least six spies in the household, not counting Keeling, if he were also involved. It wasn't such a stretch of the imagination for her to fool the boy into thinking she were also an operative of the Crown.

He looked uncertain.

"The Duke's wife is in labor and has been for some time. He won't be at liberty to see you for hours still. If this missive is important, it's best I handle it."

Cautiously, the boy said, "Britain is cold," as if that were a valid reason not to hand over the message.

No—wait! Why did that phrase sound familiar? Frowning, Lucy tugged the notebook from her reticule once more and flipped through the pages, starting at the beginning. She didn't have to look far. It was one of the copied phrases she'd purloined from Morgan's office, the basic phrase used as example in one of the ciphers.

The answer was... She flipped the page. "Only in spring."

When she glanced up, the boy's face was slack with relief. He thrust an envelope into her hand. "The Duke will want to receive this as soon as possible."

Lucy nodded. "Of course." She'd give it to him... after she had a peek herself.

Slipping back inside for a bit of privacy, she used her thumbnail to painstakingly open the envelope while leaving as little trace of her tampering on the seal as possible. She'd have to melt the wax back into place, but hopefully Morgan would be too distracted with the arrival of his first child to pay close attention.

When she folded open the letter, she discovered that it was written in code. She used one of the few blank pages left in her notebook and flipped back and forth to the cipher as she decoded it. The missive was from Lord Strickland. Clearly, he had some involvement in the spy business as well.

I know your wife is coming to term, but Monsieur V is back in London. As you know, we haven't seen hide nor tail of him since Lady Belhaven's masquerade. I need you in London posthaste, along with your best spies. We must catch this spymaster before he disappears into smoke once more. We must catch his face this time.

Lady Belhaven's masquerade? Lucy had attended that. In fact, so had Rocky, the Tenwick gardener, which she'd thought a little odd. She'd considered it odd that Morgan would lend Rocky's services over the winter even with the hothouse in disrepair. Even more bizarre had been the fact that Catt had followed Rocky into Lady Belhaven's household, though Lucy had assumed he'd only done that because he was in love with her. In a way, she had been right, seeing as they were now married.

But, if the Belhaven masquerade had something to do with the spy effort...then Rocky and Catt must be spies. And if they were spies...

The man Rocky had tasked her to watch must have been Monsieur V. Everyone, Lucy's entire family, had come running to burst into the library a moment after he'd departed. Lucy had thought their reaction a bit extreme simply to preserve her virtue for sneaking away without a chaperone. Though, given her brothers' overprotective streak, it hadn't been beyond the realm of possibility.

Now, Lucy replayed the scene. Could they have been worried about her safety, not only her virtue? The stranger hadn't hurt her...but he had seemed amused by her accusation. And he'd given her a flower, which Morgan had soon taken possession of even though the man had left it for Rocky.

What a dolt I've been.

She re-read the decoded missive, thinking. Strickland stated that no one knew what this Monsieur V looked like—but if he was the man Lucy had confronted, that wasn't true. She knew. Why had no one asked her?

Because of Morgan. A duke held a lot of clout, apparently even against Lord Strickland. Her brothers didn't want to put her in danger—even if it jeopardized the security of the nation.

She gritted her teeth. *I'm not a child.* She could do anything her brothers could do. In fact, she would. She would prove to them that she was just as brave and smart as they were. And she'd do it by finding the very spymaster they hadn't been able to locate.

As she tucked the letter into her reticule along with her notebook, a cheer roared from the family quarters to her left. Lucy lifted her skirts and hurried up the wooden steps to the balcony that abutted the quarters. She slipped through a narrow corridor, ending in an area swarming with servants. They beamed, laughed, jostled each other. Money exchanged hands. Phil must have successfully delivered her baby.

Lucy breached the ocean of servants and was able to breathe a little easier. She spotted her best friend, bouncing on the balls of her feet as Tristan and Freddie hugged next to her. When she spotted Lucy, Charlie skipped over.

"Did you hear? It's a boy!"

The future Duke of Tenwick had been born. Lucy smiled. That ought to keep her brothers occupied for the foreseeable future. She hugged Charlie tight, sharing in her joy and relief that Phil's labor had concluded successfully.

"And Phil?" she asked.

"Healthy. No complications, the physician said. They're just cleaning off the baby and mother and then everyone can go in to see him. They're naming him Oliver, after her father."

Lucy smiled. "Good. After we say hello, I want you to pack your bags."

"Why?" Charlie frowned.

"They've got so much help that we'll only be in the way if we stay here. We're going back to London."

Where Lucy would start the search for the notorious spymaster only she could find.

2

For the past three days, Lucy had relived her encounter with Monsieur V, searching for any kind of clue or starting point from which to search for him. She'd consulted the notes she'd taken from the evening's events, for future use in a book. The biggest clue toward finding him, she would think, would be his costume. He hadn't simply worn some outdated clothes—his costume had included that paunch, which would need to be specially made.

Specially made...or perhaps borrowed from a theater company. Lucy couldn't very well enter all the shops on Bond Street asking after who might have made such a thing—not with Mrs. Vale, who had accompanied her daughter and Lucy back to London to act as chaperone, constantly hovering over her shoulder. So Lucy decided to try the next best thing and attend a play. Both the Vales loved taking in the latest play.

She started on Drury Lane. The play, a matinee, was filled with bored peers who chatted lazily with one another as they claimed their boxes. As a Graylocke, Lucy had claim to the family's perpetually-reserved box on the upper right near the stage. Figures milled below, members of the audience as well as shadows behind the curtain as they set up.

Although not titled, Charlie and Mrs. Vale were such permanent fixtures of the Graylocke family that they'd started to amass the same admirers hoping to curry favor with the ducal family as Lucy had. Mrs. Vale handled the inquiries of a matron her age with aplomb while Charlie smiled and chatted with her mousy daughter exchanging a bored look with Lucy behind the girl's back. Charlie had an adventurous spirit and, while she loved the theater, she was not one to be content chatting up boring debutantes. As the true Graylocke, Lucy should greet both of them herself, but this was just the distraction she needed. With the Vales occupied, she slipped out of her booth and down the crimson-carpeted corridor toward the stairs.

Women bombarded her on the way. *"Oh, Lady Lucy, have you met my..."* Brother, nephew, cousin, it was always the same. Some young buck who wanted to be tied to the Duke of Tenwick and Lucy, as the only daughter, was the lucky lady to bear the brunt of their attentions. With over a year since her come-out, Lucy liked to think that she had enough skill and wiles to extricate herself from such conversations without arousing suspicion.

She eventually made it down the stairs and snuck into a side corridor before someone followed her. Once there, she paused to get her bearings. The chatter of the audience radiated from her left, almost drowning out the movement and voices to her right.

She followed a light down the corridor, eventually coming to a wide room teeming with actors in various states of dress. Some wore only their undergarments and the padding necessary to bring their characters to life. One wore what looked to be a long, fake nose atop their own. Another pasted on what slowly progressed to become a shaggy beard. A woman called for someone to do up the ties of her wide dress. It was miraculous, this glimpse into the creation of a character. Lucy stepped into the corner, tugging her notebook out of her reticule and taking notes as she observed. Fascinated, she watched as a wig, makeup, and a little padding and shoes with high heels turned a woman into a completely different person.

"Oi! You there! No audience members allowed back here."

Lucy jumped. She shut her notebook and turned to the speaker, a reed-thin man with a thick mustache and smutches of what looked like rouge or a dark powder along his cheekbones.

"I just wanted to ask you a question."

"No time, lady. Don't you see we've got a show to put on?"

She stepped forward, trying to catch his attention before he turned away. "I know, but—" She might not be able to sneak away later.

He pointed to the corridor. "Go on now, or I'll have Bull remove you."

Bull turned out to be a short fellow that looked a bit like a hound with a squashed face. He wore a dog collar around his neck and growled when the thin man spoke his name. Was he another actor or did he stand guard just for effect? Did the actors often have to field off inquiries from audience members? Lucy scribbled down notes in her notebook, unperturbed despite the attempt at intimidation.

When the thin man strode away, she hastened to catch him. "Wait! This will take only a moment of your time."

He looked irritable. "You've already claimed more than that." Twitching his shoulder as if to brush her off, he continued walking.

She followed on his heels into the center of the room. "I am the sister to the Duke of Tenwick. You have to talk to me."

The room hushed at her loud pronouncement. Inwardly, she winced. It wasn't precisely the most subtle spy work. She hid the reaction and stared the thin man down.

His mustache twitched. "And what will you do if I don't?"

The actors continued to prepare. One woman excused herself, removing to her dressing room. Lucy paid her no heed. If there was some kind of pecking order in the troupe, the ornery man in front of her appeared to be at the top. Besides, she didn't want to speak with an actress; she wanted to speak with someone who handled the costumes.

Donning her most impassive expression, Lucy said, "In January, I saw a costume at Lady Belhaven's masquerade that might have been plucked from one of your plays."

"You were mistaken. We don't lend out our costumes, not even to young noblewomen like yourself. Try a tailor." Turning, he glared at the men and women along the perimeter of the room, clustered near the racks of clothes or standing in front of a vanity. "Look lively! Break doesn't come until the curtain closes!"

They jumped back into motion, completing their preparation.

Lucy said, "I intend to. Try a tailor, that is. Only the person wearing the costume left before I could ask who made it and the only identifying mark I can remember is this symbol embroidered just beneath the collar." Hastily, she flipped through her book until she came to the page containing a bunch of shorthand notes and a little symbol. Four triangles, their points touching in the middle.

The man harrumphed. "Black-Eyed Joe is who you're looking for. Or Joseph Gordon, as you fancy ladies might know him. He runs a little shop off an alley near Bond Street."

Lucy smiled sweetly. "Do you happen to know the address?"

She scribbled it down as he gave it to her, verifying.

Irritable, the man snapped, "Is that all, *your highness?*"

Not the proper address for a duke's sister and he said it in far too disrespectful a tone, but she smiled anyway as she snapped her book shut. "Yes, thank you.

You've been very helpful." Before he could rebuke her further, she scampered into the hall.

There, she stopped short. A man blocked her path, the devilishly handsome sort of man that had most debutantes atwitter despite his blackened reputation. Alexander Douglass, the Marquess of Brackley, loomed as tall as her two oldest brothers, an inch or two over six feet. He was just as athletically built, with his forest-green jacket molding to his broad shoulders and lean torso. However, instead of spying, his physique most likely came from climbing in and out of women's bedrooms. He'd been to the St. Gobain house once or twice to speak with Morgan, however, so she couldn't be certain. Why would he speak with her brother?

Parliament. Business deals. Estate advice. Morgan was a duke, after all—he had been for eleven years now. Whereas Brackley had only inherited his title last year, after the sudden death of his father and older brother. Quite tragic, though the new responsibility hadn't seemed to curtail his carousing any. The one time she'd encountered him at the St. Gobain town-house where Morgan had lived since his marriage, her brother had warned her away from him.

He isn't the sort of man with whom you want to associate.

Most likely, Morgan had said that because of

Brackley's penchant for sneaking backstage at plays. Was he here to meet with a lover? Excitement ghosted through her as she met his green eyes. He cocked an eyebrow, the brow nearly disappearing beneath the artful sweep of his reddish-brown hair over his forehead. His clean-shaven mouth spread in a cat-got-the-cream smile.

Her fingers itched to jot down a description of the thrill that swept through her. Illicit, almost dangerous. She shouldn't be alone with any man, but Brackley more than most.

Maybe this was exactly what her book needed—a scoundrel.

* * *

"LADY LUCY."

Perhaps, given her brother's involvement in the Crown spy network, Alex shouldn't be surprised to find the youngest Graylocke sibling nosing around the back of a theater. But, given the duke's obvious protectiveness of her, he was surprised. And a little alarmed, quite frankly. Morgan Graylocke would never involve his sister in matters where her safety might be in question.

Unless Monsieur V was back in London.

Alex barely kept the relaxed smile on his face. He

didn't dare hope that that was the case. In fact, if it were the case, he would have liked to think that Morgan would have assigned him to the mission of swiftly bringing the fiend to the end of a noose. There was no one in Britain more driven to catch the heinous spymaster. But, confound it, Alex didn't know the man's face! Morgan suspected that the spymaster performed some weird sort of mesmerism on anyone he spoke with, mesmerism that made them forget what he looked like. None of their spies were immune.

Except, perhaps, Lucy Graylocke. Alex had been under the impression that the Graylocke women were to be kept in the dark regarding the family's spy efforts. However, if Lucy was back here...

Why *was* she back here? She held a small, leather-bound journal in one hand, a pencil stuck between the pages. Had she found a clue, something he had missed?

It had been *three months* since Monsieur V had vanished into smoke. Three months during which Alex had been chasing his tail searching for a lead. Frustrated, he'd decided to forget everything he knew and start again. The last sighting of the slippery spymaster had been at Lady Belhaven's masquerade, which unfortunately Alex had not attended, and he'd been wearing a Tudor costume. So Alex had searched the tailors, the museums, and now the theaters. Had Lucy found something pertaining to the case?

Ask her.

He couldn't. He couldn't know for certain that Morgan had assigned her to chase Monsieur V. In fact he wouldn't, not without a partner. Alex had been reprimanded more than once for looking into matters without a second person to watch his back.

No, more likely she was here to chase some other thrill, flirt with the actors or some other banal activity. Who knew what ladies did these days for entertainment? Alex certainly didn't. After all, he hadn't kept their company for well over a year, barring the occasional female partner during a mission for the Crown.

Oh, he'd kept up appearances, for the sake of his cover. But he hadn't continued his rakish ways past his brother, Camden's, death. Now, he was walking in his footsteps in every way except perhaps the most pivotal —an untimely death. The moment he'd laid his father and brother's bodies to rest, Alex had pledged himself in service to the Crown. Something, perhaps, that he should have done while his brother had still been alive.

At least then, he would have been able to watch Camden's back. The golden boy, apparently too foolhardy to know when he'd gotten himself into too deep trouble.

What would his father have to say about him, now?

As the young woman in front of him curtsied, spreading her lilac skirts, Alex shook himself from his reverie and inclined his head in answer.

"Lord Brackley." Her mouth, with its wide lower lip, curled up at the corner, mischievous. Her coffee-dark eyes twinkled, only a shade or two lighter than the black curls affixed to her head.

Lady Lucy Graylocke might pretend innocence—at least enough to arouse such a protective instinct in her brother—but in that moment, Alex knew her for a very dangerous woman. Dangerous to a man's sanity. And, given the way her brothers guarded her as zealously as lions, dangerous to a man's health, no doubt.

"I must admit, I didn't expect to find you here." Her voice was laced with amusement. She clutched that notebook to her chest as though it were a life raft.

What did she have hidden in those pages? *Was* she investigating Monsieur V on behalf of the Crown and if so, what had she found?

Alex burned to know. The desire was so swift and sudden that it was nigh undeniable. If she hadn't been holding the book so tight, he might have snatched it out of her hand, hoping to read the secrets contained within.

Monsieur V... Alex would catch him. He'd see that the man got what he deserved.

He pretended innocence. "At the theater?"

Her smile grew. "Backstage."

"I imagine I'm here for the same reason you are." Was he? Those words were the closest he dared come to asking if she were on assignment for the Crown.

But if she were, where was her partner? One of the Graylocke brothers would have been hanging on her coattails.

Her eyes widened with feigned innocence, the act given away by the smirk affixed to her lips. "You came to ask the actresses for cosmetic tips?"

Cheeky little minx.

He raised his hand to his heart and played along. "You've found me out! I do hope you'll keep it a secret. My sparkling reputation, you know."

Judging by the strangled sound she made, she stifled a laugh. Her eyes were alight with amusement. As she stepped closer, her hips swayed, drawing his attention to her figure.

Don't look. He couldn't help himself, and given the look of satisfaction on her face, she knew it, too. She was beautiful from afar, but lively and breathtaking up close.

And clever. Maybe even conniving, because she used his attention to her benefit. She whispered, forcing him to lean closer in order to catch her words.

"Don't worry, my lord. Your secret's safe with me. I wouldn't want your friend to get the wrong impression."

She thought he was meeting a lover. He grinned before he caught himself and sobered his expression. How wrong she was. But she intrigued him. Most women in her position would be scandalized, or disapproving at the very least. But the look she gave him was almost...encouraging. As if she egged him on simply to see what he would do.

Sorry to disappoint. He wasn't here to meet with a lover, after all.

She tipped her face up to his. "Do you always sneak by before the performance? It seems to me that you'd be better off waiting until the end."

He laughed. Was she giving him advice on how to conduct a liaison?

"My dear, you have the wrong impression of me."

"Do I?"

She narrowed her eyes, drawing his attention to her thick, sultry eyelashes. Her lips pursed, begging for a kiss.

He couldn't give it to her.

"My brother's warned me about you."

"Has he?" Morgan had warned him as well—

explained in far too explicit detail what would happen if Alex were ever found in a compromising position with Lucy.

A position such as being alone with her in the back corridor of a theater. He took a subtle step away from her and the heat of her body.

He couldn't help but tease her, though. "Perhaps you ought to listen to him. It's a thin line you're treading, associating with a man of my reputation. It could be dangerous."

Dangerous for him, that was. He wouldn't harm a hair on Lucy's head, regardless of her brother's threat.

Oh, but she reminded him of the game of seduction. Making himself out to seem just dangerous enough to get a woman's heart pounding, making himself into the thing she shouldn't have. And then, leaving her with a bit of mystery, walking away. In the end, he rarely had to pursue them again. Eventually, when they searched for a bit of excitement, they always came crawling to him.

With a wink, he inclined his head again. "If you'll excuse me, my lady, I believe I ought to search out my seat before the performance begins." Without waiting for an answer, he turned away and strode down the corridor.

That was reckless. Even if the lure had been too much to deny. Could he tempt a woman like Lady

Lucy? Better he not know. If she sought out his company, he'd be a dead man. The Duke of Tenwick had made himself perfectly clear. Lucy Graylocke was the one woman Alex could never have.

But her activities today were suspicious, nonetheless. She might bear watching. If he were lucky, she could lead him straight to the man who had torn his family asunder.

3

*T*he seamstress, a pretty young thing smattered with freckles, smiled at Lucy, Charlie, and their chaperone Mrs. Vale and asked, "Have you given any thought as to the style of the dress you'd like?"

Charlie picked one out of the book straight away while her mother hovered over swatches of fabric, lifting them to check the color against her daughter's porcelain skin. They each seemed distracted.

Before the seamstress turned her attention back to Lucy, Lucy said, "Drat. Charlie, why don't you get fitted first? I have a sketch in my notebook, but I must have left it in the carriage. I'll only be a moment."

Mrs. Vale glanced up with a frown. She looked from Lucy to her daughter, clearly conflicted. Lucy pasted on a smile. "The carriage is waiting just down the street. I won't be long at all."

Charlie, unperturbed, held up a swatch of vibrant pink that made her look like a ghost. Lucy frowned. Charlie knew that color made her look ghastly. Then again, that was probably why she'd chosen it. The last thing Charlie wanted to do was attract a potential husband. "What do you think, Mama? This is pretty."

Lucy breathed a sigh of relief as Mrs. Vale turned away. Before either Vale woman paused to pay more attention to her, Lucy slipped out the door and into the thin, dreary drizzle seeping from the sky. She pulled the hood of her pelisse up over her curls and strode briskly down the street—in the opposite direction from the ducal carriage.

It had taken a bit of persuasion, but she'd convinced the Vales to try a different seamstress from the one the Graylocke family usually used. Although not as reputable as their usual seamstress, this shop had the benefit of residing closer to the tailor to whom the costumer had referred her. She didn't have long—after all, the carriage wasn't far and if she didn't return soon, Mrs. Vale would undoubtedly grow suspicious and come looking for her—but hopefully, she would have enough time to question the tailor and learn more about Monsieur V.

Her story about forgetting her notebook in the

carriage was pure drivel. As she slipped between two brick buildings into an alley so narrow she nearly brushed both shoulders against the walls, she pulled the little book from her reticule and readied her pencil. At the end of the alley was another street, too narrow for a carriage, that ended in a row of squashed little shops. A wooden sign hanging from above one plain door depicted four white triangles, each meeting in the middle to resemble the blades of a windmill. Her heartbeat sped. This was it! Composing herself, she reached for the handle and stepped inside.

The interior of the shop was as squished as the outside. A long counter divided it neatly lengthwise down the center. On the far wall, a faded crimson curtain separated the front room from another in the back. The space in front of the counter was filled with displays of the tailor's work, primarily replica historical garments like one might wear to a masquerade. The hodgepodge of eras reminded Lucy of the portrait hall at Tenwick Abbey, where all the family's old heirlooms had been stuffed out of sight. The shop was otherwise empty.

"Hello?" Lucy called. Was the tailor out? If so, he would do better to lock his door. "Is anyone here?"

The curtain rustled. A little man, as squat as the shop, bustled from the back. Joseph Gordon was clean-shaven and kept a neat appearance. His hairline was receding and he had deep wrinkles around his eyes, nose, and mouth. Lucy didn't understand why the theater's costumer had referred to the tailor as Black-Eyed Joe, however; from her position by the door, his eyes appeared a pale blue or green, as far as she could tell.

"Hello, young lady. How can I help you? Looking to make an impression at your next ball?"

Lucy couldn't decide if the man guessed her social status by her clothes or if the only people who ever came into his shop were women looking for masquerade clothes. If the latter, he ought to be able to point her in Monsieur V's direction without preamble.

"Actually, I've come to ask you a question."

As she approached the counter, the tailor looked disgruntled. He glanced over her shoulder toward the door, as if hoping that her chaperone would soon step through and take her to task. *No such luck, my friend.*

"It'll only take a moment," she added. After all, she didn't have more than a moment to spare. Every second that she spent here ticked in her head like the echoes of a grandfather clock.

Black-Eyed Joe grunted. "What's your question?"

"About three months ago, I met a man at a masquerade who wore an exquisite King Henry costume. It had your symbol right about here," she demonstrated with her hands, "under the collar. Do you remember that costume?"

Or the man, she added silently.

"Ah. He said you'd be in. It's about time."

Wait...what was about time? Who was he— Monsieur V? Lucy clasped her hands hard around her book as she struggled to rein in her whirling thoughts. Had Monsieur V been watching her movements in London since she'd returned?

Perhaps she should reach out to her brothers, after all.

"Wait right here," the tailor said, interrupting her thoughts. Without waiting for an acknowledgement, he spun on his heel and slipped behind the curtain once more.

Lucy waited. She tapped her toe. Why had he suddenly left?

Ice chilled her as a thought dawned. He might have sent a runner to the infamous spymaster in order to corner her! Lucy turned, abandoning her quest for information. Her heartbeat sped. As she reached the door, the tailor shuffled into the main room again, the curtain swishing.

"Here you are. It's all made to the right specifications, but if you'd care to try it on, I can make some alterations."

What? Her ears ringing, Lucy turned around.

The tailor set a wide, round box on the counter. The lid sported his recognizable four-triangle signature. He lifted the lid to display a mass of dove gray and periwinkle blue fabric beneath, dotted with seed pearls. When he lifted part of it to drape over his forearm, Lucy recognize the length of fabric for a dress.

But she hadn't ordered one. She'd never even been here before. With a weak smile, she approached the counter again. "Are you certain that's meant for me? I never ordered it."

His attitude businesslike, he shut the dress away in the box once more. "Young lady with black hair, brown eyes, and bearing of a peer. I don't get many that meet that description in my shop. He's already paid for it, if that's what you're worried about. Oh, and he left this, too." The tailor tugged a crinkled envelope from his jacket pocket and tossed it atop his symbol on the box. It slid a little off-center.

A letter. From Monsieur V?

"Jibberish, if you ask me, but he paid me to pass it along, so there it is."

He'd read the letter? It must be in code. And if it were in code it was almost certainly from the spy she chased. She dipped into her reticule and found a shilling to tip the man.

"Thank you for your time." Hefting the box—and,

more importantly, the letter—she turned away. She juggled her package as she exited the shop.

The moment she stepped out into the little square, she shut the door behind her and huddled in the over-hanging eaves to keep out of the rain. She wrestled the letter open and pinned it to the box with her thumb as she skimmed it.

To the untrained eye, it likely looked a fright. The letter was a long one, filled with a string of banal sentences that jumped from one topic to the next without reason or meaning. However, as Lucy looked it over, she noticed that several words were misspelled. In fact, the letter was riddled with misspelled words.

It was a code. One she'd certainly copied from Morgan's office. Awkwardly, she juggled her notebook onto the top of the pile and started to flip through the pages. Drops from the eaves plunked on the edge of the round box. She pressed herself against the door, trying to protect it and herself from the falling moisture.

Where was the cipher? She reached the end of her notebook and swore under her breath. She must have copied it into a different notebook. It had been several months ago. The notebook in question might not even be in London, though she was usually careful to pack them all, seeing as they held snippets of research and plot ideas that might prove useful at one time or another. Did she bring the letter home and decipher it there?

The spellings were key. She remembered that much. Unwilling to admit defeat, she combed through the letter and copied each misspelled word into her notebook in order. Then she stared at the page. The cipher... Once it had clicked, she'd thought it rather simple. But what had the trick been?

Ah. As she remembered, she held her lower lip between her teeth and deciphered the code. She brimmed with triumph as she read over her finished note. She crossed out and modified two words before she was satisfied with the result.

Midnight, Leighton's west terrace, opening night. Wear the dress. Come alone. Tell no one. I'll know if you do. M.V.

Lucy's lungs ached. As she realized she was holding her breath, she let it out in a rush. Cool, moist air flooded her lungs as she inhaled. Opening night... opening night of what? She was missing something, some integral piece of the puzzle, and if she didn't find it in time, she would miss this opportunity. Monsieur V was handing her the opportunity to speak with him again in the flesh!

Stuffing her notebook into her reticule, she fisted the note and pulled open the box just wide enough to slip her hand inside. She groped through the muslin until she felt something hard and rectangular. She pulled out a card.

An invitation to Lady Leighton's house party. The invitation wasn't addressed to her by name. Presumably, all she had to do was present this to Lady Leighton's butler in order to be invited into the house. This was it! She could catch him.

But wait—she only had one invitation. Did that mean it would only admit herself, not a chaperone like Mrs. Vale or even one of her brothers?

Morgan. Guilt and anxiety swamped her as she realized that she needed to tell him about this. It was one thing for her to venture to London in order to undertake some investigative work, but she couldn't arrest someone on his behalf. Assuming that spies were permitted to arrest others. She'd never asked.

She'd send him a letter. No, wait, she couldn't. *Tell no one. I'll know if you do.* Those were the words Monsieur V had written. They could be a bluff but... what if Morgan had an enemy spy in his midst and didn't know about it? Any letter she sent him might be intercepted and she didn't have time to drive down to Tenwick Abbey and return in time for the party.

She squared her shoulders. She could rely on no one but herself.

You're not a dimwit. You can do this. Her insides quivered with mixed excitement and trepidation.

Ignoring the flutter, she stuffed the letter and the invitation into her reticule. The small bag that hung from her wrist bulged as she forced the two articles in alongside her notebook and other personal artifacts. The strings wouldn't pull shut, but she tightened them enough that the letter and invitation wouldn't slip out.

Then, turning the box sideways, she turned toward the alley. If she hurried, she should be able to stash the dress in the boot of the carriage and neither Charlie nor Mrs. Vale would be any the wiser. But she'd dallied long enough already.

A figure separated from the shadows of the doorway across from her as she started toward the alley, back the way she'd come. Lucy jumped, her heart speeding. She clutched the box in front of her like a shield as she turned to him.

Brackley. His auburn hair was dark with moisture, a bit flat as it curled across his forehead, as though he'd been standing out in the rain a while. The collar of his greatcoat was turned up to shield his neck, but he didn't have a hood.

"Lady Lucy." His tone was laced with amusement. "What do you have there?"

Reluctant to remain out in the rain, Lucy stepped into the doorway of the nearest house. The square beneath her shoes was slippery with grit-turned-mud over the cobblestones. The stoop was raised a bit, necessitating that she pay attention to where she rested her feet as she stepped onto the ledge, out of the falling drizzle.

Brackley stepped up after her, squeezing into the narrow doorway with her, under the eaves. His broad shoulder stuck out, catching the drips from the overhang. The constricted space meant that in order to fit, he was pressed nearly against her body. Only the wide, flat box served as any barrier between them. Since the doorway didn't quite match his height, he was forced to stoop, bringing his head closer to hers.

Lucy swallowed. "You shouldn't stand here."

He arched an eyebrow. Had he leaned even closer? A shiver coursed through her, one she tried hard to suppress.

"I shouldn't stand out of the rain?"

"You shouldn't stand so close. It's..."

His mouth curved, a clear sign of his amusement. He said nothing as she grasped for a word.

"Improper."

"Ah, yes." He nodded, solemn. "We should tell your chaperone at once."

She gritted her teeth. "I am not a ninny. I don't need someone standing over my shoulder at all hours of the day."

"No?"

She glared up at him. "No."

He wouldn't dare harm her. Hers was a close-knit family, and everyone knew it. If he so much stepped a toe out of line, she would tell one of her brothers and that would be the end of Alexander Douglass. There were benefits to having overprotective brothers, after all. One of them was that every gentleman, whether he found himself alone with her or—far more likely—not, treated her with respect.

Brackley, on the other hand, didn't seem at all concerned with his pending plight.

"You still haven't answered my question."

"It's a dress," she snapped.

"An odd location for you to choose a tailor." He waved an ungloved hand at the doorway to the shop she'd come from, the gold signet ring on his finger winking in the light. His eyes danced, as if he suspected her of lying.

Perhaps she wasn't telling the whole truth, but she certainly wasn't lying. She did have a dress in the box. Only it had been gifted to her by a notorious traitor.

She kept that particular tidbit to herself. If she was to handle the slippery spymaster, she would have to prove herself by handling one far-too-curious marquess.

"Are you getting a dress as well?" she asked sweetly.

He laughed. "Hardly. I buy my cheroots from a

man down this lane."

"You could have them delivered."

"You could have had the dress delivered, too."

He had her there. Very well, they were at an impasse. She straightened her spine, intending to renew their battle of wits. Brackley's breath teased a lock of her hair. Her lips parted. When had he moved so close? The eaves shadowed the look in his eye. His face was intent as he slanted his head, almost as if he meant to kiss her.

No. He wouldn't...would he?

"Brackley."

He paused, an inch away from her face. His body leaned into hers, the heat emanating from his form. "Yes, my lady?" His voice was as rough as gravel.

Kiss me.

No...don't. Lucy couldn't make up her mind. She'd been kissed before, of course, so she'd be able to accurately write it in one of her books, but she'd never craved the taste of someone's lips the way she did now. Her head all but spun with the overwhelming desire.

He was a scoundrel, a rake of the worst caliber. She'd encountered him only yesterday on his way to meet with a mistress. He might be sneaking around this little-known street with the same intent in mind! Two women in two days...

And yet, the lure was undeniable. She'd revisited

their encounter over and over again in her mind. Writing it down hadn't purged the thrill, nor the shiver she'd gotten when he'd winked at her. Now, to know what it would be like to be kissed by someone so masterful...

He stepped out from under the doorway. "You should hurry back to your chaperone, Lady Lucy. It wouldn't do for you to be caught unawares by the wrong sort of person."

As his boots clicked on the cobblestones while he strode down the lane, Lucy turned to stare after him. What had that been about?

She pressed her lips together and tried not to be disappointed that he hadn't kissed her. After all, she didn't know where his mouth had been recently. And she didn't want to know, either.

ALEX'S SHOULDERS burned from Lucy's gaze as he strode away. *Don't look back, whatever you do.* His shoulders weren't the only part of his anatomy that burned, either. His mouth felt as though he'd set it aflame.

He danced a dangerous line. Lucy was beautiful, young and guileless, headstrong and passionate. Kissing her would be a death sentence. Even if Morgan didn't exact revenge personally, he had in his power to assign Alex to the most dangerous assignments in the most violent neighborhoods. Never mind that Alex was a titled peer; he was under no illusion that if he laid a hand on Lucy that he would walk away unscathed.

She tempted him all the same. If he hadn't needed to get so close to learn her secrets, he would have taken himself far away. But, where the matter concerned Monsieur V, Alex couldn't simply walk away. Not even if it would mean trouble for him later.

As he ducked into a shop down the line, he shut the door and pulled out the folded note and card he'd filched from Lucy's reticule while they stood so close. The invitation, blank as to the recipient, seemed innocuous enough. A house party.

At first glance, the letter seemed just as innocent. However, Lucy had helpfully used her pencil to underline the misspelled words in the rambling note. It was a simple code, cycled out of use months ago by the French once the Crown had deciphered it. Alex decoded the message in his head.

As he finished, he smirked. This was it, the moment he'd been waiting for. He knew precisely where Monsieur V would be, and he would be there first to intercept him.

Then he would finally get his revenge.

hat devious, black-hearted scoundrel! Lucy upended her reticule on the settee at the end of her bed, next to where a servant had delivered the box containing her dress. A few shillings clinked together as they fell next to her notebook, pencil, handkerchief, and a few other scattered items.

No note. No invitation.

She clenched her fists. "I'll show you what happens when you cross a Graylocke."

If she'd been in any doubt that Brackley was a spy, it had been erased. The only question was: for which side? Had her brother tasked him with following her and removing her from the investigation, or was he acting on his own? For a moment, with him all but pressed up against her, so close that she could feel the touch of his breath, she'd thought for certain that he would kiss her. A thrill had coursed through her and she'd thought, from his expression, that he'd been just as desirous to succumb to temptation.

But no, it had all been a ruse so he might steal from her! That blighted man! How could she hope to follow the clues and catch Monsieur V if she was denied entrance to the location where he would be?

Perhaps that had been Brackley's design. Perhaps Monsieur V had only been toying with her, holding his location just out of her reach and then taking it away again. That did seem to be the more likely recourse. After all, why would such a wily spymaster submit to meeting with her in person?

But, if Brackley had removed the note to stymie her efforts on Monsieur V's behalf, then that meant that a British peer was a French spy. Why would someone with such a noble lineage turn their back on their family and country? She couldn't fathom it.

Simply because she could never imagine anyone of her acquaintance committing such an atrocious act of treason didn't mean that it wasn't true. Did she have two spies now to apprehend, not just one? Perhaps she should take her chances that Monsieur V might be telling the truth about having eyes on Morgan's correspondence and attempt to contact her brother anyway.

It would be admitting defeat. Morgan would shut her away as far from the investigation as he could manage and her brothers would see that she remained there. Hell and damnation, she wasn't a child! She could do more than twiddle her thumbs. No, she didn't even know for certain that Brackley was involved in this at all. Perhaps he was only curious and had filched the letter only to find that it contained indecipherable nonsense.

Lucy stuffed her belongings back into her reticule and turned her attention to the box. A quick peek inside proved that her lady's maid hadn't yet found the time to put away the dress. Lucy decided to do that herself, taking the opportunity to examine the garment in more detail, just in case Monsieur V had left her a clue on the dress itself. Perhaps Brackley didn't have the entire story, after all.

If the spymaster had ordered some kind of code or clue be affixed to or embroidered into the dress, Lucy couldn't find it. Just as she admitted defeat and crossed to her wardrobe to put away the dress, Charlie stuck her head into the room.

"There you are." The blonde frowned. She tugged on one of her ringlets as she stepped into the room proper. "What do you have there?"

"A dress for Lady Leighton's house party."

The corners of Charlie's pink mouth turned down

even farther. "Lady Leighton? When did we receive that invitation?"

Lucy stuffed the dress into her wardrobe and turned, a smile curving her lips. "We haven't yet, but we will."

After all, she was the sister of a duke. She could gain entry anywhere in England, if she chose.

GAINING entry to Lady Leighton's London townhouse posed no problem. The moment she passed the butler her card, he whisked her and the Vales into a parlor near the front of the house. It was a bit frilly for her tastes, overdone in frothing white doilies and pale pink furnishings, but she took a seat and waited nonetheless. The tea service arrived before the hostess, and a maid poured the tea.

Charlie jiggled her leg as she waited, impatient. She nearly sloshed her tea over the rim of her white cup. Mrs. Vale, seated on the settee next to her, laid a restraining hand on Charlie's knee. She said nothing, but the young woman pressed her lips together and tried harder to hide her impatience.

Lucy fought to retain a calm exterior as she waited. She finished her tea cup before Lady Leighton presented herself. Didn't she know she entertained a member of the ducal family? Since Lady Leighton wasn't one of the many who hoped to marry one of her relatives into the Graylocke family, apparently Lucy's presence carried little weight. At least, less weight than Lucy had hoped.

Eventually, Lady Leighton sailed into the parlor. The slender woman, in her early forties, wore a prim expression. Not a hair on her head was out of place. Each golden-brown lock was pinned neatly into place. Not a thread on her blue dress dared to fray. Next to her, Lucy felt a mess, ink stains on her fingers and more than one stray strand tucked behind her ear. She folded her hands on her lap and tried not to show her feelings of inadequacies.

A viper like Lady Leighton would undoubtedly capitalize on it. Although she was unfailingly polite, it was common knowledge in the gossip mill that the lady only kept her friends according to the fashions. If someone fell out of favor with the *ton* at large, so too would they find themselves barred from Lady Leighton's presence. She had no notion of family; in fact, many whispered that the reason she had never provided her husband with children was on purpose, so she might keep her figure.

Although, after witnessing the pain through which

Phil had suffered in order to give birth, Lucy wasn't entirely certain that she could blame Lady Leighton for choosing not to bear a child. Children were cute... but although Phil had seemed content, even radiant after the delivery as she held her son in her arms, Lucy had to wonder if it all was worth it.

Fortunately, she didn't plan on marrying any time soon, not to a man who saw her as little better than a brood mare or who sought to curry favor with her family. Lucy had her book to write, and now she had a nephew upon which to dote as well. Perhaps, with luck, Tristan or Giddy's wives would grant another such little miracle in the family.

With a little simper, Lady Leighton claimed the chair across from Lucy. "So sorry for the wait, Lady Lucy, Mrs. Vale, Miss Vale. I had some business that simply couldn't wait."

Liar. The woman had only wanted to feel superior by making them wait. Lucy gritted her teeth and tried to appear unaffected.

"It's quite all right," she lied. "We were just admiring the furnishings." She kept her smile sweet, matching the edge to the hostess's voice.

No matter what machinations Lady Leighton attempted, couched in a demure demeanor, Lucy refused to let her get the upper hand. Compared to the complexity of puzzling out Monsieur V's next move, this subtle, edged dance between peers was laughable. She played it for as long as necessary, leading the conversation on the weather and delivering the news of Morgan's son.

Finally, after nearly an hour of brainless chatter, Lucy was able to circle the conversation back to her reason for calling. "I hear you're planning a house party."

Lady Leighton fanned her fingers over her chest. "How remiss of me! I assumed that you and the rest of your family would remove to the country for the rest of the Season."

That might even be true. Truthfully, Lucy wouldn't care to receive the invitation if Monsieur V wasn't to be in attendance. She fixed her smile in place as she met the viper's eyes. Was she in league with the French? Lucy wouldn't know without further investigation. But in order to do that, she needed to secure an invitation.

"I'm afraid we'd only be in the way, there. My sister-in-law has more than enough help, what with my brothers' wives and my mother. I have returned to Town for the foreseeable future."

Although Lady Leighton matched Lucy's smile, her eyes were cold. It was an empty expression. "Then you must come to my house party." She veered her attention briefly to the other two women in the room.

"All three of you. I'm certain you'll find it quite diverting."

"Thank you. We would be happy to accept."

Lucy masked the surge of satisfaction that rose within her upon uttering those words. *Brackley, you are going to regret stealing from me...*

5

*N*ever before had a week crawled by with such insufferable slowness. Although Lucy had at one time considered spying to be a thrilling enterprise, she was forced to amend that opinion. Spying was not thrilling or entertaining or at all worthy of being added into a book. It comprised of more waiting than investigating, for until she met with Monsieur V, she had no clues to follow.

She spent that time agonizing over what her brother would want her to do in regards to this mission —other than remain safely at home, that was. Would he want to kill the spymaster to prevent him from causing further harm to England? Lucy didn't know if she had the mettle, let alone the means to do such a thing.

No, a spymaster must be more valuable to Morgan alive than dead. He knew information about the enemy, didn't he? Her brothers could be very persuasive, when the mood overtook them. Therefore, when she met with Monsieur V in a few moments, Lucy had determined to capture him. She'd stuffed silk ties into her reticule for just that purpose.

Lady Leighton's manor was the height of sophistication. Her ballroom was dressed in the neoclassical style, with pillars reminiscent of ancient Greece framing the perimeter of a marble dance floor. Potted plants in Oriental vases dotted between the pillars. In separate rooms that adjoined the ballroom, card tables had been set up, as well as a buffet table. A crystal chandelier shimmered two stories overhead, where a fresco had been painted on the ceiling.

For all the manor's splendor, the number of guests was limited. Only the elite were invited to Lady Leighton's house party, and even then, only so many as she could fit in her guest rooms. Although she'd granted Lucy her own room, she'd put Charlie and her mother in a neighboring chamber together. If she'd done so with guests with connection to a duke, Lucy could only imagine that she'd resorted to the same thing with other debutantes and their chaperones. Lady Leighton's country estate, for all its fashionable architecture and furnishings, was less than half the size of Tenwick Abbey.

Much of that size seemed to be eaten up by a ballroom that could have comfortably fitted another fifty people, especially considering the number of men and women who had shut themselves away in the card rooms. Less than twenty people mingled and danced. The small number made it exceedingly hard for Lucy to lose herself in the crowd.

But she had to try. At any minute, the grandfather clock would chime the hour and she would be due to meet a notorious spy out in a corner of the terrace. Even though she knew Charlie loved an adventure, she couldn't very well drag her best friend or her mother into the danger. She had to do this alone.

Monsieur V had instructed as much. For all that she intended to thwart his plans and arrest him instead, first he had to show up to their arranged meeting. Lucy didn't want to jeopardize that by stepping even a toe out of the lines he had set. She wore the gray-and-periwinkle dress, had her hair pinned up off her neck so it didn't fall into her eyes, and had spoken to no one about the meeting. Not a note, not a whisper. She hadn't even pretended to have a lover so that Charlie might keep watch and ensure that no one followed. Lucy was on her own.

But first, that meant she had to trick her dearest

friend into looking in the other direction while she slipped away. Strolling arm-in-arm with Charlie around the perimeter of the room did not make that an easy task. At least Mrs. Vale remained seated near some of the other chaperones. Once Lucy devised a way to free herself of Charlie's company, she should be able to slip away with relative ease.

"So," Charlie murmured, "why did you want to attend this party so desperately? You don't like Lady Leighton."

Apparently the answer that Lucy had given her the first six times she'd asked over the past week—that she was bored of the same old thing in London or that she'd heard that such-an-acquaintance was coming—wasn't believable enough. Nevertheless, Lucy tried again.

The moment she opened her mouth, Charlie added, "You never run out of things to do in London. You have more to research there than here. And you had to leave Antonia behind."

Lucy usually preferred to keep her parrot with her whenever she traveled, but in this case it had been unavoidable. Lady Leighton would never have permitted a pet onto the premises, let alone one who often insulted people at random.

A gift from her brothers. Lucy would never have taught the bird to be so rude.

She tried again to answer Charlie's question, but her friend cut her off.

"None of your friends are here, after all. Perhaps you heard wrong."

"Perhaps I did. But now that we're here, we might as well make the most of it. We might make new friends."

Charlie looked dubious.

Pointing across the room at a young gentleman in a walnut-brown tailcoat, Lucy added, "What about this fellow? He's been staring at you all evening."

Charlie glanced over, then frowned. "I have noticed him looking, but I think he's been staring at you, not at me. I'm nobody."

"A beautiful nobody," Lucy teased. "Perhaps he'd like to make you into a beautiful somebody."

Charlie laughed. "Well, I'm not looking to become a somebody to any man. We're young yet!"

Lucy smiled. "Yes, we are."

"I still think he's been staring at you."

As the young man in question started striding across the room to intercept them, Lucy pinned her smile in place. "I suppose we'll find out." She hoped that Charlie was wrong.

The young man stopped to gain the company of the hostess on the way. By the time the pair reached them, Charlie had donned a sunny smile that Lucy couldn't hope to match. They were like night and day, Charlie a blonde beauty in a rosy dress and Lucy no doubt fading beside her with her more muted shade of garb and her dark hair.

Once again, Lady Leighton's smile didn't reach her eyes as she introduced Robert Hale, the heir to Baron Langford. "And this is Lady Lucy Graylocke, sister of the Duke of Tenwick."

Lucy didn't much care for the way the woman emphasized her connection to her brother. She curtsied nonetheless. The young man gave a half-bow in response and immediately turned his attention to Charlie.

"Lovely to meet your acquaintance, Lady Lucy. And who might this gem be?"

Lucy bit the inside of her cheek to hide a smirk. She had been right. If they hadn't been standing in front of the hostess, she would have shot her friend a triumphant look.

Reluctantly, Lady Leighton introduced Charlie before excusing herself. As Mr. Hale struck up a conversation with Charlie, Lucy slowly inched away.

Her friend noticed. With a frown, she turned as if to call Lucy back or include her in the conversation, but Mr. Hale chose that particular moment to ask Charlie if she was free for the next set and Charlie couldn't possibly refuse without being impolite.

Lucy slipped away.

Unlike the ballroom at Tenwick Abbey, this one did not adjoin the gardens. It was located in the center of Lady Leighton's manor, with the other wings of the house surrounding it. As Lucy slipped into the hallway, she fished her notebook from her reticule and flipped to the page where she'd sketched a crude map earlier. After a moment's hesitation, she continued down the corridor and made a left.

No one, guest or servant, stopped her as she exited the premises, if anyone even noticed her. She shut the door quietly, pausing to let her eyes adjust. Unlike the hallway, lit at intervals, the only light outside was that of the moon.

Distantly, she heard the chime of the grandfather clock. Midnight. She swallowed the lump in her throat, lifted her skirts, and hurried around the perimeter of the mansion until she found the terrace. Gooseflesh rose on her arms beneath the cool spring air. The air was calm, and the sky mostly devoid of clouds, but the air tasted moist.

As she walked, she reviewed her plan silently. Wait for Monsieur V. Talk to him, perhaps get him to follow her to a more confined location. Then she'd have to find something to subdue him with unless she could devise a way to trick him into allowing her to tie him up. He wouldn't be likely to come peacefully, would he? Oh, dear. She should have thought harder on the mechanics of enacting her plan. In her head it had seemed simple: arrest Monsieur V, take the carriage and deliver him to her brother. But how, practically, was she to do that? She should have nabbed one of Phil's inventions. Her sister-in-law was always concocting fanciful devices. In fact, her inventions had been the inspiration for the heroine's in Lucy's story.

Unfortunately, Lucy had nothing except her wits and a couple of silk ties. Considering that she hadn't thought through this portion of her plan, Lucy considered her wits to be rather dull at the moment. She faltered in mid-step. Should she return to the ballroom and find a last minute accomplice? Perhaps a servant or Charlie's new dance partner.

But she couldn't. The hour of their meeting was already upon her. She had no time. She had to meet Monsieur V—now.

Think of this as a research opportunity. Anything and everything could be used in her book. What would her heroine do in her situation, if she were caught needing to capture someone but with little means to do so?

The heroine would wait and try to sneak up on the person. Though, she would also probably be armed with one of her self-made guns, whereas Lucy had no weapon at all.

She would figure something out. She was a story-teller, after all. She didn't lack for imagination.

She slowed as she neared the edge of the terrace. Leafy bushes grew next to the stairs, tall enough to conceal her when she crouched. The terrace was a semi-circle jutting from the side of the manor, composed of flagstones, with a gravel walkway near the bottom and steps at intervals leading to the ledge. Sneaking up, Lucy used a bush for cover as she peeked between the stone rails, carved like Grecian pillars. No one yet.

She pressed her lips together. Should she stand and reveal herself? It might be that Monsieur V wouldn't emerge until he saw that she had come alone. She could scour the gardens for him, but the light was dim and she might easily overlook a clue. No, she had no choice but to face him on even ground and keep her escape route open. With so many exits from the terrace, if something went amiss, she could easily run and lose herself among the twists and turns of the many walkway gardens.

Her decision made, she stood, tended to her appearance, and mounted the steps.

Strong arms gripped her from behind. One, wrapped around her waist and trapping her arms in place, pulled her back against a man's muscular physique. The other clamped over her lips, muffling her shriek. She thrashed as the figure hauled her away from the terrace. Blind panic gripped her as the man half-dragged and half-carried her across the lawn. She dug in her heels, but only managed to lose her shoe. When she thrashed, the man swore under his breath, a voice she swore she recognized. Her head was fuzzy with fear and she couldn't place it. Her heart pounded angrily in the base of her throat. She tried to bite him, but his hand was pressed too firmly for her to open her jaws wide enough.

He hauled her into a building. A shack, really. Four wooden walls and a roof. Shadows loomed, horrifying torture devices with hooks and blades that glinted in the meager moonlight. When the man released her, she stumbled. He shut the door, cutting off the light.

"Release me," she demanded. "Or I'll have your freedom." If not his life, for daring to kidnap a Graylocke. Her brothers would see to that.

Movement rustled and she balled her fists, prepared to do violence if he came any closer. Instead, the scratch of flint and steel was followed by a flood of light as the man lit a lantern. The light threw the shadows back, illuminating the gardening tools along the walls. As he turned, Lucy caught sight of his profile and recognized him instantly. Not Monsieur V, as she'd half-feared.

The Marquess of Brackley crossed his arms, using his bulk to his advantage as he barred the door. Trapping her inside the shed with him.

Hell and damnation! Why hadn't Lucy stayed home? Alex had stolen her note and the invitation to gain her access to the event. She should have remained in London—cursed him, perhaps, but remained. Instead, she'd somehow used her wiles to gain access to the event. Since neither the butler nor the hostess had looked askance at Alex when he'd presented himself at the house, Lucy had likely gained entrance for the same reason; her family connections.

But the fact that she was here—that she was, in fact, pursuing Monsieur V on her own—was troublesome. Not the least because, in order to get her out of harm's way, he'd sacrificed his one chance to meet Monsieur V on even ground.

The thought that he might not corner Monsieur V after all fanned the anger building in his chest. But what was he supposed to have done, leave Morgan Graylocke's sister in harm's way? Morgan knew that she was in danger from the spymaster. Where were her protectors? Her brother couldn't possibly leave her unattended. And trained spies ought to be able to follow her when she strayed out of sight. Unfortunately, since he hadn't spotted anyone lurking in the gardens to ensure her safety, that lot had fallen to him. Lucy might have cost him...everything.

No, not everything. She was stubborn. Even now, the glint of the lantern reflected off the steel in her eyes. She balled her fists, ready to do battle with him if the need arose. Might there be more to her than what met the eye? Although Alex would never underestimate Monsieur V's capacity to manipulate young women into doing his bidding, he had to consider that Lucy might not be as innocent as she seemed.

Was she in her brother's employ? Or was she in league with Monsieur V? *Lawks!* He didn't even want to consider it, but the slippery spymaster *had* sent that missive directly to her. She'd known to go to that costume shop directly to get it, too. Could she be a traitor?

No. It was...unfathomable. Her entire family was in service to the Crown!

He had to be certain. Muttering an oath under his breath, he squared his shoulders and donned his most impassive expression. The only way to know for certain whether or not Lucy was a French spy would be to interrogate her.

If Morgan Graylocke ever learned of this, Alex would be a dead man.

6

When Brackley took a step forward, his broad shoulders seemed to fill the meager space in the shed. His expression might as well have been carved from stone, for all the emotion it expressed. Only his eyes proved that he was, indeed, a flesh-and-blood man. They glinted with something other than hardness. Hesitation, perhaps. It was hard to tell in the light.

Lucy held her ground, her heart pumping as he closed the space between them even further. She licked her lips and refused to move back. Her body prickled with the awareness of his.

"Here's what we'll do," Brackley said, his voice soft and composed. "Before the night is over I'd like to see you back safely in your room."

Lucy offered him a sweet smile that belied her racing pulse. "Then why don't you do that now?"

He shook his head. She supposed it had been too much for her to hope. Why would a man kidnap her only to set her free again a moment later? If she'd written such a scene into one of her books, the villain would need to have a reason in order to do so. The heroine would offer him something he couldn't refuse, or apply leverage to force him to let her go. Unfortunately, Lucy couldn't fathom how she could do either of those things.

She couldn't offer him money; he had plenty of his own. He was a titled peer, nearly as exalted as a duke, all but untouchable when it came to threats. She knew none of his secrets, save perhaps about the mistress he kept at the theater. Though, now that she found herself in this situation with him, she had to wonder if she'd been correct about that. This was the third time he'd shown up on her trail while she was pursuing Monsieur V. It couldn't be coincidence.

What did he want with her?

Brackley re-crossed his arms, a solid barrier between her and escape. "Before we do that, you're going to answer some questions for me."

An interrogation? She'd never thought to find herself in quite that situation. If her brothers had been nearby, they never would have allowed it. But, despite the shiver of fear that trembled through her, Lucy embraced the thrill. This was the perfect opportunity to research for her book!

Brackley narrowed his eyes. "What were you doing outside on your own tonight?"

She raised her eyebrows. "You stole my letter. Since you were there, I assume you can decode it. You know precisely what I was doing."

What he had interrupted her from doing. Had he been trying to thwart Britain's efforts to counter Monsieur V?

Brackley grunted. How verbose of him. He was worse than Morgan when he got in a snit.

"Are you in your brother's employ? Did he send you here tonight?"

Are you? If Brackley had been working with Morgan, wouldn't he have known that Lucy was not? She hesitated, turning the answers over on her tongue before she offered one.

"I'm working under my own direction."

She was the only person who could identify Monsieur V by his face. Logically, she should have been inducted into the ranks of spy months ago. If her brothers weren't so stubbornly overprotective, she would have been. She was certain that, if it had been Giddy or Tristan who had crossed paths with the spymaster instead of her, they would have been told the truth of the matter immediately. Morgan only sought to shelter her because she was a woman.

He should know by now that she was just as capable as any of her brothers. She would have thought that her escapades in the name of research would have convinced him of that, seeing as she'd endured various circumstances that her brothers thought too crude for her delicate sensibilities and she hadn't swooned once. Nor had she been reduced to hysterics or been irrevocably scandalized or any other nonsensical thing that a man wanted to pretend a lady would do in such situations. The world consisted of more than balls and afternoon tea, and Lucy could handle all its aspects.

Try convincing her brothers of that, though. She had, to no avail. Perhaps when she delivered Monsieur V into their grasp, they might change their opinion of her.

If, in fact, she could still capture the man. She hadn't shown up to the meeting where he'd expected her. She had no other clues to follow. If he disappeared, she would have to start again, with even less of an idea of where to look.

She glared at Brackley for thwarting her plan, though he didn't appear to be paying attention. Instead, he muttered under his breath. Something that sounded near to, "That explains it."

His expression hardened again. "Explain your contact with Monsieur V."

She battled the urge to roll her eyes. "You know the answer to that question. You read the letter."

"That was your only contact?"

She hiked up her chin. "Yes."

"How did you know to find it at the shop off Bond Street?"

"A lucky guess."

It *had* been lucky, come to think of it. How had Monsieur V known to leave it for her? If she'd arrived at that line of inquiry a week later, she would have been too late to attend this house party. It seemed like a risk he couldn't possibly have known would pay off.

Unless the man she'd spoken to in the theater had been in Monsieur V's employ. But, if so, how had the spymaster even known that she would approach him? She might have gone to any number of theaters. The one on Drury Lane had just happened to be performing a play that Mrs. Vale had particularly wanted to see. It had been sheer coincidence.

"Do you know where to find him now?"

Something in Brackley's countenance bespoke of desperation. The set of his jaw had an edge to it. His eyes glinted like steel. Lucy refused to be cowed, even by his sharp tone.

She countered, "If you hadn't dragged me away,

you would have been able to find him on the terrace. Perhaps it might not be too late to catch him." She waggled her fingers, sending him off.

Not that he budged by even a hair. It seemed he suspected just as much as she did that Monsieur V was long gone. When she hadn't arrived as expected—or worse, when he'd witnessed Brackley bodily remove her from the premises—he would have made himself scarce. If he had been the type to be easily caught, her brothers would have done so ages ago. She had faith in their abilities. They were none of them simpletons. Brackley ought to have known that, too.

Unless... Perhaps the reason he was so assured that Monsieur V was gone was because he was working for the man, keeping an eye on Lucy on the spymaster's behest. Perhaps this interrogation was made on behalf of Monsieur V, to assure himself that she knew nothing.

Unfortunately, she didn't. She had nothing to hide.

"What about your notebook?"

She bristled and clutched her reticule to her chest. "What about my notebook?" It was hers. It held her most sacred thoughts, as well as all the research she had gathered of late.

Brackley scowled. "What are you hiding in it?"

"I'm hiding nothing. I keep notes in it for the novel that I'm writing, that's all."

He looked dubious. "Show me."

"No. Why should I?"

He closed the distance between them. As she tried to back away, she stumbled over a fallen rake. The shed was such a tight, enclosed space that when she lost her balance and reached out behind her, she touched the wall and was able to right herself.

Brackley wrestled her reticule from her wrist.

"Give that back," she snapped. "That's my personal property."

He held it high over her head as he fumbled with the ties to open it. If he thought she hadn't been shown that tactic countless times by her much taller brothers, he was wrong. She stormed up to him, all but pressing herself against him as she jumped to try to snag her bag once more. No luck. She stomped on his foot, hoping it would make him lower it.

He swore and took a step back as he pulled the leather-bound notebook from the bag. He tossed the bag at her, taking advantage of her momentary distraction as she caught it to flip through her prized notes.

She stuffed the reticule onto her wrist again. "Give that here," she demanded.

He made a face. "It's in code. What's the cipher?"

"Not code. It's shorthand. It takes up less space if I don't have to write out all the letters to every word."

Frowning, he continued to flip through the notebook. He paused at a diagram she'd sketched. "Is this a gun?" he asked with a raised eyebrow.

Lucy craned her neck. "Yes."

The second eyebrow lifted to join the first. "You design weaponry?"

"I don't. My heroine does. She's a princess-turned-swashbuckling inventor." Most people, upon hearing about Lucy's story, made a polite comment that masked their disbelief that she could or would write such a thing at all.

Brackley shut the book and handed it back. His face didn't hold a shred of disbelief. It appeared that he believed her about the notebook's contents now.

"How long have you been involved in Britain's spy efforts?"

She narrowed her eyes. "I haven't." It was the truth.

"How long have you known about them, then?"

"Months."

"When you saw Monsieur V's face?"

Why did he want to know? Lucy gritted her teeth, holding her ground as he loomed closer. When he stopped a foot away, she hated to admit that she wouldn't mind him stepping even closer. The heat of his body was seductive. She battled the urge to close her eyes and savor the awareness of his body.

Was this what her novel needed? A love affair?

She stifled a laugh. No, not love. Lust, maybe, but her princess-turned-pirate heroine was too hard-hearted to fall in love. Especially with someone bound to treat her as if she was the pampered woman everyone thought she should be.

Keeping her voice even, Lucy answered honestly. "I knew about the spy network, but I didn't know who he was until later."

Until recently.

Brackley didn't seem pleased with her answer. Just what did he hope to discover from her? She didn't know whether he hoped she knew more about Monsieur V or that she didn't. She pressed her lips together and stared him down, waiting for his response.

"If you were to guess where Monsieur V is right now, where would you say?"

She released an exasperated breath. "I honestly have no idea. You just foiled my only clue!" She gritted her teeth and crossed her arms.

"Very well. Then you're free to return to the ball now."

Did he sound disappointed about that?

As she moved toward the door, he didn't budge, still firmly in her path. He caught her gaze and held it. "You'd do better not to let anyone know that we spent so much time alone together."

No one...including her brothers? She narrowed her eyes. "Why?"

"Considering my reputation, it might prove damaging to yours."

He was right, but there was more to it than a black stain on her reputation. He didn't want her to spread the word for some other reason, a reason she would uncover.

That, or he was unwilling to pay the price if the truth did emerge. Either way, perhaps she would do best to keep their meeting to herself, after all.

She smiled, falsely sweet. "It will be our secret."

7

*B*rackley accompanied her back to the house, giving Lucy no opportunity to sneak off to the terrace on the off chance that Monsieur V had lingered. The stubborn man even waited in the corridor, where everyone could see him, as the sounds of the concluding ball wound down. At any moment, guests would spill out into this very corridor on their way to their rooms, and he and Lucy would be discovered. Given his adamancy over keeping their association a secret, Lucy would have thought that he would want to avoid just a scenario.

Apparently, he preferred to irk her instead. For a long moment, she caught his gaze, calling his bluff. The echo of footsteps and voices emanated, growing closer. Bollocks! He wasn't going to back down.

Turning on her heel, she scampered up the stairs. A moment before she turned her back, she thought she caught the beginning of a smirk on his face. She balled her fists and stormed into her room.

The moment she reached that sanctuary—a small yet elegantly-decorated haven including a bed, a chair, a dressing screen, a wardrobe, and a vanity—she sighed with relief. She toed off her shoes, having stopped along the way to collect the lost one, and set her reticule on the vanity. Once she retrieved her notebook and pencil from inside the bag, she curled up on the bed and scribbled every detail of the interrogation, including the way it had felt, into one of the precious last few pages in the book. By the end, the small page was crammed with notes, more pencil markings than blank page.

A knock came from the door. She glanced up. "Come in."

The door opened a crack and Charlie's blonde curls peeked through. "So you are in here, after all." She opened the door wider and stepped inside.

Her mother followed, a frown turning down the corners of her mouth.

"Where did you disappear to?" Mrs. Vale asked. "I thought you might have snuck off to the library, but when I checked I couldn't find you. I was worried."

Charlie perched on the edge of the bed. "Were you

here the whole time? I thought you wanted to attend this house party."

Lucy bit the inside of her cheek and forced a smile. "I got an idea for something to include in my book and had to write it down. See?" She flashed the page of her notes to the pair, thanking her forethought in scribbling it all down the moment she returned to the room.

Mrs. Vale looked dubious. Didn't she believe Lucy?

Fortunately, Charlie seemed to accept the explanation readily enough. She tucked her heels to the side as she rearranged her skirts into a more comfortable position. "What idea did you have?"

Lucy's smile turned genuine as she confessed. "I think my heroine needs to take a lover."

"A lover?" Charlie giggled. "Whatever gave you that idea?"

Lucy gave her a sly smile. "Maybe a certain gentleman who seemed bent on following a certain lady."

Charlie blushed. "Mr. Hale is well enough, but don't think anything will come of it. I'm not looking to get married right now, you know that."

Good, she thought that Lucy meant her. In actuality, she thought of Brackley. Why *had* he followed her? His questions had given little insight into his motives, and only some insight into his skills. Obviously he had a working knowledge of codes and the spy network. But where did his allegiance lie? And what did he want with her?

As Lucy and Charlie moved on to an enthusiastic discussion about what kind of man would attract a princess-turned-pirate, Mrs. Vale excused herself and left the room. As she shut the door behind her, Lucy couldn't help but relax a bit. Mrs. Vale had accepted Lucy's lie, after all.

Hadn't she?

* * *

ALEX LINGERED in the shadow of a doorway as the guests milled past and ascended the same staircase Lucy had taken. The look in her eye still haunted him. Challenging, confident. Luckily, he could be just as stubborn, because he suspected that if he left her alone for a moment, she would go looking for Monsieur V.

That was his job. No, more than a job. The day he'd learned of his brother's death, he'd made a vow to himself to rip Monsieur V from his pedestal. And that was precisely what he would do. He didn't care if Morgan assigned him to the mission or not. This was personal.

How personal was it for Lucy? She seemed bent on throwing herself in harm's way. All in pursuit of a man she'd met but once. Was she in over her head? Perhaps he shouldn't, but Alex believed that what she'd told him was the truth. She didn't have prior association with or knowledge of Monsieur V. Which could only mean that he was manipulating her to some end that neither of them had yet guessed.

Nevertheless, once was more often than Alex had found himself face to face with the man. Whatever Lucy's connection to him, Alex needed her. He'd taken a chance last night in choosing to interrogate her over waiting to confront the man himself. He'd hoped that she would know how to make contact with Monsieur V, that Alex could set his own trap...

As much as he wanted her answers to be lies, he *did* believe her. He had been in this spy game long enough to know when he was being lied to, and Lucy was far too free with her emotions. The women he encountered in his line of work were jaded. They didn't see the value in telling the truth, not unless it benefitted them in some way. In comparison, Lucy Graylocke was like a breath of fresh air. Guileless and innocent. If she remained in Monsieur V's vicinity for much longer, she would undoubtedly lose that. As Alex mounted the now-vacant stairs, he wrestled with the irrational urge to preserve Lucy's guilelessness, to keep her from being tainted by the sorrows of the world.

He couldn't protect her because he needed her if he was to exact his revenge.

As he reached the landing, he expected the corridor to be vacant. The top of the steps branched into a long corridor; women roomed on the right, men on the left. However, as he parted from the shadows, he discovered that he was not alone.

Mrs. Vale stepped into the light. The flickering flame glinted off her hard gaze, masking the expression in her eyes. Her face was as cutting as a blade, her mouth no more than a thin line.

She stepped closer, the click of her heels sharp in the silence. "I didn't expect to find you here, Brackley."

He offered her a bland smile. "I was fortunate enough to receive an invitation." Albeit indirectly. For all Lady Leighton's groveling upon his arrival, he doubted that he would have been invited on his own merit. Alex's wild reputation from before his brother's demise had carried over into his succession of the Brackley title. Lady Leighton wasn't the type to invite scandal to her house party; though, now that he was a marquess, she couldn't turn him away and earn his censure, either.

Mrs. Vale, on the other hand, wasn't as concerned with drawing his displeasure. She crossed her arms. "Are you here on business?"

"Aren't most house parties for pleasure?"

She raised her eyebrows as if demanding a better explanation. He offered her none.

Her frown deepened into a scowl. "Stay away from her."

So Morgan had warned Lucy's chaperone to keep him clear. Alex was touched that the man held him in such high esteem. Before he'd crossed paths with her in London, Alex had never entertained the notion of approaching Lucy. Her brother was far too overprotective of her, if his hackles rose because Alex had happened to glance in her direction one time while meeting with Morgan.

Now that he knew her connection to Monsieur V —or, if nothing else, the spymaster's affinity for toying with her—Alex couldn't promise to stay away. He needed Lucy if he was to draw out the traitor. Monsieur V slipped through his fingers tonight, while he'd been wasting time interrogating Lucy. Even if she was innocent, he couldn't afford to steer clear on the chance that she'd stay that way.

He might need her for bait.

"Goodnight, Mrs. Vale," he said, his tone clipped. Without another word, he strode in the opposite direction, away from the woman and the women's chambers. One of which housed Lucy.

He couldn't rid himself of the confident look in her eye. He smothered a wayward desire to protect her, keep her safe of Monsieur V's machinations. He couldn't do that.

Nor could he allow himself to be drawn to her, even if he hadn't felt this lure to a woman since his father and brother had died. Letting himself succumb would be the height of folly. It would be dangerous not only to his self-imposed mission, but also to himself.

8

The warbling songbirds didn't seem to understand that this sunny morning was not the time for celebration. It was a morning filled with frustration and aggravation. Dew clung to the leaves of the bushes framing the terrace. Droplets fell onto the gravel walk, crunching beneath Lucy's shoe as she circled the area for the sixth or seventh time, searching for a clue.

She'd found the area where she had hidden easily enough. Her shoes had bent the grass and left a depression near the bush. That had given her heart, made her think that maybe she would be able to find some clue from Monsieur V even if she hadn't been able to meet with him after all.

She'd been wrong. No matter where she looked—on the terrace, through the garden paths, or the trail ringing the steps and railing—she couldn't find a single piece of evidence to support that Monsieur V had shown up to their arranged meeting at all. The only disruption to the ground that she could notice was her scuffle with Brackley and where she'd crouched near the bush to watch the meeting spot. Even those, she might only have discovered because she knew where to look. In her book, she'd assumed that finding evidence of someone's presence where they ought not to be would be easy in nature. Perhaps she needed to revise those scenes, because she couldn't find the faintest echo of Monsieur V.

Damn Brackley! If not for him, she would have been here to meet with the notorious spymaster. If not for Brackley, she might have been on her way to Tenwick Abbey with the traitor in her custody even now. Instead, she was rooting around in the dirt searching for clues that didn't exist.

She blinked hard as she straightened and turned her face up to the brilliant blue sky. The weather seemed to defy her mood, more cheerful than it had been in days whereas she felt like a rag wrung out too many times. What now? Did she...give up? Return to London or to Tenwick Abbey and turn over her findings to her brothers?

No. If she were writing a book about this, it couldn't end that way. It wouldn't be satisfying. Squaring her shoulders, she took a deep breath and mustered her resolve. She knew Monsieur V's face. If he had been invited to this house party, she would know it. She would find him.

"Enjoying the fresh air?"

Lucy jumped. She whirled on the speaker, Brackley. How had he approached without her noticing the crunch of his footsteps? He was as silent as a cat. He stood on the terrace, bent forward with his forearms resting on the stone railing as he watched her. When she turned, he offered her a lazy, smug smile.

The scoundrel. She gritted her teeth, composing herself before she climbed the steps to stand next to him. She wouldn't act the demure damsel around him. Better he know that he nettled a woman every bit as clever as he was.

When she reached his side, he straightened, though his air remained casual. His gaze swept over her bare collarbone and the scoop of her gown. Goose-flesh rose in its wake.

"It's a bit cold out this morning to be walking around dressed like that, wouldn't you say? Didn't you bring a shawl?"

And have it snag on one of the bushes? She was in

danger enough of doing that with her skirts. She hadn't wanted any added deterrents.

"It's invigorating. It keeps me alert."

He raised his eyebrows. "And did that alertness grant you a fresh perspective?"

"As a matter of fact, it did," she lied. She crossed her arms and didn't break eye contact.

He chuckled. "Don't let me keep you, then, if you're still looking."

She pressed her lips together, but couldn't think of a good retort. Turning away, she batted her braid over her shoulder once more.

"What brings you out so early? I thought none of you titled peers rose before noon."

"Does your brother give you that impression?"

Not at all. Morgan was always the first in the family to rise, except perhaps Giddy. Though, sometimes, Giddy got so wrapped up in his plants that he forgot to sleep, so he didn't count.

"That depends to which brother you're referring." Tristan tended to lay abed past noon and stay up all night. Anthony... Actually, Lucy didn't know what her second-youngest brother's sleeping habits were these days because he was leagues away in the middle of the ocean, in service to the Royal Navy.

For all that they had remained in England, her

brothers had chosen a profession that was no less dangerous, if few knew of the danger they put themselves in. It was no less important, either, which was why Lucy couldn't simply give up because she'd missed the meeting yesterday. She had to find Monsieur V. She might be the only person who could.

Brackley smirked. "I thought you noblewomen tended to lay abed past noon, as well."

Considering that she had been up past two in the morning, Lucy usually would have slept in a bit longer. This morning, however, she hadn't wanted to run the risk of someone having trampled all over her evidence. Unfortunately, even if someone had, she would be no closer to finding a clue. If Monsieur V had been there last night, he had left no clue behind. No footprints, and certainly no note.

She stifled a sigh. With a falsely bright smile, she told Brackley, "I didn't want to miss the beauty of the morning."

A groove deepened next to his mouth, his expression amused. When he leaned closer, her breath caught. He lowered his mouth next to her ear, and she breathed in his manly scent. Cedar with a hint of starch. Her heartbeat quickened. His breath tickled the shell of her ear.

"Do let me know if you find anything, would you?"

Without waiting for her to agree—not that she would since she still didn't know on which side his loyalties resided—Brackley turned on his heel and entered the manor by way of the terrace doors. Light reflected off the glass as he shut the lattice doors behind him. Lucy squinted. When the glare from the reflection abated, he was nowhere within sight.

Good, she told herself as she rubbed her sweaty palms against her skirt. Now she had time and privacy to concoct some semblance of a plan to find Monsieur V. If he was among Lady Leighton's guests, Lucy would know by the end of the day.

THE LUCKY THING about house parties was that all the guests were, at one point or another, crammed into the same room. Such was the case later that afternoon. Lucy had lingered in the breakfast room, drinking far too many cups of tea as she'd tried to glimpse the face of every man to enter. When that had still left some lingering doubt as to whether one of the guests had snuck out for a morning ride or hunt, Lucy had dragged Charlie and Mrs. Vale on a tour of the manor in search of diversion. In Lucy's case, the only diversion she was interested in was a man who she recognized. She didn't find him.

As the day wore on, the sky frosted over and the wind picked up, chasing anyone who thought to go outdoors back inside. The party congregated in the biggest of Lady Leighton's parlors, where she served tea and seed cake and played a parlor game.

Monsieur V wasn't in attendance. Lucy stared at the male guests with such intensity, just in case one had disguised his true appearance beneath cosmetics the way the actors had at the theater, for so long that most likely thought her addled. Unfortunately, everyone seemed to be wearing their genuine faces. None were the man for whom she searched.

Sighing inwardly, Lucy chose a spot at the edge of the room by the window, hoping to be overlooked as she peered outside. It was difficult to do when Charlie insisted on including her in the game.

Movement caught her eye. A figure outside. Was that...Brackley? She turned, surveying the room, only now realizing that she hadn't felt that prickle of awareness indicating his presence. She'd been so focused on finding Monsieur V that she hadn't thought to look for the other man dogging her footsteps.

But why was he out there, in the deteriorating weather, when he should have been in the house with everyone else? When Lucy turned her attention to the window once more, she found Brackley crouching over something near the edge of the property. He stood, surveyed the house, and then walked on.

Just what was he doing? Her instincts buzzed, insisting that this would be well worth uncovering. But first she had to excuse herself from the game.

She sidled closer to Mrs. Vale, murmuring, "I don't feel quite the thing. I think I might lie down for a spell before supper."

A furrow formed between the woman's eyebrows as she glanced at Lucy. "Maybe a walk outside might do you some good."

Lucy nodded. If she wasn't destined to be allowed to sneak off to speak with Brackley herself, taking her chaperone with her was the next best thing. Ever since she'd woken up this morning, Mrs. Vale had kept an unusually close eye on Lucy. Apparently, she hadn't believed Lucy's tale of writing in her notebook instead of attending the ball. Even if it was partially true.

Charlie, seated diagonally, twisted to look over her shoulder. "What are you whispering about?"

"Lucy is feeling a bit off and would like to take a tour of the gardens."

The grounds, was more like it. She'd already thoroughly investigated the gardens and terrace without finding clues to Monsieur V. Brackley, having encountered her there, knew as much. Why had he wanted her to tell him of her findings? So he could thwart her efforts or take them over himself? She still didn't know for which side he played.

What use could he have examining the edge of the property like that? Lucy didn't know, but as Charlie eagerly added her wishes to join them out of doors, Lucy inwardly smiled. One way or another, she was going to discover Brackley's secrets.

ALTHOUGH THE OPEN invitation to Lady Leighton's party would suggest that Monsieur V had influence over her—a guest or a servant perhaps—Alex had been chasing the spymaster's shadow for long enough to know better. Monsieur V was a master at disguise, at blending in to any scenery and blurring the memories of those who encountered him using little more than his words. However, he wouldn't be able to hide in plain sight at this house party; not so long as Lucy was in attendance. For whatever reason, Monsieur V's usual tricks hadn't seemed to work on her. Or so Morgan suspected. And, for all that the man seemed bent on keeping Alex away from Lucy before Alex had given him any cause, Alex didn't think the Duke of Tenwick a fool. He would wager his eyeteeth that Lucy still remembered every detail about the encounter. She was, after all, a novelist. Given the way she'd seemed to revel in the interrogation, paying rapt attention to him despite the air of danger he'd been trying to cultivate, Alex suspected that she made a habit of memorizing moments and conversations to scribble down in that little book of hers.

If Monsieur V couldn't risk attending the party, disguising himself as a servant was equally risky. Lucy could turn down the wrong corridor at the wrong time and find him out. Therefore, the most logical course of action that the spymaster would have taken would be to sneak onto the property while the ball was in full swing to mask his actions.

Never, for a moment, did Alex believe that Monsieur V had gone through the trouble of leaving Lucy the note and instructions only to miss their meeting. The spymaster wanted something from her, even though Alex hadn't yet puzzled out what that something might be. Unless, of course, the fiend hoped to use Lucy against her brother. Would it work? Undoubtedly. Alex had never witnessed a family as close-knit as that of the Graylockes. He and his family certainly hadn't given each other the time of day. In fact, he'd gone out of his way to disappoint his father. Now that both he and Camden were dead, Alex regretted those actions deeply.

Kidnapping Alex and holding him for ransom probably wouldn't have done a damn thing except make his father angrier at him. Capturing the youngest Graylocke sibling, on the other hand... Morgan would stop at nothing to see her safe return.

A small part of him whispered of another possibility, that Lucy was in no danger at all. That she had been meeting with Monsieur V because she was in league with him. A Graylocke, a traitor? He couldn't fathom it. Maybe it was his own folly in falling for a pretty face, but he believed her when she said that she had no prior contact with Monsieur V.

With a sigh, he continued his search of the perimeter of the property, checking for signs of intrusion. The wind, blustering harder and harder throughout the afternoon, cut through his coat. He endeavored to ignore it as he worked. Unfortunately, there were far too many places where Monsieur V might have slipped onto the property unnoticed. A grove of trees approached far too close to the terrace, scarcely fifteen feet away. It would provide cover for someone skilled at concealing himself.

As Alex turned, he spotted the figures of three women striding toward him. *Bollocks.* He recognized Mrs. Vale in the rear, two steps behind the two women whispering with their heads together. Despite the glare he received from the chaperone, he waited to greet the women. Lucy had a gleam in her eye as she steered her friend toward him. The wind tossed the wisps of her hair falling free from her braid. It turned her cheeks pink with vigor.

As the women came within speaking distance, Alex smirked and gave Lucy a full mocking bow, as if he was being presented to the Prince Regent. "Lady Lucy, what an unexpected pleasure. Mrs. Vale, Miss Vale." He inclined his head to each. "You ladies appear rather chilled. Shall I accompany you back into the manor."

Lucy cocked up her chin. If she was trying to look down her nose at him, she would have to grow at least a foot taller. His smirk widened at her attempt at indifference. From the way she'd led the others directly to him, her main purpose in venturing out of doors had been to encounter him. At least, that had certainly become her purpose once she'd spotted him, if it hadn't been before.

Her companion, Miss Vale, crunched her nose and asked, "Have we been introduced?"

Alex fought the urge to glance at her mother. Although he knew Mrs. Vale, mostly by reputation rather than a more personal acquaintance, he had never been introduced to her daughters. Or, come to think of it, to Lucy, either. He'd steered clear of the proper *ton* events as much as possible, yet another source of outrage to his father. Before he'd inherited a title he'd never thought would fall to him, Alex had eschewed polite company in favor of associating with the degenerates and derelicts of Society.

"Forgive me," he answered Miss Vale. "I guessed your identity from your companion." He nodded to Lucy.

He half-expected her to challenge his propriety as well, but instead she neglected to comment on the nature of their association in favor of addressing his previous comment.

"Thank you for your concern, Lord Brackley, but we are not at all cold. In fact, I find the weather quite stimulating."

He met her gaze, struggling to contain his amusement. "Do you?"

Her eyes sparkled with mischief. "I do. That is why you're out here, isn't it, my lord? Enjoying the brisk fresh air?"

"That I am. It is quite stimulating, as you've said."

"There are many delights to be found on a stroll out of doors."

Was she attempting to quiz him on what he'd found? He glanced at the Vales, trying to discern whether or not they caught Lucy's game. Miss Vale was frowning at her friend, though she hadn't released Lucy's arm. Mrs. Vale looked pensive, perhaps even suspicious.

Although Alex didn't want to arouse her suspicions further, he couldn't help but tease Lucy with shreds of the truth. They couldn't speak plainly without the others catching onto their game, but this volley of half-truths couched in polite chatter held a certain challenge.

And Lucy was a worthy opponent. Quick of mind, and quick with a retort.

"Many delights to be found, indeed. What a large property Lady Leighton has."

"Not so large. Tenwick Abbey is two, if not three times the size."

Her companion, Miss Vale, added, "More than that, I think, if you count the lawn."

The comment was innocent enough. She didn't seem to realize that his and Lucy's conversation had a deeper meaning. He offered a smile as he amended, "I meant compared to the size of the household. Tenwick Abbey has many more servants." Seeing as it was a training ground for new spies, to the best of his knowledge, the Tenwick ancestral estate had more servants at any one time than it needed. Most were engaged in activities that had little to do with the estate.

Miss Vale nodded, seemingly accepting that answer. Mrs. Vale, on the other hand, watched with narrowed eyes.

Turning his attention back to Lucy, who struggled

to conceal a smirk and failed, he added, "A household this small must struggle to keep up with the grounds."

Did she understand what he was trying to say? Although perhaps it was imprudent to share the details of his investigation, he found a perverse sort of pleasure in couching his meaning in their innocent chatter.

Lucy's eyes gleamed. Her fingers twitched as if she yearned to reach for her notebook and pencil. "There isn't much in the way of grounds to maintain. The trees encircle it."

"Quite right. They nearly abut the terrace 'round the side there." Without taking his eyes off Lucy, he gestured toward the corner of the manor.

She lifted her eyebrows and pursed her lips. "Such a shame Lady Leighton has no children. It sounds like a marvelous place to play hide and seek."

Alex didn't know for certain whether that had been Monsieur V's point of entry. He abandoned the secret conversation in favor of teasing Lucy outright.

With a grin, he asked, "Were you considering starting up a game? I should warn you, you haven't the faintest chance of going unseen. You're far too noticeable a woman."

From the way she narrowed her eyes, she didn't appreciate the comment. In fact, he suspected she was moments away from resorting to a juvenile retort like sticking out her tongue. The notion of rendering her so incapable of speech made him fight an even bigger smile.

She turned to her companion. "You know, now that I've been out of doors for more than a moment, I think I *am* chilled. Charlie? Are you ready to go inside?"

Alex bit back a laugh. Retreating so easily? They'd barely started. He caught the shrewd look on Mrs. Vale's face and tried to contain himself.

Unlike the previous times when they'd met, he and Lucy were not alone. He wasn't at liberty to act freely with her. If he did, the others might notice the magnetic pull between them. As much as Alex fought to conceal it, he couldn't keep his awareness of her in check. The way a strand of her hair batted against her cheek from the wind. The way her eyes sparkled and her mouth pursed as she spoke. She was beautiful, but that was only the tip of the iceberg to her allure. Her liveliness, her cleverness drew him as much as or more than her beauty.

Not that he could act upon it. Doubly so while under Mrs. Vale's watchful eye. He'd already been warned away from her once.

So he restrained himself as Lucy led the trio back toward the manor. The wind continued to whip at him, sending cold fingers down the collar of his jacket.

He stared after her a moment more before collecting himself and continuing his inspection.

One way or another, he was going to find Monsieur V. And he shouldn't allow himself to get too close to Lucy—because he might need to put her in harm's way in order to do it.

9

*B*rackley was trying to hide something from her, and Lucy was determined to discover what. This afternoon, even after she'd gone inside, he'd remained outdoors. He'd teased her with only a bit of information...if, indeed, that had been information he'd been passing, disguised as banal chitchat. Perhaps she'd read more into it than had been intended. He might simply be an uninspired conversationalist.

In all the other times they'd encountered each other, he hadn't bored her, so she liked to think that he had been trying to communicate with her. That he'd been trying to tell her that Monsieur V had hidden in the forest near to the terrace as he waited for her to arrive for their meeting.

Or had that been where Brackley had lain in wait,

only sneaking around behind her after she'd dallied by the railing?

The surest way to discover what Brackley was hiding was to search his room. Unfortunately, that might also be the surest way to ensure that she be forced to marry him. Despite the sparks of attraction that flew between them, rekindled every time they met, a marriage to Brackley was the very last thing Lucy wanted. Charlie wanted to enjoy her freedom a little longer, and Lucy couldn't blame her. Her experience with her brothers was that they tended to act overprotective of her and tried to shelter her as though she was a child.

Brackley doesn't do that. Lucy's brothers never would have shared information about an ongoing spy mission; they hadn't even told her they were spies. Brackley, on the other hand, had hidden the information in a seemingly innocent conversation. Not only sharing it, but presuming that she was intelligent enough to understand what he was saying.

As thrilling as it was to decipher such information and be let in on the mission for once, that still was no reason to marry him. If Lucy was to search his room for signs of his allegiance, she had best do so undetected. The consequences to her reputation otherwise might prove irreversible.

Gritting her teeth, she tried to keep the agitation

from her body as she slipped onto the staircase leading toward the guests' quarters. Although the guests were otherwise occupied—the men in the library, drinking port and smoking cheroots with Lord Leighton, and the women working on their needlepoint with Lady Leighton in the front parlor—the servants still milled throughout the house. For all Brackley's talk of Lady Leighton keeping a small household, Lucy couldn't seem to step out of a room without encountering someone.

Miraculously, when she reached the top of the stairs, she found the corridor deserted. Her heart hammering, she knew she didn't have much time alone. Smothering the small voice in her head that told her this was a poor idea, she turned away from the women's quarters and strode down the men's. She'd seen Brackley disappear into one of these rooms earlier when the entire party had ventured upstairs to change for supper.

Counting the doors until she found his, she tested the latch and found it unlocked. She slipped into the room and shut the door behind her, pressing her weight against it to keep it closed.

The interior of the room was dark and cold. Clearly, it hadn't been used since before supper. Lucy waited, the blood roaring in her ears and obscuring the sound of any other occupants. No movement stirred that she could see. Slowly, her eyes adjusted and she was able to make out the silhouette of the furniture in the room. The chamber, not much bigger than hers, was crammed with furniture. Was that a candle on the writing desk? After pressing her ear to the door to ensure that no one was coming, she slipped closer to the desk and groped for the item. It was a candle, and a tinderbox, too.

When she lit the candle, the warm orange glow lit the room. She considered what she had to work with and decided that there wasn't much here that would consist of Brackley's personal belongings. The furnishings were provided by Lady Leighton, and therefore were unlikely to contain any hidden compartments. Lucy checked for some anyway, starting in the writing desk before moving on to the drawers in the armoire and the posts of the bed. She had discovered the hidden compartments in Morgan's desk, so she liked to think that if there had been anything to find, she would have done so.

Brackley didn't appear to have used the writing desk at all, but Lucy rifled through his clothing just in case he'd hidden his letters there, instead. If he was corresponding with anyone in the spy network, there was no trace of it.

Just as she finished searching the bed frame for hidden compartments, finding none, the creak of a wooden board out in the corridor caught her ear. Her breath hitched. Had Brackley returned?

Desperate, she searched the room for a hiding place. There weren't many options. What would he do if he found her in here? She still had found no notion of his allegiance, nothing to tell her on which side he resided. For all she knew, he might be working alone.

But if he was, how had he learned the code to read the note she'd received from Monsieur V? And why had he visited Morgan? Though perhaps that *was* due to his title and not his service to his country, after all.

Regardless, Lucy didn't think it boded well for his discovering her in his room. Her heart pounding, she snuffed out the candle, dropped to her belly on the floor, and rolled under the bed. She whisked her skirts out of sight behind her. As the door opened, she held her breath.

Footsteps. The man left the door ajar, letting in some of the light from the corridor. Enough to reflect off his polished black boots as he crept forward. Trying not to make a sound, Lucy adjusted her position to peek beneath the lip of the bed.

It wasn't Brackley. One of Lady Leighton's servants bent over the bed, doing something to the coverlet or pillows. They hadn't been out of order; not to mention, tidying the bed would likely be the maid's domain, not a footman's. What was going on?

Mustering her courage, Lucy dared to peek a bit farther. Her angle didn't allow her a glimpse of the servant's face, but she caught the shape of his physique. Athletic, tall. Could it be Monsieur V? She couldn't catch sight of the man's face to tell for certain. As he stepped back from the bed, she slipped farther into the shadows, hoping not to be caught. His footsteps resonated along the floor as he retreated to the doorway once more. There, he paused to glance out into the hall. When she snuck a glimpse, holding her breath in the hopes that she wouldn't be discovered, she caught sight of his profile.

It was difficult to tell his identity when she could see no more than the shape of his face, but she didn't think the man was Monsieur V—unless he'd cosmetically altered the shape of his face, with padding and such like the actors had used.

The servant shut the door. A moment later, muffled footsteps indicated his departure.

Lucy's limbs went watery with relief. She laid limply beneath the bed as she fought to catch her breath. Her heartbeat thundered in her ears. That had been close.

What had the servant done to the bed, and why? She crawled out from under the bed and stood, first brushing herself off so that she looked presentable again for once she left the room. No one must suspect that she'd spent some time hiding beneath a man's bed. Once she was assured that she was presentable again, she found the tinderbox by feel and used it to light the candle once more.

The bed appeared pristine, the same as it had been before the servant had walked in. But he hadn't come in to straighten it, so what had he been doing? Lucy ran her hands over the coverlet, feeling for something amiss. When she found nothing, she checked beneath the pillows.

A note. She pulled the folded page from beneath the pillow and opened it. It was written in code. The hairs on the back of her neck rose as she examined the page.

This code wasn't the lengthy letter with misspellings. This one, to an observer who didn't know it was a code, would have been gibberish. Did Lucy have the cipher in her notebook? She'd copied quite a few in there from Morgan's desk, thinking that they might come in handy for her book writing. Despite the fact that she'd begged a moment upstairs to fetch her notebook, she always had it in her reticule; that had merely been a plausible excuse. Fishing the little book out, she flipped through the pages, comparing notes with the message laid out on the nightstand. Finally, she found the translation. She decoded the message on the margin of that page with her pencil.

Stay away from L. Graylocke.

Lucy stared at the message, uncomprehending. When the servant had entered Brackley's room, she'd assumed he was Monsieur V. Or, if not the spymaster himself, certainly working for him. But why would the French warn Brackley away from her? It didn't make sense.

Could the servant be employed by Morgan instead? If so, he likely already knew what she was up to. If he didn't come to collect her himself, he would send one of her brothers. She'd hoped that the new baby and the fact that she'd withheld the missive from Lord Strickland might have bought her some time to investigate on her own. Now, she had to wonder.

Giving herself a mental shake, she folded the note once more and laid it beneath Brackley's pillow. After returning the candle to the writing desk and blowing it out, she left his room behind, almost exactly as she had found it.

Unfortunately, her search had raised more questions than it had answered.

10

*L*ucy battled a yawn as she turned down a narrower corridor that wasn't quite as well-decorated as the rest of the house. The walls were plain, no adornment of any kind or any other sort of decoration in niches. Finally, she'd reached the servant's wing of the house. If only she wasn't battling to keep her eyes open after the second night of staying up late with the guests and yet dragging herself out of bed before they rose.

She had work to do, after all. If Monsieur V wasn't among the guests, there was a chance that he had hidden himself among Lady Leighton's servants. As the only person who knew his face, Lucy needed to catch a glimpse of all the servants if she was to find him among them.

That was, if he was still there. He might have fled shortly after she'd missed their meeting two nights ago. While she questioned the servants today, she would have to ask after men who had mysteriously disappeared. Though, to be honest, she hoped that he hadn't fled. If he had, she might have trouble leaving the party to follow him. She had not only accepted, but pressed for an invitation. If she left early, she would arouse the hostess's suspicion—perhaps even incense her. Although Lucy had been willing to risk it if she'd had a notorious criminal in custody, she couldn't put her family's reputation on the line simply to follow a clue. She would have to wait.

Had Monsieur V given up on her when she hadn't arrived for their meeting? She couldn't fathom why he'd wanted to meet with her to begin with. Perhaps he'd try again to make contact, if only she was patient and waited.

Lucy had never been skilled at showing patience. If she couldn't fathom waiting until the spymaster sent her another message, she would go out hunting for him instead—or, at the very least, the man who had infiltrated Brackley's room last night.

Unfortunately, being the sister of a duke had its detriments as well as its benefits. Among the servant class, she found herself shut off by a polite wall. The servants curtsied or bowed, addressed her as *my lady* despite her repeated corrections, and provided her with no useful information. They didn't bar her from their domain but it was clear from the polite masks they wore while in her presence that she was unwelcome.

If no one would tell her what she wanted to know, Lucy would at the very least search for the man she'd seen last night. But, as it turned out, identifying a man from his profile was more difficult than she expected. Although she searched the face of every servant to enter or leave the corridor, she left defeated. The hard-eyed woman who had deflected the bulk of Lucy's inquiries seemed relieved when she gave up.

She'd have to try again later, because quitting was not in Lucy's vocabulary. One way or another, she would find the man she was looking for. Unlike Monsieur V, she knew this man was in the house.

As she turned the corner to return to the guests' quarters—with luck, before Charlie and Mrs. Vale awoke to wonder where Lucy had run off to—Lucy found herself face to face with the very man she was looking for. Not Monsieur V—that would be far too good a stroke of luck—but the spy who had snuck into Brackley's room. Lucy recognized the shape of his nose and chin immediately.

Triumph shone through her as she blocked his

path. The man looked wary as he bowed, tugging on his forelock. "My lady, how may I be of service?"

You can tell me why you infiltrated the room of a peer last night. But no, she already knew the answer to that. He'd done it to deliver the note.

What *did* she want to know? She hadn't stopped to think past finding the man. Now that she had him in her sights—in fact, at her mercy, considering that no other servants or guests populated this corridor for the moment—she realized that she had no idea what information she wanted to draw out of the man. It would help if she knew for whom he worked. If he was her brother's man, then she likely couldn't use him at all. If, on the other hand, his allegiance belonged to Monsieur V, she might be able to extract a clue as to the spymaster's whereabouts.

How did she discover the allegiance of a stranger without him realizing that was what she searched for? If he *did* work for Morgan, she didn't want her brother to hear that she had caught on to his underling. Her brothers seemed determined to treat her as though she was too fragile and empty-headed to have learned about their involvement in Britain's spy network. They wouldn't be happy to hear otherwise. Better they learn of it *after* she'd proven that she could handle the rigors of spying.

Donning her sweetest smile and batting her

eyelashes, she tried to draw the information out of the man by flirting. Men always felt gratified when a woman paid them extra attention, especially men approaching their fifties, like him. Lucy played to the weakness she'd observed in other men as she attempted to pry the information out of him.

"Have I seen you around the guest wing?"

His expression hardened. "I doubt that, my lady. My duties confine me to the ground floor."

Lucy bit back a smirk as she stepped closer. She'd gotten him to admit that he shouldn't have been in that area of the house to begin with. Now, how to coax him to tell her why?

What was it that Lord Strickland's messenger had said to Lucy, the code phrase to identify her as an ally? She fought not to frown as she recalled it. Her fingers itched to check her book, but she couldn't do that in front of him. Instead, she flipped the pages in her mind's eye until she thought she might remember.

"Britain is cold."

Was it Britain or England? Oh, drat! He looked confused. It must have been England.

The echo of booted footsteps bounded down the corridor a moment before a man latched onto her elbow. "Lady Lucy, what a pleasure to see you awake so early in the morning."

Without paying any attention to the servant at all,

Brackley towed her down the corridor. When he stopped midway, he continued to hold her elbow as he stared over her head. When she glanced over her shoulder, she was just in time to catch the spy hurrying out of sight around the corner.

Blast! How long would it be before she found him again? Let alone without her chaperone so she could speak freely?

She turned to glare at Brackley.

Before she could say a word, he said dryly, "It seems you make a habit of rising early."

"As do you," she bit off.

He smirked. "It appears early mornings do little to sweeten your temper. I hear a cup of tea does wonders to brighten the day."

If she'd had a cup of tea at that moment, she might have upended it in his lap. He was deliberately trying to nettle her. More so, he was having *fun* doing so!

Although there was no one else in the corridor, she stepped closer and lowered her voice. If she didn't make an attempt to bridle her annoyance, she feared their conversation would evolve into a shouting match.

"You had no right to interrupt," she snapped. "That was a private conversation."

He cocked an eyebrow. "A private conversation with a servant?"

Lucy was friends with some servants. The

Tenwick gardener, Rocky, for instance. And she was friendly towards others, such as Bess, her middle-aged lady's maid. Nothing precluded her from having a conversation with someone.

"Yes. Do you have a problem with that?"

His second eyebrow rose to join the first. "Frankly, I'm surprised you do not. I was taught that it would mean the devastation of a young lady's reputation to be found alone with a man—any man—not related to her."

Lucy fought the urge to roll her eyes. "He's a servant." It wasn't as though Morgan would force her to marry a servant, even if she'd been caught in a more compromising position than a mere conversation. No, she would more likely be married off to one of her peers.

If someone caught her speaking alone with *Brackley*, on the other hand...

She narrowed her eyes and clenched her fists to keep from jabbing her finger at him. "I was safer with him than I am with you."

His smile turned wolfish. That rakehell enjoyed putting a woman's reputation in danger, didn't he? It was part of the thrill for him. Lucy refused to play his game.

She crossed her arms. "Thank you for your concern, but I believe I'll be the judge of my associates."

"Associates like the one you meant to meet two nights ago?"

She smiled up at him sweetly. "I don't know what you're talking about. I spent the night with you, remember?"

The playful look on his face fell into something more serious. "I recall." His gaze dropped to her mouth before he brought it back to her eyes.

In a light voice, he added, "Do you have anything you'd care to share about your morning?"

"Other than spending it with you yet again?"

He teased, "You really should be more discerning about your companions."

"Indeed. You made me miss a very important appointment." Lucy might even call it pivotal. If she wasn't able to pick up Monsieur V's trail…

She would. She had to. This wasn't only about proving to her brothers that she could be every bit as clever as them. She was the best person, perhaps the only person who could see this criminal to justice.

If Brackley stopped getting in her way. Was he doing it on purpose? She didn't have anything to share about the investigation, but even if she had, perhaps she would do better to keep it to herself. If he was keeping her away from Monsieur V on purpose, he would use anything she told him to stop her from catching the spymaster.

The scoundrel smirked. "I made you miss an appointment with whom?"

He knew very well whom. Either he was working for the man or he had intercepted Lucy's message and thought to go in her place.

Personally, she didn't think the dress Monsieur V had insisted the recipient wear would look very flattering on Brackley.

"My lover," Lucy lied, since apparently this morning they were going to dance around the truth.

His smile grew. "You're a very poor liar, Lady Lucy."

She hadn't been trying. "Perhaps you're bad at reading people," she countered.

He shrugged, unconcerned. "Very well. You were meeting with a lover. What would you have done with said lover if you had kept the appointment? Kissed him?"

Kiss a notorious traitor? Lucy had been face to face with him once—not that she'd known his identity at the time—and she hadn't been the least bit tempted. The thought of kissing the man she conjured in her mind's eye, Monsieur V, held little appeal for personal reasons. But for her book... How thrilling it would be to kiss a traitor! She wouldn't be able to describe it properly unless she did it.

And Brackley... although he may not be a traitor

himself, he might be in league with one. He was dangerous, rakish. If Lucy wanted to learn what it felt like to kiss someone she shouldn't, he might do just as well. In fact, considering the sparks that flared to life under her skin whenever he looked at her, he might do even better.

Before she thought better of it, she leaned up on her tiptoes, gripped him by the back of the neck, and kissed him. As her body flared to life, she surrendered to the kiss, savoring it and committing every last detail to memory.

he Duke of Tenwick was going to kill Alex. Rip him limb from limb as he stared with those colder-than-ice eyes. But at that moment, as Lucy's warm mouth brushed over his, Alex couldn't bring himself to care. He could never kiss her again, but he would damn well enjoy it now.

Lucy Graylocke kissed like she processed every new experience; with eagerness and meticulousness, as if going over every detail and committing it to memory to write down later. So Alex gave her something to write about.

He pulled her flush against him, splaying his hand in the small of her back to hold her to him. He deepened the kiss, conquering her with lips and tongue. The taste of her, a hint of sweet like she'd indulged in a cup of chocolate before setting out on this mad and dangerous investigation, made him lightheaded. How long had it been since he'd lost himself to a woman's touch? And none of them compared to the heady kiss of a woman he shouldn't have.

A year ago, before Camden had died, he would have taken what he'd wanted without regret. He also would have been drawing as much negative attention to him as he could manage, creating scandal after scandal to cause his father more grief. Camden, the golden boy, had tried to reason with him more than once. To convince him to do right by his family.

Unfortunately, it had taken their deaths to convince Alex of the sensibility of Camden's advice. Since that day, he'd sworn off his wild ways, rededicating his life to finishing what his brother had started. In other words, finding Monsieur V and seeing that the heinous man got what he deserved. Although his reputation had served as a cover for several spy missions, Alex hadn't drank more than a glass of spirits, hadn't gambled when not on mission, and hadn't so much as looked at a woman for his own pleasure.

Not until Lucy, at least. Knowing he couldn't have her even if he allowed himself to want her didn't seem to suppress his desires. If anything, it made the urge to possess her even stronger. As he kissed her, stoking their passions until she fisted her hands in his hair, the pinpricks of pain telling him that he made her every bit as wild as she made him. He longed to unleash his passion, to lose himself in the pleasure of her kiss. Every bold stroke of her tongue against his tested his limits.

When a rhythmic clicking wormed its way into his senses, he thought for a moment that it was the beat of his heart. No. That sounded like...footsteps?

Hell and damnation, he was kissing Lucy in the middle of the bloody corridor, where anyone could happen upon them! As he broke the kiss, she swayed toward him as if hoping for more. He stepped back and watched her eyelashes flutter as she opened her eyes, confused.

Then she, too, registered the footsteps. Alarm crossed her face and she jumped back.

They didn't say a word. Rather, they locked gazes and, by unspoken agreement, turned and dashed for separate exits. Lucy slipped into the nearest room. Alex strolled down the corridor toward the approaching footsteps, hoping to keep whoever they belonged to busy for long enough for Lucy to escape. He ran his fingers through his hair, trying to tame it back into place after Lucy's eager response. He hoped the evidence of their kiss wasn't marked on his face.

The owner of the footsteps turned out to be a plain-faced young maid. She paid him no mind aside from dipping a quick curtsey as she stepped out of his path. Once he passed her and turned the corner, he lingered near the junction as he calmed his fiercely-pounding heart.

That had been foolish. Beyond foolish, in fact. British spies, all reporting to Morgan, riddled London. It wasn't such a stretch to imagine that he might have eyes inside Lady Leighton's country estate as well. If he and Lucy had been witnessed, Alex might be on his way to a noose—whether the parson's noose or some other, he couldn't imagine. Morgan had been quite forbidding in cautioning Alex to keep away from his sister.

He wasn't the only one. Aside from her chaperone, Mrs. Vale, who had apparently been warned by Morgan though Alex couldn't fathom why, Alex had received a baffling note last night. Why would Monsieur V care whether or not Alex spent time with Lucy? Then again, Alex hadn't yet reasoned out how Lucy had known to receive the initial letter from Monsieur V at a secluded costume shop, nor why the spymaster had singled her out. There was something more going on, but he couldn't figure out what, precisely. If she was telling the truth—and with her guilelessness, Alex couldn't fathom believing other-wise—then she had no inkling of why the spymaster had targeted her, either.

Or why he appeared to be as protective of her as her brothers. The coded message he'd found beneath his pillow last night could be from no one else. A British spy would have sent a different code.

Upon finding it, Alex had burned with anger and frustration. Not at the note's contents—although it didn't bode well for the blackguard to be taking such an interest in Lucy—but at the fact that Monsieur V had been in his room. Not being on official assignment from Morgan, Alex had brought no sensitive material with him to the house party, but the fact that his privacy had been violated in such a way made his blood boil. Monsieur V was taunting him, toying with him as much as he was with Lucy. Alex didn't know if the spymaster was aware of the festering hatred Alex harbored for him, but this warning did little to dispel that feeling.

Lying in bed last night, Alex had imagined Monsieur V standing there, over the mattress, close enough for Alex to strangle had he been there. Logically, he didn't believe that the spymaster had left the note himself, but that didn't stop Alex from entertaining the fantasy. Alex had mulled over the information as he'd lain awake, staring at the ceiling. If Monsieur V hadn't entered Alex's room to leave the note, then someone else in the house must have done it. Someone who had access to the guest wing.

Only one man, the aging Earl of Euston, had been absent among the guests during the time when the note must have been left. Unable to sleep, Alex had risen early to keep watch for when the man, a known early riser, departed his room.

Alex had followed him to the servants' wing of the house, only to be blindsided by Lucy's presence. The moment he'd seen her alone with a man, albeit a servant—and flirting, no less—Alex had forgotten his initial reason for venturing to this part of the house. Even now, he had to fight the urge to find Lucy and ensure that she found her way to the safety of her chaperone. If a notorious traitor was showing undue interest in her, the very last thing she should be doing was venturing out alone.

By will alone, he managed not to turn down the corridor in search for her. Instead, he prowled the servants' wing, hoping that Euston might still be around. If Alex had lost him, he might have to wait until tomorrow to learn what the old bloke did every morning. He certainly didn't care to be among the guests much.

A woman's giggle bubbled from a room farther down the corridor. Frowning, Alex quickened his step. The giggle didn't sound familiar, but his mind jumped to Lucy all the same. As movement caught his eye from the shadow of the servant's stair, he paused. He closed the distance slowly, trying not to draw attention to himself as he searched out the occupants.

A broad smile capping his jowls, Euston towed the giggling maid up the steps to the floor above. There it was, then. The man was a randy womanizer, not a spy.

Then who had left the message in Alex's room? A servant? If so, Alex had no means of tracking their movements after the fact.

He'd never been very good at admitting defeat and moving on, not even when he knew he should.

He arranged to find himself alone in the company of one of the maids. He chose a plain-faced young woman, hoping she would be flattered at the attentions of a marquess and he could charm the information out of her.

Not that there was much information to be had. He knew that even as he aimed his best smile at the utterly forgettable young woman. "Do you happen to know who was up in my room yesterday? I seemed to have misplaced my favorite cravat and I wondered if someone might have taken it for laundering or some such."

A bald lie. Not only did he not care a whit what cravat he wore, but it would be his valet's duty to see it washed, not one of the maids in the household he visited.

Nevertheless, he hoped that by probing, he would

gain some insight into who might have ventured near his room.

The maid curtsied, meek as a mouse. "The guest quarters fall under my domain, my lord, but I assure you I haven't touched your cravat."

"Are you certain? I had it laid out near the foot of my bed before I went to supper." As he delivered the lie, he studied her face for signs of deception. If she'd been in his room while he was away yesterday evening, she would have known that he'd done no such thing.

She didn't widen her eyes in surprise or narrow them with suspicion. In fact, she barely batted an eyelash. Inclining her head and giving another little curtsey, the maid informed, "Then I'm quite certain no one can have touched it, my lord. Our duties are finished by that time of the night. Could your valet have misplaced it, my lord?"

Despite the fact that he could have her reprimanded for accusing his servant of wrongdoing, she delivered the statement with a straight face. He suppressed a sigh at the evidence that he wouldn't be getting any information out of her.

"He's adamant that he hasn't. If you happen to learn of anyone who was in my room and might know, I would be grateful if you'd let me know."

"Of course, my lord." She looked up through the

veil of her eyelashes. "Is there anything else I can do for you, my lord?"

Was she trying to entice him into a more lecherous bent? She'd have better luck with Euston. Alex's mouth still throbbed from Lucy's kiss. He still tasted her on his tongue. If he was going to misbehave with anyone, it would be her.

After all, she had initiated the kiss. She might be open to another. Why *had* she kissed him? He'd been teasing her, but not flirting, exactly. However compelling he found her, magnetic with the sparkle in her eye and always armed with her ready wit, he knew he couldn't have her.

Apparently, she hadn't been told the same thing. Running his hands through his hair, he realized that the maid was staring at him, waiting for him to say something. He'd forgotten what she'd asked. "Thank you," he said simply, hoping that solved the matter. He turned on his heel and strode away before he made a bigger fool of himself.

He needed to stop thinking about Lucy. The taste of her kiss, the feel of her body pressed against him, he needed to wash it from his mind. If he didn't find a way to flush her from his thoughts, he might find that Monsieur V had slipped through his fingers for good.

And he could never let that happen.

12

*A*lthough Lucy's stint in the servants' wing had largely been unhelpful to her mission, she had learned that no servants were believed to have gone missing. At least, not that any of the staff had mentioned. They had been cold, evasive, and as a whole, unwilling to confide in her. Having no other recourse, and not having glimpsed the man whom she sought, Lucy had no choice but to believe that Monsieur V had not hidden himself among the servants in order to meet with her. Since he wasn't among the guests, either, that meant that he had to have come to the house from outside—perhaps, as Brackley had suggested, through the grove of trees abutting the terrace.

The thought of Brackley conjured the memory of his kiss. She'd used up the last few precious pages in her notebook describing that kiss in lingering detail, bringing it to life as she would in her novel when she returned home. The way her pulse had pounded, the pressure of his lips and stroke of his tongue, she'd committed it all to memory.

The problem was, she wanted more. This was supposed to have been for research only, but if he attempted to kiss her again, she feared that she would let him. The passion between them had been nothing short of incendiary, lighting her in ways she hadn't thought possible. Now she understood better how a strong woman like Phil had allowed herself to be swept up in Morgan's orbit and put herself in such pain to deliver him a child.

Lucy understood. That still didn't mean that she would succumb to the same weakness. Certainly not with Brackley. She didn't even know if the man was loyal to Britain!

What should trouble her far more than Brackley and his questionable allegiance was the whereabouts of Monsieur V. Regardless of the way Brackley's mouth had felt against hers—and the impossibility of succumbing again—the spymaster was still at large. She forced her focus to return to him.

If he wasn't among the staff or guests, then he must keep lodgings somewhere. They were over a day's ride from London. He had to sleep at some point. The closest place to do so would likely be the inn in the village Lucy had driven through on her way here. At her estimate, it didn't reside more than an hour's walk away. Perhaps less, if she walked briskly.

Gathering Charlie and Mrs. Vale, Lucy proposed just such a walk. Charlie was always willing to find delight in a new shop, even one in a small village, and agreed readily. However, once the three women had collected their pelisses and bonnets, Lucy's companions balked on the doorstep.

The day wasn't the most inviting. Clouds frosted the sky, darkening to a gloomy gray that promised rain to come. Although no rain appeared to have fallen yet today, the air was heavy, humid, and damp.

"Perhaps we ought to stay in and try again tomorrow," Charlie suggested, her voice small.

Blast! If Lucy waited another day, her already cooling trail toward Monsieur V's whereabouts might have turned entirely cold. She was already two days behind him, having dallied too long searching the house and being detained by the activities arranged by the hostess. If the day were any more pleasant, it was entirely possible that Lady Leighton would already have planned something for the guests and Lucy might never make it to the village.

"I can't stay in this stuffy house any longer," she informed. "I need a walk. Maybe one of the ladies' maids..."

"Perhaps I may be of service," Brackley said as he joined them in the entryway. He didn't wear his outerwear, but as he raised his hand to the butler, it was quickly produced. He shrugged it on as he added, "It would be my pleasure to accompany you ladies wherever you may care to go."

Lucy locked eyes with Brackley. The awareness of their kiss crackled in the air between them. Her mouth tingled with the memory. Could the Vales read it on her face?

When Brackley smiled, the tingle spread from her lips into her extremities. She curled her toes in her shoes.

"Now, where will I be escorting you ladies?"

"To the village," Lucy said decisively.

Her answer earned her a sharp look from Charlie, who sighed and tilted her head up to the clouds. "I hope it doesn't rain."

"You can stay here if you'd rather," Lucy said.

Charlie made a face and turned to examine Brackley. "I'll go with you."

"Splendid." To be honest, Lucy did feel a bit

relieved. If she and Brackley were alone, with the memory of their kiss this morning hanging between them, she didn't know what she'd say. He probably wouldn't understand why she'd done it. He would make some sly comment about her research or her book. The men with whom she'd associated in the past all tended to do that, to make themselves feel clever.

Never mind that most of the things she did, she did only in the name of research. Brackley... Very well, once that had started, it had become very pleasurable indeed. But she no longer had the excuse of research to hide behind. Their kiss couldn't be repeated.

Surely he knew that, even if he had returned the kiss with passion. She'd had the name of research to hide behind. Why hadn't he stopped her?

"Shall we set off, then?"

His deep voice shivered through her. She looked away, afraid of what he or the others might read in her expression should she look at him.

He didn't offer his arm as they descended the steps. Did he not want to single her out? Or was he trying to put as much distance between them as possible since their kiss in the corridor? She wasn't likely to demand he propose over something as innocent as a single kiss. Especially when she'd initiated it.

Nevertheless, she matched his aloof demeanor as they strolled along the rut-marred dirt road toward the village. The conversation was tense and uninspired. When the houses sprang into view, Lucy released an inner sigh of relief.

As they came abreast of the cluster of houses, Lucy searched for anything that might resemble an inn. A row of buildings squashed together each held a wooden sign over the door with a pictorial depiction of what the interior held. Lucy counted a milliner, a shoemaker, and a general store. The sign depicting a frothy pint of ale must be the inn.

Charlie tugged at her arm and pointed to the row of shops. "That looks like a milliner's! Let's go see what it has to offer."

Lucy cast a longing look at the inn. "Are you certain you wouldn't like to eat first?"

Charlie made a face. "We just ate before we left."

With the faint trace of a smirk, Brackley inclined his head. "I fear I'll be of no use in a milliner's shop. I'll await you over there at the inn."

Lucy glared at him. That scoundrel! He knew that was where Lucy aimed to go. He might have taken her side and tried to convince the group to venture there. Instead, he flashed her a look of mixed triumph and challenge as he departed. Lucy watched him go, balling her fists.

When she returned her attention to her companions, Charlie was frowning.

Lucy forced a bright smile. "Let's go to the milliner's."

Charlie stopped her from moving forward with a restraining hand on her arm. Leaning closer, the blonde whispered, "Have you gone mad?"

Lucy frowned. She flitted her gaze between her friend and Mrs. Vale, who watched the street as if she hadn't heard. Given the way she canted her head, she was listening to every word.

Returning her attention to her dear friend, Lucy shot back, "I don't know what you're trying to say."

When she jerked her head toward the inn, Charlie's blonde curls bobbed. "Him. Why are you courting his attention?"

Had she not been involved in the same conversation as Lucy during the way here? Lucy and Brackley had barely spoken to one another directly on the way here. Although they'd each contributed to the conversation about the weather of late and their opinions about Lady Leighton's house party thus far, she hadn't directly answered anything he'd said.

"I am not courting his attention."

"No?" Charlie raised her eyebrows and pursed her lips. "Then why did you ask him along?"

"I didn't ask him along. He invited himself!"

"And you encouraged him by accepting."

Lucy gritted her teeth. He had been a means to an

end, that was all. And right now, at that very moment, he might be inside gleaning information that she should be present for—or else warning his treacherous employer that she was on her way. Arguing about it was losing her time!

"It was the polite thing to do," she said simply, not quite looking the Vales in the eye. "Next time, I promise to decline."

Mrs. Vale harrumphed, but added nothing beyond that disbelieving sound.

"I won't accept," Lucy insisted, looking from one woman to the other.

"Good," Charlie quirked a brow. "You know of his reputation."

"Of course I do." Everyone in the *ton* knew of the notoriety of the new Marquess of Brackley. The gossips collectively held their breath as they awaited a hasty marriage when he got some poor woman enceinte. It hadn't happened yet, but there were likely bets on when that inevitable day would occur.

That dangerous reputation of bewitching women was precisely why it had been so thrilling to be held by him, to be kissed. He certainly knew how to bring a woman's body to life. It had been the perfect fodder for her book.

Charlie persisted, "Then you know the harm that he can do to your reputation."

Why was everyone suddenly so concerned over her reputation? It seemed to be the only thing people spoke to her about these days. She was more than a sacrificial virgin.

"I'm not courting his attention," she repeated, for all the good it would do. "We barely even spoke on the way here."

"Exactly."

Charlie's eyes glittered with triumph, though Lucy didn't know what about her sentence had led her friend to think she'd won this argument.

"You always contribute to a conversation. You make a point of answering whomever you speak to, to present a gracious representation of the Graylocke family. Didn't you tell that to me once?" Charlie shook her head. "Since Lord Brackley is a marquess, you'd think it would be more important for you to represent the Graylocke family in a gracious light, no?"

Lucy narrowed her eyes. "Like you said, he has a black reputation." She bit off her words.

"He does." Charlie hiked her chin up by an inch. "Did something happen between you? You both seem to avoid speaking or looking at one another."

"Maybe we don't like each other."

Charlie scoffed. "The truth, Lucy. The other day when you were absent from the ball, did you sneak off to meet with him? And what about last night when you left the parlor?"

Lucy swallowed, hardening her expression before she answered. "I was in my room, writing. You found me there, remember? And last night, I forgot my notebook in my room. You know I don't do needlework. I needed to get it."

Lies, all of it. But she willed her closest friend to believe them, anyway. For all that she had found herself in Brackley's company that first night, she hadn't deliberately set out to do it.

Charlie didn't seem convinced. She touched Lucy's arm. "I just don't want you to get hurt. He isn't the sort of man who cares which woman keeps him company. You're a challenge, nothing more."

"I'm not even that," Lucy said firmly. "Lord Brackley and I are nothing to each other. Barely even acquaintances. Your worries are noted, but unnecessary."

This time, she seemed to get through to Charlie. After the young woman exchanged a wary glance with her mother, she murmured, "Very well. Let's see this milliner's shop."

Lucy relaxed. "Yes. Let's." She didn't dare bring up the possibility of going to the inn afterward. Charlie would only see it as an eagerness to find herself in Brackley's company once more.

She would have to find another way to slip free of the Vales. Because if there was one thing Lucy knew for certain, it was that she would not—could not—give up her search to find Monsieur V.

ALEX FELT the lingering effects of Lucy's hot stare piercing between his shoulder blades long after the door to the inn and tavern had swung closed behind him. He paused to get his bearings, looking around the surprisingly crowded common room. The neat array of tables were nearly all filled, with only a chair here and there yet unclaimed, and several stools along the counter were filled as well. A serving maid a few years older than him expertly navigated between the tables, pausing to deliver a drink or take an order for another. Despite the amount of people vying for her attention, the serving maid maintained a cool head as she meticulously traversed the length of the common room in a winding path and made her way back to the counter once more.

Although he needed to secure someone's attention, he didn't think that she would have the loosest tongue if he were to try to take her away from her duties. Instead, he strolled to the counter and claimed a stool near the end, searching for someone else. The owner, perhaps.

A man near double his age with a thick mustache approached and asked, "What can I do you for, my lord?" Even when Alex didn't announce his heritage, he was often chosen out of a crowd unless he took pains to alter his manner of dress and appearance. In his case, he hoped the extra attention would help him.

"A pint, please. Your best."

He slid a few shillings onto the counter and the man, presumably the innkeeper, left to find his drink. When he returned, Alex took a sip from the mug. As he set it down, he commented, "I didn't expect to find you quite so full."

"I can vacate a table for you if you'd like, my lord."

Alex waved away the suggestion. "I'm happy to sit here. Is it usually this busy?"

The man's mustache bobbed as he nodded. "Every year at this time, my lord. With spring upon us, we have renewed interest in folks traveling to London for business or pleasure."

Alex took another sip of the ale. It was just bitter enough to meet with his approval. "Do many people stop to spend the night as well, then?"

Another nod. "I'm afraid we're near full up, but if you've an inkling to stay the night, I can see that there's a room made available for you."

"I'm staying at Lady Leighton's manor, but thank you for the offer."

"Ah," the man said, "part of that house party, then."

"Yes. I've come to meet an acquaintance, actually. A tall fellow, about six feet, with brown hair and an athletic build."

The innkeeper looked dubious. "You just described near half my patrons. Can you be any more specific? What's this fellow's name?"

I haven't the faintest idea. Monsieur V had a wide array of aliases. Most recently, before he'd fled London, it had been Benjamin Faulkner. Alex didn't think the man would be bold enough—or foolish enough—to use that moniker again.

"I'm afraid I only met the man the other night at Lady Leighton's ball."

If only that were true. At least then he would have been able to describe him better. Even though most people who crossed paths with Monsieur V mysteriously forgot the details of his face—including several British spies and the sole high-level French spy they'd managed to catch and question—Alex would feel far better if he'd come face to face with his nemesis. After all, Alex wasn't likely to forget the face of a man who had destroyed his family. In fact, if he'd met with Monsieur V that night on Lady Leighton's terrace, the traitor wouldn't be alive to use the eerie mind-tricks he employed. One way or another, Alex would put an end to the destruction he caused.

"Is there anyone who has spent a particularly long time at the inn recently?" After all, if Monsieur V was still around, he would have needed to remain nearby for long enough to set up his plan and monitor its progress. He might even be lurking in this very room.

Alex surreptitiously glanced around as the innkeeper answered. As the man had said, he found too many men who might loosely fit Monsieur V's description.

"I'm afraid not. It's been folks stopping by on their way to London, as I've said."

Damn and blast! He needed Lucy. She would be able to tell for certain whether or not Monsieur V lurked beneath their very noses. He took another swig of his ale as he wracked his brain for anything that might lead to the reveal of the spymaster's whereabouts.

As he lost himself in thought, the door to the inn opened. He glanced over and nearly choked on his ale as Lucy strolled into the common room. He waited, but she shut the door behind her quickly. Her chaperones did not miraculously appear. That woman had a singular talent for finding herself alone in places she should probably not be alone. Although the common room seemed innocent enough, if the wrong gossip spotted her here without escort, her reputation would be tarnished.

Not that she seemed to care a whit whether people thought her angelic or not. Keeping an eye on her, he sipped from his mug.

Lucy paused to get her bearings. She scanned the common room, but must not have seen Monsieur V there, because her attention didn't linger until she reached Alex. Her eyes narrowed and a smirk lifted one corner of her mouth. She seemed pleased to have found him. What, precisely, had she thought he would be doing?

She traipsed up to him and claimed the vacant stool next to him. She took a moment to rearrange her skirts before she pulled the notebook out of her reticule and fished the pencil out after. Did she go anywhere without those two objects? As she started to flip through the book, she hailed the innkeeper with a hand.

"What can I do for you, miss?"

Apparently, whereas Alex appeared lordly, Lucy didn't show her ducal heritage. Alex fought not to smile. He took another sip of his ale, thinking to watch her at play before he interrupted. She hadn't even asked what he'd already learned. Did she not trust him to tell her the truth?

"I'm looking for a man," Lucy began.

The innkeeper glanced toward Alex. Hesitantly, he said, "I don't know if I'll be able to help with your search. As I told my lord here, we've been busy of late. No shortage of men passing through."

Upon finding the right page, she smoothed the notebook and turned it toward the older man. The two pages comprised of densely-packed notes, indecipherable at first glance due to the shorthand she used. A symbol that looked a bit like a windmill rested beneath an amateur pencil sketch of a man's face.

Alex held his breath. Had she committed Monsieur V's face down on paper? Why hadn't Morgan mentioned this, used this? Unless she'd kept it to herself. But why would she do that? He believed her when she said she wasn't working for him. If she'd known that she knew the face of a notorious criminal—had, in fact, drawn it—then shouldn't she have given that information to her brother? Morgan would have circulated it to the spies searching for Monsieur V. Alex could have had him in his sights weeks ago.

He swallowed thickly around the lump in his throat.

"Have you seen this man?" Lucy asked.

Although it was difficult to memorize the sketch upside-down, he did his best. The drawing wasn't completed by an expert touch, that much he could tell from the lines and poor shading, but it was a damn sight better than he could have done. Lucy had a talent, one she likely didn't foster often or she might have been more accomplished at it.

The innkeeper lifted the notebook and turned it from side to side. "Hard to tell. As I said, any number of men come in here." He squinted, then passed the notebook back to Lucy once more.

As she turned it in Alex's direction, he took the opportunity to study the figure more closely. The set of the eyes, the thickness of the eyebrows, the nose and mouth, the shape of the jaw. How accurate was the sketch? Even if it wasn't exact, he had a much better idea of the man for whom they searched.

In fact, he probably didn't even need Lucy's assistance anymore. If he could identify Monsieur V himself, there was no need to involve her in more danger than she already put herself in. Then again, for some unfathomable reason, Monsieur V seemed to have developed enough of an attachment to her to warrant warning Alex away.

"The sketch looks a bit like a gent who stayed here a few nights. He left this morning, though."

Lucy's face fell. "Thank you for your time."

"Is there anything else I can get you, miss?"

Lucy shook her head. She spun on the stool, looking glum. Her eyelashes formed crescents on her pale cheeks. When she lifted her gaze to meet Alex's, her eyes were hard, glittering. Although they hadn't discovered Monsieur V's whereabouts, she didn't look likely to give up the search.

Neither would Alex. There had to be another clue.

13

"*I* missed something. What did I miss?"
Lucy slid the book back onto the shelf
with perhaps a touch more force than necessary. She
immediately winced and checked to see that it was
undamaged. Once assured that the spine, cover, and
pages were all in pristine shape, she replaced it on the
shelf. Gently, this time.

Only then did she allow herself a frustrated sigh.
She balled her fists, her fingernails digging crescents
into her palms. What had she missed?

Monsieur V had left a very specific message for a
very specific person—her—in a place other people
hadn't known to look. The only reason that Lucy had
known to find that particular costume maker had been
because she had been in Monsieur V's presence. That

message had led her here, where she hadn't come face to face with him again and it appeared as though he had given up on the possibility that she would. He wasn't among the servants or guests and he was no longer in the neighboring village. At her best guess, he had returned to London.

Which meant that she had missed her chance.

Lucy shook her head as she perused what else Lord Leighton's library had to offer. Thus far, he had seemed to have an interest in horticulture. Thanks to her brother, Giddy, Lucy knew far more on that topic than she would ever find useful. She hoped to find a thrilling work of fiction, something that would take her mind off her debacle—and the fact that she might have made a mistake that would cost her the glory of capturing the spymaster.

As she ran her finger along the spines of the books, her mind wandered once more. As much as she yearned to hasten back to London and start the search anew, she couldn't simply leave Lady Leighton's house party. It would be the height of rudeness. Not to mention that Charlie and Mrs. Vale were already suspicious about her motives for attending the house party, after they'd found her in her room on the opening night. Now Lucy was squirreling herself away from the guests, hiding out in the library instead. She was certain to hear of it later, when she rejoined her chaperone. If she were to leave the party and return to London, Mrs. Vale would certainly wonder why she had bothered to secure an invitation in the first place. Lucy had enough trouble sneaking away without her chaperone keeping an even closer eye on her than usual.

So, with a sigh, she continued to peruse the titles and resigned herself to days of socializing without the thrilling mystery of unearthing a French spymaster to keep her entertained. Seeing as she was a guest, she couldn't even continue working on her book. She'd left the rough draft in London, in any case.

Lucy finished reading each of the spines—more horticulture books—and started to turn away. Something niggled at her, like a word at the tip of her tongue that she couldn't quite think of. She turned back and ran her finger quickly along the shelf. She paused at the second to last book.

Lilium. That meant lily, didn't it? She nibbled on her lower lip as she tried to recall why that flower in particular caught her interest. She preferred tulips, personally, but there was something about a lily. She ran her finger up and down the spine, leather-bound but dyed to a deep purple. A purple lily...

Her heart skipped a beat as she remembered the last time she had seen someone with a purple lily. Monsieur V had twirled one between his fingers as he spoke, over and over again. It had been a bit mesmerizing, the way the curve of the flower had went around and around.

Mesmerizing, but ultimately unimportant. It was probably just a coincidence that she now found a book about lilies that happened to have a purple cover.

Although...purple was a far from common cover for a book. When she'd gone to the costume shop, she had at first thought it to be a coincidence that had led her there as well. But it hadn't been, had it? No, Monsieur V had arranged for a pivotal message to be left with the tailor.

Could he have done the same thing with the book?

Careful not to dislodge anything, Lucy eased the book from its slot on the shelf. Just in case, she pulled out the books to either side, shook them out, and ran her hand over the wood shelf between to ensure that the book hadn't left anything behind. She replaced the other two books and picked up the purple one.

The cover gleamed with gold lettering, proclaiming the title in Latin. When Lily opened the book, the very first image, set just inside the cover opposite the title page, happened to be of a purple lily.

That had to be more than mere coincidence. Was the book a code? A cipher? Had Monsieur V scribbled on one of the pages for her to see? Frowning, Lucy flipped through the pages one at a time, carefully examining the margins of each page and trying to decide if there were any underlined or altered words.

When she reached partway through the book, it fell open to reveal a small folded note. Lucy smirked. She thumbed open the note.

Numbers, in sets of three. In fact, the first number of the first set was the very page she was open to. On a hunch, she counted down the line number and then moved over to the appropriate word in the line. It couldn't be so simple, could it?

She fished out her pencil and tried decoding the note that way. By the time she was finished with the sets of numbers, she had a legible note.

Water garden. Nine to more old eve.

She frowned at the message. Perhaps it wasn't as legible as she'd hoped. Though, given the book, perhaps the options were limited. Nibbling on her lower lip she tried to decipher the note further. If, in fact, that had been the code, "water garden" could mean a pond. Was there a pond on Lady Leighton's property?

Or—wait. Perhaps it meant water in the garden. A fountain. Lady Leighton had a fountain in her garden, a rather distinctive one, in fact.

Nine to more old eve.

Nine o'clock tomorrow evening? That would likely be during the evening needlework, after supper, before the men rejoined the women for the evening entertainment. All Lucy had to do was slip away.

The note wasn't signed, but considering that she had found it in the purple lily book, Lucy was confident that it was from Monsieur V. She had a second chance to catch him! And she wasn't going to squander it this time.

"That must be a riveting book."

Lucy jumped. She shut the book, flattening the note between the pages once more. Clutching the volume to her chest, she turned to face Brackley.

Perched on the arm of a well-stuffed chair near the hearth, Brackley crossed his legs at the ankles and raised his eyebrows.

"How long have you been there?"

He straightened and closed the distance between them. "Long enough. Like I said, the book must have been riveting for you not to notice my entrance."

Had he watched her decode the note? She couldn't tell him about it, and not only because she didn't know with which side his allegiances resided. The last time, he had interfered with her meeting with the spymaster. He might do so again. She couldn't take that chance. This might be the last time Monsieur V would contact her.

She couldn't fathom why he had singled her out the first time. For him to do it again was a stroke of luck. This time, she wouldn't let Brackley get in her way.

His amused expression faded as he stopped within arm's length. "What did you find that so enthralled you?"

He knew. She didn't know for how long he'd been watching her, but even if he hadn't witnessed her flipping through the book to decipher the code, he suspected that she'd found a clue. Why not confront her about it? Was he giving her a chance to prove her trustworthiness by telling him the truth?

He couldn't trust her. And she couldn't trust him. She wished for such a test that she could put him through in order to discover whether or not she was alone in her hunt for Monsieur V. As zealous as she had been, striking out on her own, the fact that she always seemed to be one step behind the notorious spymaster gave her pause. An extra pair of eyes could be of use to her, if she could be certain that he wouldn't seek to overshadow her or edge her out of the investigation "for her own protection." Not to mention that Brackley was better able to overpower Monsieur V physically. He could be an asset to her.

If she could trust him. Which, at the moment, she could not. So she held her tongue on what she'd learned.

"It's only a book. Do you read, Brackley?"

"Alex," he corrected. "I'd rather you didn't call me by my title."

"You still haven't answered my question."

"And you didn't answer mine."

She shielded the book so he couldn't read the title. She didn't know for certain that he would make the same connection she had, pairing Monsieur V with purple lilies, but she couldn't take the chance. No matter what, she must attend the meeting tomorrow. He would only get in her way.

"It's research. For my book."

Alex raised an eyebrow. "Does your heroine want to change professions again and become a botanist?"

Frankly, Lucy was surprised he recalled enough about her story to comment. "No...but perhaps she meets a scoundrel interested in botany."

Alex smirked. "Perhaps she's the scoundrel, and she tempts a golden-hearted boy."

She narrowed her eyes. Was he trying to give her a genuine suggestion for her book—albeit, one she wouldn't use—or was he trying to insinuate something entirely different? For instance, that she was tempting him.

On impulse, she licked her lips. They tingled as he dropped his gaze to her mouth. Did she tempt him? Did she want to? Their kiss...

Was for research only. She knew what it felt like now.

Unfortunately, that didn't help to smother the desire to repeat it. They were utterly alone in the library. No one would know.

Except him. As much as he might like to pretend, he was far from golden-hearted.

"Do you have an interest in botany?"

He laughed. "Not in particular. Do you have a lust to sail the seven seas?"

"Perhaps. It would be good research." Imagine how authentic a book she would be able to write if she could only see the locations where her heroine adventured! Alas, that particular research was impossible. Morgan had purchased her books on the subject instead.

Alex inched closer. The heat of his body burned into hers. "Do you do everything in the name of research?"

Was he asking her if she'd kissed him because she'd wanted to? She had, but she would never have given in if she hadn't had the excuse of her book to hide behind. How could she expect to write a good book if she wrote about things she knew nothing about?

"Not everything, but near enough."

He raised his gaze to meet hers once more, though his voice remained intimate as he asked, "And do you always show such enthusiasm for your research topics?"

Her cheeks burned. Was he asking about the book or about their kiss?

"Of course. Why do something if you aren't going to be passionate about it?"

He made a strangled sound and took a step back. "In that case, enjoy your book, Lucy. Goodnight."

Lucy gaped as he turned and strode from the library without another word. Was he going to give up on gleaning what she'd learned so easily? She hadn't thought he was the type to turn his back on something he wanted, no matter the deterrent.

Perhaps she shouldn't question it. Opening the book once more, she slipped out the code and replaced the book on the shelf. She tossed the slip of paper into the fire, watching it blacken and curl until there was nothing left. Her mind had already turned to what would happen on the morrow.

She had a lot to prepare if she was to ensure that Monsieur V didn't escape this time.

14

The very last thing that Alex was about to do when he was certain that Lucy was hiding something was to leave her unattended. He lingered in the downstairs parlor until after she went to bed, then shut himself in his room with the door cracked open so he might hear if anyone passed through the corridor. Unfortunately, too many people came and went, even at night, and Alex found his dozing to be restless. It seemed as though every few minutes he roused again to check the corridor. If Lucy went out that night, she managed to sneak past him.

The following day she spent an inordinate amount of time out in the garden, much to the apparent consternation of her companion, Miss Vale, if he read their body language correctly. Alex sequestered himself in the parlor adjoining the terrace and watched from the doors, where he went unnoticed and stayed dry to boot. A cool mist seeped from the dull gray clouds overhead, too fine to properly be called a drizzle. Nevertheless, it likely soaked Lucy through to the skin within half an hour. From the way Miss Vale danced and tried to keep to the shelter of the hedges, she was acutely uncomfortable. Still, despite Lucy's repeated gestures telling her to go inside, the young woman stubbornly stuck to Lucy's side.

What was Lucy's fascination with the garden? Was she hunting for clues to Monsieur V? The rainy weather overnight and drizzle during the day would have washed clean all evidence. Not to mention, he had already combed through the gardens and discovered nothing. If she'd cared to share what it was she was hiding from him, he would have been able to tell her that much and save her the trouble of getting wet.

Although she eventually gave up and returned inside, he imagined that her companion was well and truly irritable by that point. At any rate, he had to endure the glares of both when he joined them in Lady Leighton's parlor that afternoon. He kept his distance. Lucy made no attempt to speak with him.

In fact, she avoided his gaze all afternoon and during supper as well. She had to be hiding something. He had to determine what.

When the men meandered behind Lord Leighton toward the library, Alex pretended to follow. He lingered near the back of the line, widening the gap between him and the other men. When he thought no one paid him any mind, he stepped into the shadow of a doorway for a moment. Once their footsteps faded, he doubled back.

He loitered in the shadow of a servant's stair down the corridor from the parlor where the ladies did their needlepoint. The soft chatter of female voices washed over him, none particularly distinctive or decipherable until one in particular moved closer.

"I've run out of pages in my notebook. See?"

That was Lucy's voice. He straightened and strained his ears to hear more.

"I have more paper up in my room. It will have to do for now, since I won't be able to start a new notebook until we return to London. I'll only be a moment."

A figure—Lucy—slipped out of the parlor and immediately turned toward the main staircase leading to the second floor and the guests' quarters. Since Alex should have been in the library at that moment, he remained still, his heart pounding as he waited to see if anyone would follow. No one did.

He slowly eased into the corridor. At the bottom of the stairs, Lucy paused. When she started to turn to look over her shoulder, Alex quickly hid again. Her footsteps resumed—away from the staircase. He counted five steps before he slipped into the corridor to follow her. Where was she going?

It shouldn't have surprised him when she exited the manor by a door close to the gardens. Obviously, she'd left something unfinished there. He shadowed her, making certain not to be seen. For all her cleverness and determination, she did not have a spy's training because it was far too easy to follow her without being noticed. Although she paused before changing direction or exiting the house to check for anyone trailing her, she made no attempt to look behind her while she walked. All he had to do was time those key moments so that he was hidden when she looked. Once she found herself a lantern, it was even easier to follow her path.

She led him to the gardens. Lady Leighton's garden, like the rest of her manor, was decorated in the height of fashion. This meant a row of shoulder-height hedges forming a labyrinth of sorts. A gravel path wove between the greenery, opening wider in nooks that contained benches and clusters of carefully-groomed, flowering plants. So early in the season, he spotted daffodils, for the most part.

Ahead, the path widened to accommodate a distinctive fountain. A statue of Aphrodite poured water from her cupped hands. The liquid gave a musical lilt as it fell into the wide basin of the fountain. Algae and lily pads floated on the surface of the water. Despite the brooding clouds overhead and the dampness in the air, the effect was peaceful. Neatly-placed stones in a mosaic ringed the fountain and along the edges, between flowerbeds and bushes, benches faced the fountain.

Unfortunately, such a wide area provided him with no place to hide. When Lucy stopped in the center, he froze in place. He glanced behind him, but the nearest nook was twenty feet behind him.

"Brackley."

Lucy said his title in a dark voice. Given her tone, he suspected she called him by it because he'd confessed that he hated it.

He faced Lucy with a disarming smile. She stood by the fountain, arms crossed. Was she cold? Her pale blue dress left her arms bare. He approached her, thinking to offer his jacket. Her dark eyes simmered with hostility.

"Are you following me?"

He ran one hand through his hair. "You wouldn't believe that I've decided to take a walk in the gardens at the same time."

She hiked up her chin. "No. I would not."

"Are you cold? You can have my jacket."

As he started to shuck out of it, she snapped, "I don't need your chivalry. I'm perfectly fine on my own."

"Perfectly fine doing what, precisely? Meeting with Monsieur V?"

She didn't deny it.

He gritted his teeth. He'd known she was hiding something, that she'd found some clue he'd missed. Why hadn't she shared it with him? He'd been forthcoming with her about his search of the perimeter.

Not that that had yielded any clues.

"You shouldn't be out here alone."

"Why? Because I'm a delicate flower?"

"Because you're meeting with a criminal who has eluded the Crown for nearly a year!" Now more than ever, Alex was sure Lucy was acting alone. Any spy assigned by Morgan or the Lord Commander of Spies, Lord Strickland, would be assigned a partner. If not someone to openly accompany them, then at the very least someone to lie in wait and observe in case something went awry.

Lucy narrowed her eyes. "I can handle myself."

Against Monsieur V? Not a chance. Since she was clearly untrained, perhaps she didn't understand the gravity of the situation. She was clearly too stubborn— and brave—for her own good. Alex stepped closer and lowered his voice.

"Monsieur V is not one of the polite gentlemen with whom you are accustomed to associating. He isn't even the scoundrel you seem bent on naming me. He is a fiend, a monster, and there is no telling what he would do to you if you found yourself in his presence alone."

Lucy scoffed. "I've already found myself in his presence alone once. He didn't do anything to me. In fact, he didn't even threaten me. You're worrying for nothing."

He was not. When a spymaster who continually slipped through the fingers of spies far more experienced than Lucy decided to contact her directly—perhaps more than once—Alex had cause to worry. Perhaps Lucy hadn't yet learned what Monsieur V was capable of, but Alex had. And he wasn't about to have to explain to Morgan why they had to bury his younger sister.

"You're wrong. This is dangerous."

"I know that," she snapped. "I've taken precautions."

What sort of precautions, exactly? She'd left Lady Leighton's manor without so much as donning her pelisse to ward away the chill. She had nothing on her save for what she could stuff into her reticule, which given its size likely held little more than her notebook, and her bodice clung to her chest in far too much loving detail for her to have hidden a weapon in there. Even if she'd stuffed a gun beneath her skirt—he would be surprised, given the lack of a discernible bulge—she wouldn't be able to reach it in time to do any damage. He tried not to picture her pulling up her skirt in order to collect such a hypothetical weapon.

"Your precautions should have included someone to watch your back. Mrs. Vale, if no one else."

Irritation flashed across her face, quickly hidden. "I don't think having a chaperone will help the situation at all."

"No, this is far more serious than a smirch to your reputation. One misstep and you could wind up dead or worse."

Given the confused look on her face, she didn't understand what might be worse than death. Alex did. He'd seen the hollow-eyed, deadened looks of spies that had been captured and tortured. That was, if there was enough left of the spy afterward to find. Alex was certain that the Graylockes would move Heaven and Earth to rescue Lucy before she succumbed to such treatment, but it would be better if no one was put in that position at all.

"I told you, he hasn't threatened me."

"*Yet.*" Alex stressed the word. "Why is he contacting you? Have you thought of that?"

A frown pulled down the corners of her mouth. She said nothing.

He continued, "You shouldn't be out here with a partner."

"And where is *your* partner?"

She had him there. Since he hadn't been officially assigned to find and arrest Monsieur V, he hadn't been given one. In fact, he likely had a note awaiting him in London from Strickland or Morgan assigning him some other duty. For all that it would earn him a reprimand later, he couldn't abide the thought that Monsieur V was back, under his nose, and Alex was doing nothing to catch him. This time, he would take his revenge on the spymaster.

That, he vowed.

Lucy snapped, "Don't tell me it's different because you're a man or more experienced or some other drivel like that."

He opened his mouth to counter, though he didn't know quite what he'd say. The cocking of a gun stilled him. Every muscle in his body went rigid. He didn't dare move, not even to turn around. Doing so might shift him out of the path of the bullet and put Lucy in danger instead. His hands twitched to retrieve his gun, which he'd carried with him since Lucy's evasive behavior had aroused his suspicion, but there was no way he would remove it from his pocket in time. From a shadowed path across the fountain from them, a woman emerged with a gun in hand. The same servant he'd tried to wheedle information from regarding who had planted the note in his room. It seemed that mystery had been solved.

"See?" he muttered under his breath. "*They* came as a pair."

He should have anticipated this.

15

*L*ucy cast a sidelong glance at Alex. A muscle twitched in his clean-shaven jaw as he walked a half-step behind her, angling his body so it half-covered hers. His efforts made no difference to their predicament; between the plain-faced woman and the man, who happened to be the same who Lucy had caught in Alex's room, neither Alex nor Lucy could sneeze without being shot.

Her heart pounded, almost like the beat of a thrilling, vigorous dance. She'd never caught herself wondering what it might be like to be held up at gunpoint—after all, there were some things she was sensible enough not to try even in the name of research —but she couldn't deny the lure of the rush that filled her. Every moment seemed more acute, more tangible.

She heard the wet grass whisper beneath her shoes and the brush of Alex's arm against her sent a shiver through her.

However, as much as she enjoyed the sensation, the fear that invoked a surreal sense of being alive, it was largely unhelpful. Whenever she turned her thoughts to trying to get them out of this situation before they were killed, she couldn't think properly. Thoughts fluttered in and out of her head, there one minute and gone the next. She couldn't muster the concentration to examine each idea properly and decide whether or not it was a good one.

What did the traitors intend to do with them? Lucy had no doubt in her mind that they were traitors. Had they been with Britain, they would never have held her at gunpoint, nor would they be forcing her and Alex to march away from the manor. The only thing looming in front of them were the shadows of the trees. If she squinted, she thought she could make out the small shed where Alex had interrogated her the first night they'd arrived.

Lucy glanced over her shoulder and into the man's cold eyes. He had divested her of the lantern and carried it himself. The light flickered off the metal barrel of the gun aimed at her back. His companion, the woman Lucy didn't quite recognize but who must almost certainly be a servant as well, wore just as cold and hard an expression.

"Why are you doing this? Don't you know who I am?"

No, she could see that playing her heritage was not the right move in their case. If anything, the hatred in their eyes deepened. Lucy knew that many, if not most peers treated the servant class with disdain, but Lucy's family was different. Not that it was worth wasting her breath to tell them. She doubted they would believe her.

Was that why they had given their allegiance to France? Did they think that the French, who had ousted and executed their nobility, had the right way of it? Lucy didn't know how many in England shared such an outlook, but she didn't think it boded well for them if many sympathized. Perhaps that was why Morgan insisted on treating everyone, man and woman, noble and servant, with respect.

She tried again, catching the man's eyes and saying, "I thought we had a connection." She sounded like a broken-hearted, weak-willed debutante begging a rake to take her to the altar. But if it saved her life...

Alex cleared his throat. "Don't taunt the nice man with the gun," he muttered under his breath.

"I wasn't taunting him," she shot back.

He made a noise of disbelief.

"Quiet," the woman snapped. "Keep walking."

She, like the man, had a British accent. Were they British, born and bred? Or had they infiltrated this country from France? Lucy didn't want to contemplate how many of her countrymen had switched their allegiance so easily. Forget that she'd once suspected Alex of having done so—clearly, she'd been wrong about him. Elsewise, he would have been the one with the gun, walking her ahead of him, rather than being in this cock-up with her.

Lucy pressed her lips together as they continued to walk. The blood roared in her ears. Once they reached that shed, would the traitors shoot them and stuff them inside? Or would they continue out into the forest instead? She swallowed heavily, trying to think.

There had to be a way to dissuade them from this course of action. Or, at the very least, to distract them once they reached the shed. If Lucy had been alone, she would have tried to use some distraction and the bulk of the shed to shield her as she ran into the forest. Tenwick Abbey had a large enough forest abutting the property that she'd played in as a child for her to be reasonably confident that she could elude the French spies if she darted into its cover.

But what about Alex? She still didn't know whether he worked for the Crown, but given this recent turn of events, he certainly didn't work for the

French. She couldn't just leave him to die. It wouldn't be right.

What would her heroine do?

Lucy tried to catch Alex's eye, to communicate with him silently, but he wasn't looking at her. His posture was rigid, his jaw set. His hand twitched as though he wanted to punch one or both of the spies who had captured them.

This had been so stupid of her. Earlier in the day, she'd stashed the things she'd thought she might need in order to capture Monsieur V, including the ties to hold him. But she hadn't considered that he would send armed spies in his place. Hadn't he wanted to speak with her?

Apparently not. Right now, with her head spinning and her breath coming fast, she couldn't begin to decipher the spymaster's motives. It felt as though he was toying with her. But if he was, wouldn't he want her alive? This seemed more like a march to her death.

They reached the shed. The woman shoved her gun into Alex's back. "Hands in the air!"

Alex's right hand twitched, then he lanced at Lucy and put his hands up.

The man stepped over and patted him down, producing a gun from his pocket. "Thought you might use this, eh?"

Keeping her gun trained on Alex, the woman

stepped to the side and gestured to the shed door. "Open it."

Alex met her gaze. "She's innocent in this. She doesn't know what she's gotten herself into. Just let her return to the manor and she'll stop sticking her nose where it doesn't belong."

Was he talking about Lucy? She bristled. She could speak for herself! And she knew exactly what she'd gotten herself into when she'd taken this assignment upon herself instead of handing it off to her brother like he would have expected her to do. She didn't need to be coddled or sheltered.

The woman gestured brusquely with the butt of the gun. "Open the door."

"No. Shoot me here, if you're going to do it."

Lucy's heart jumped into her throat. Was he suicidal? Or perhaps just criminally stupid. He told her not to taunt the spies, and yet that was precisely what he was doing. Perhaps she should leave him to his own devices and run.

The woman's mouth narrowed into a thin line as she trained the gun on him. She looked like she might do it.

Lucy stumbled forward. "I'll open the door." She unlatched it with shaking fingers. When she pulled it wide and released it, the door banged against the wall of the shed. The light of the lantern was impeded by her body, only a halo showing around her shadow as it stretched into the dark interior.

"Get in," the woman commanded.

Lucy glanced toward the tree line. Should she run instead?

Alex stepped closer to her. His body jostled hers and she stumbled to the side, into the threshold of the shed door. She caught her balance against the door frame.

Thumps and grunts echoes as a scuffle ensued. A shot rang out and for a second, Lucy's heart stopped beating. But it must have gone wide because it didn't stop the fight for even an instant. The light guttered as the man dropped the lantern. Lucy blinked against the erratic light. Alex struggled to subdue the woman.

Unfortunately, it was two against one. When the man entered the fray mere seconds later, while Lucy still tried to process the scene, the pair overpowered Alex. They shoved him into the shed. His body impacted Lucy and she stumbled. He caught her, staggering a bit to keep them from landing on the floor of the shed. Her body was pressed intimately against his for a moment before he released her and turned toward the door.

It slammed shut behind him. The darkness weighed on her eyes. A grating sound scraped from the other side of the door. The two spies spoke in rapid

French—at least, that was the language Lucy thought they spoke. She'd learned French, but they spoke far too quickly for her to catch more than the scattered word.

When the voices faded, Alex tested the door. The sound of it connecting with the frame, a light thump, sounded overly loud. It didn't open. He swore under his breath.

They were trapped, but they weren't dead. They could get out of this...somehow. Lucy nibbled on her lip. The shed was completely dark, but she shut her eyes and tried to recall what gardening tools had been held in here. Anything that might help them to escape. The shed held no light whatsoever, enclosed on four sides without windows.

Alex crossed to her. He nearly bowled her over before he caught her by the upper arms. His palms were warm. He murmured an apology, then turned his back again.

A moment later, an impact thudded. It was followed by a rattle, like that of metal. Alex must have charged the door. Judging by his resultant groan, it hadn't worked in the least.

"Use your head," Lucy snapped. She could barely think straight and all his banging wasn't helping. "Brute force is obviously not going to get us anywhere." If it had, his efforts would already have worked. "At least we're alive."

For a moment, that had been in question. That gunshot...

Her breath caught. "You aren't injured, are you?"

"No. She fired over my shoulder when I rushed her." Cloth rustled as he moved. "If we don't get out of here quickly, those spies will be long gone. And so will Monsieur V."

"We thought he had left upon departing the inn. It seemed we were wrong." She stepped closer and gasped as her breasts brushed against his coat. She hadn't realized that he was standing so close. She took a small step away again, but couldn't banish the awareness of his body that the encounter provoked.

"So you think. We didn't see him. Unless that man..."

"No. He wasn't Monsieur V." That, she could say with utmost certainty.

Cloth rustled again as he shifted. He swore under his breath. "Then we have to get out of here."

"I'm aware of that." It seemed, with the situation they were in, that he'd conveniently forgotten his earlier concern regarding her reputation. She had not. If they remained in this shed, alone, for someone to find, then they would be forced to marry. Nothing else would appease the gossips, and even that solution was questionable.

However, the notion of her tattered reputation mattered far less than the preservation of England. Why was she even thinking of it?

She shook her head and tried to think of a plan. "The door opened from the outside."

"Yes. I could bloody well kick it down if the latch didn't appear to be secured with something. A padlock, perhaps."

Lucy released a frustrated breath. "If it opens to the outside, that means the hinges are on the outside, away from us."

Alex paused. After a moment, he ventured, "Yes."

"Is there enough of a crack between the door and frame for us to use something like a lever to pry it open?"

"I doubt it, but it's worth a try. Can you find a rake?"

Despite the situation, a wicked thrill overtook her. She stepped closer, close enough to feel the heat of his body once more. "I thought you were one," she teased.

"I meant a gardening tool."

His tone was not amused. Apparently, he didn't think it the proper time for jokes. Maybe it wasn't, but if she didn't joke, she feared she might succumb to the urge to enact more research. Lucy might need to write her heroine into a dark corner, unable to see, only able to feel. She'd never kissed a man under such circumstances.

She wanted to kiss Alex again. But that wouldn't solve their predicament. If anything, it would only make his mood worse. While they kissed, the enemy spies would be getting farther away.

She forced a smile and quipped, "You mean you've never charmed the hinges off a door before? I'm disappointed." Her voice was a bit breathless.

When she started to move past him to search the walls for the rake he requested, her arm brushed against him. He caught her elbow, holding her near him. The air charged with promise as she turned her face toward his. Did he want to kiss her, too?

He slid his hand down her bare arm to her wrist. Shivers coalesced across her skin in the wake of his hot touch. She gasped as she lifted her face, hoping he would lower his head.

The influx of air brought the taste of something... singed. Frowning, she sniffed again. "Is that...smoke?"

Her heart quickened and her throat burned. The enemy had set the shed on fire!

Alex swore under his breath and dropped his hand. "The rake. Now. You check behind you and I'll search this wall."

Lucy couldn't see where he gestured when he gave

the command, but she assumed that he meant the wall behind him. She turned, starting to search her end as quickly as possible. More smoke stung her nose. Just a thin amount at first, but it thickened the longer she took. She didn't see any evidence of flames, but the smoke seemed worse near the back.

"I found one!" She coughed as she pulled the rake down from its nook on the wall.

"Bring it here, quickly."

She did as he asked. When she approached where she estimated the front door was, she said, "Where are you? I don't want to hit you by accident."

The rake in her hand jostled as he groped for it. "I have it. You can let go."

He did some fiddling. Lucy stepped back. She pulled a handkerchief out of her reticule and held it over her nose and mouth, breathing through the perfumed fabric. She felt useless, standing and doing nothing.

"Can I help?"

"Grab the end and try to use it like a lever."

When she did as he asked, the pointed tips popped free of the crack where he'd lodged it. The tines scraped across the wood of the door.

Alex swore profusely. "That's it. We don't have time. Stand back. I'm going to try to kick it open." Under his breath, he added, "I hope."

He kicked at the door and Lucy saw the slat of light grow wider. He was making progress but not fast enough.

"Wait." Lucy pulled the rake aside and stowed it against the wall. "I found a pick-axe in the back. Maybe we can use that to break the door away from the latch. It's only attached in that one area, right?"

"It's worth a try." His voice was brusque. "Get the pick-axe."

Lucy started to feel heat as well as the sting of smoke. The shed was definitely on fire. She fumbled to find the tool on the wall. When she pulled it down, she immediately crossed the short few steps to Alex's side. She groped along his arm until she could hand it to him. "Here." He was stronger than she was.

"Step back."

When she complied, he set to work hacking at the door. It took him a couple minutes, but he made progress. The thin line of light seeping from the opening told her that much. She held her breath as more smoke stung her throat. Her eyes watered. She blinked rapidly, not wanting him to think she was crying.

This was almost over. They were almost out...

Alex swore. He stepped back and kicked the door. It flung away from the latch with a snap, swinging on its hinges to slam into the wall. Alex dropped the pick-axe. He took Lucy by the hand and towed her through the opening. Around the still-intact latch was a ragged semi-circle of wood. She avoided the jagged edges. As she staggered into the night air after him, she clutched his hand tighter and gulped in the clean air. She glanced behind her, but the only thing she saw was the faint halo of flame and a thick column of smoke coming from the shed.

They were free, but as predicted, the spies were nowhere in sight.

he dampness of the grass and shed had saved them, of that Alex was certain. Although the wood had taken a while longer to light than it might have if dry—and had churned out more smoke than fire in so doing—the fire drew the attention of someone in Lady Leighton's manor as or before he and Lucy stumbled clear of the edifice. As he gulped for air, his throat and eyes still stinging, servants poured from the manor. They were like ants. One spotted at first, then two or three, then the swarm descended. Shouts rang in his ears as the housekeeper called for water to be pumped from the well and brought around.

With the amassing of the servants, so too was the hostess's attention caught. And as she spilled into the night air, she brought with her a parade of guests hoping for a bit more titillating excitement for the evening. Alex, blast it all, found himself in the middle of the spectacle with Lucy by his side.

The lanterns of the servants and guests lit the scene as bright as day. Lucy, with her black hair escaping its coif in rebellious wisps, turned her face down and wrapped her arms around herself. She tried to stuff a handkerchief back into her reticule with one hand. This time, Alex didn't bother asking for her permission. He shucked out of his jacket and wrapped it around her shoulders.

She turned her face up to his as he secured the jacket in place. Although her expression was emotionless, composed, there was something in her eyes that begged for his help. If he didn't think quickly, her reputation would be in tatters. He dropped his hand before he lingered a touch too long to appease the gossips.

Perhaps the tarnish to her reputation was deserved. When he'd touched her, temptation had overwhelmed her. Given a moment longer, he would have pulled her into his arms and kissed her senseless. Never mind the enemy spies who might lead him to Monsieur V—the moment he'd felt the soft skin of her arm beneath his hand, he could think of nothing except tasting her velvet-soft lips again. If she hadn't noticed the smoke, he might have been blind to the danger.

If he'd kissed her, if they'd been discovered together in the shed, more than her reputation would have been in jeopardy. Her future, perhaps, as well—and his, too. He would have no other recourse but to marry her. That was, if her brothers didn't kill him before he made it to the altar.

Strangely enough, the idea didn't repulse him the way it used to—marriage, that was to say, not death-by-angry-Graylocke. The latter he'd still like to avoid. But marriage... a couple years ago the notion had thrilled him not at all. Then again, a couple years ago, the light-skirts with whom he had kept company weren't precisely the sort one started a life with. And he hadn't been fit to be a husband, either.

The sudden deaths of his father and brother had changed that. In an evening, his role in the world had been flipped on its head. Instead of pleasure-seeking, he waded through a mountain of responsibilities. The biggest responsibilities in the eyes of his staff appeared to be that he find himself a wife and beget an heir. He'd ignored them, finding a new purpose in his life.

A purpose that, even if marriage no longer gave him a shiver of repulsion, he must adhere to first. From the moment he'd signed on with Morgan, that purpose had been to find Monsieur V and ensure that the traitor got what he deserved. And now, thanks to Lucy, he might finally be close to doing that.

If he could concoct a reasonable explanation for being out here with her that would appease the hostess and the other guests. Until he took care of that, he wouldn't be at liberty to chase after the French spies and follow them to their employer. His heart raced as he scrambled for an explanation as to their behavior that didn't end in him accompanying Lucy to the altar.

Not, strangely, that he believed a marriage to Lucy would be the same as what he had always imagined. The debutantes of his acquaintance were usually mousy little things who simpered and boasted of their accomplishments and showed off their figures while they danced. That sort of woman bored him within five minutes. But Lucy... He suspected that any marriage to Lucy wouldn't be the quiet affair demonstrated by his peers. She was far too curious, far too brazen. Lucy Graylocke would keep the man she married on the tips of his toes.

But that man wouldn't be him. It certainly wouldn't be today. The only reason he was keeping such a close eye on her was to catch the man who had torn apart his family. No more, no less.

Therefore, when the hostess demanded to know what had happened, he concocted a plausible tale.

"I came out for a bit of fresh air after supper. I find a walk to be particularly good for the digestion, you see, and you have such well-kept grounds that I couldn't resist the desire to see them in moonlight." Not that there was much of a moon to be seen; the clouds clotted the sky. "As I was strolling past, I noticed the fire and called out to see if anyone was inside. Lady Lucy cried out for help, so I broke down the door and whisked her out. Your servants must have noticed the fire at the same time I did, for they were upon us immediately. We were scarcely alone for thirty seconds," he lied.

Lady Leighton glanced from Alex to Lucy, who—blast it, was she glaring at him! It seemed that she didn't much care for being cast in the role of damsel in distress, even if it was the story that was most likely to be believed.

The hostess asked her, "Is this true?"

A dark expression on her face, Lucy opened her mouth. For a moment, his heart skipped a beat as he feared that she would contest his claim. If they argued about the tale, no one would believe a word to emerge from their mouths. He caught her gaze, begging her to see reason. She might not like the explanation he'd given, but as long as everyone else accepted it for truth, it didn't matter.

"Indeed." Lucy bit off the word.

The tension melted out of Alex's shoulders. He slowly released the breath he'd been holding.

When Mrs. Vale elbowed her way to the front of the gathered crowd, who whispered his tale to one another, spreading it amongst themselves like wildfire, Alex stiffened once more. The older woman caught his gaze, her eyes like steel. When she turned her gaze to Lucy, he couldn't help but release a breath of relief.

"How did you find yourself in that shed? You said you were going up to your room to find paper."

Blast! Why couldn't she have waited to interrogate her charge until they no longer had an audience?

Alex held himself rigid, praying that his expression was impervious as Mrs. Vale turned her cutting gaze on him. Surely, she didn't believe that he had whisked Lucy away in order to romance her? He had more sense than that.

As much as he sometimes wished he didn't.

Lucy's eyebrows knit together as she glanced from him toward her chaperone. Lady Leighton looked at her expectantly. The guests awaited the answer with bated breath.

Say something. Anything.

"Well, you see, there was a cat."

Perhaps anything but that. A cat?

As Lucy launched into her tale, Alex reminded himself that he wasn't in the presence of a trained spy, who would know to make the lie short and simple. No, he had decided to keep company with a bloody storyteller. And a story, she certainly did weave.

It was a heart-wrenching tale involving a surly little black cat with a limp who apparently had a thieving bent, for when Lucy went to pet it, it stole her favorite pencil. And she was not content to let the little thief—no longer hurt, it seemed—keep her pencil. No, she had to follow the cat. The feline apparently led her on a merry chase through the gardens, where she neither noticed nor encountered Alex, before running into the shed.

"'Aha,'" Lucy exclaimed, apparently adding dialogue into this tale, now. "'I've got you!' But when I entered the shed, I found it so dark and the cat's fur so black that I couldn't see him at all. There are a great many tools to find in that shed, and I soon found my way to a tinderbox and lantern. Once I lit it, it threw back the shadows, and I was able to find the cat, who still held onto my pencil, I'll have you know. I tried to corner the scoundrel—"

She paused to shoot Alex a triumphant glance. How that helped her tale, he didn't know. Apparently the thieving cat was an allegory for him, never mind that he'd never once tried to steal her pencil. Hopefully the others crowded around, listening to the tale with expressions of varying amusement, took it at face value.

Lucy continued, "He outsmarted me. I nearly had him, but he scurried out the door and it fell shut behind him. I don't quite know how he managed to lock it—"

Oh, Lucy. Why did you feel the need to add that implausibility? Perhaps no one would have connected her fanciful tale with the fact that the shed door had been locked.

He interrupted. "Perhaps it wasn't the cat who locked the door, but someone else?" He raised an eyebrow. "It seems much more likely that a servant happened upon the shed, noticed that the lock had been forgotten, and fastened it promptly."

"Oh. Perhaps." She waved her hand in dismissal as she turned back to her waiting audience. She seemed to thrive on the attention they were giving her.

If his freedom hadn't been at stake, he would have found the scene amusing. Perhaps even heartwarming. Clearly, she was destined to be a storyteller. In fact, he was surprised that she didn't already have her name on the cover of a book. As she recounted her tale, she delivered it with excitement, intrigue. She played on the audience's rapt attention to build tension and relieve it later with an amusing antic from the cat. The concept was a bit beyond what someone might believe, but it had all the good makings of a fine story.

Unfortunately, he wasn't in the midst of a novel, and her lie would never stand up to questioning. Could she even recount the details a second time? More likely, she'd add in more and more fanciful aspects to the tale and it would unravel with the least bit of prodding.

Lucy continued, "In any case, I found myself trapped, with no other recourse than to hope that some hero would happen upon me." She batted her eyelashes at him with a smirk.

This was retaliation for making her the damsel in distress, wasn't it? He tried to keep his expression neutral.

"I was so stricken at being unable to find my way out that in my distress, I knocked over the lantern and the shed caught fire! If not for my lord, I surely would have perished."

She batted her eyelashes at him again like a lovesick milksop. He gritted his teeth.

Keep this up and you'll find us married.

For a moment, all was silent as Lucy finished her tale. Then, in a dry voice, Mrs. Vale echoed, "Indeed. How fortunate we were that he found you in time."

Alex highly doubted that a single member of the party believed such a far-fetched tale, not the least because of the chaperone's incredulous tone, but no one contested it. Wickedness must run in the Vale blood because the young Miss Vale, who during the tale had meandered to find her way next to her mother, felt a need to comment.

"Did you reclaim your pencil in the end?"

"Oh, yes." Grinning, Lucy opened her reticule and pulled it out for all to see. "The cat left it behind in the shed while he ran out."

"How fortunate," he said, fighting to keep the dry humor from his voice. "The world would be deprived if you were unable to commit your talent for recounting a tale to paper, Lady Lucy."

"It is fortunate. And it all ended well, despite that terrifying bit in the middle."

Yes, he suspected he would have nightmares about that as well. For a moment, his life had flashed in front of his eyes and he'd been reminded that he had nothing. On paper, he had a lot—multiple estates, more money than he could have gambled away even at the rate he was going, and a title that put him at just a touch less important than a duke. However, at the end of the day, his life was empty. The only purpose to his life was to catch Monsieur V.

And yet, for a brief moment, the thought that Lucy would die alongside him had agonized him more than the thought that he wouldn't avenge his family.

She flashed him a pretty smile as she slipped his jacket from her shoulders. She held it out to him. "Thank you for your assistance this evening, my lord. I don't know what I would have done without you."

As Lucy made her excuses and allowed her chaperone to herd her away to bed, and likely a scolding, Alex bit his tongue.

He doubted that Lucy would continue to thank him when she found herself shackled to him for life. Once Mrs. Vale reported back to Morgan, Alex had no doubt that that was where their lives were headed.

Of all the excuses, why had she had to choose a bloody *cat*?

17

*A*lex didn't need to approach Lucy in order for her to deduce that he wanted to work together to investigate the two French spies who had nearly killed them. The looks he gave her—in the parlor for the evening entertainment that Lady Leighton had insisted that everyone attend, even Lucy despite the trauma she'd weathered—spoke volumes. However, even if Lucy had trusted him enough to join forces and investigate the spies together, they had no opportunity. Lady Leighton, determined to avoid scandal during her house party, watched them like a hawk. Lucy didn't even dare to stroll within arm's reach of Alex for fear of the repercussions. Somehow, they'd avoided being forced to the altar, and she wanted to keep it that way.

The next day, the clergyman droned on about morality in Church, no doubt at Lady Leighton's behest, and Lucy found herself pinned beneath the sharp stare of her chaperone, Mrs. Vale. She couldn't sneeze without Mrs. Vale appearing at her side with a tissue. Lucy had no hope of sneaking off to investigate.

Fortunately, Alex appeared to be at the same disadvantage. Lady Leighton had tasked her husband with occupying the male guests, particularly the man who had managed to sneak off and find himself alone with one of the women invited last night. Upon eavesdropping on her way out of the church, Lucy caught snatches of conversation involving the prospect of a ride. She smirked. Now all she had to do in order to catch the spies' trail before Alex was slip away from her chaperone.

She played meek during lunch, spending more time nibbling on her food than talking. Afterward, when the ladies retired to their rooms for a nap before afternoon tea, Lucy simmered with excitement. Now was her chance. She pretended to retire to her room as well, knowing that it would separate her from both the Vales. Although she suspected that Mrs. Vale would be keeping an ear out to hear if she stirred, Lucy bided her time. She sat at the vanity and pressed an ear to the wall, mulling over the changes she would make to her novel once she returned to London. The moment she heard a snore, she smiled. Charlie snored like thunder when she found herself in an unfamiliar bed. Mrs. Vale couldn't hope to hear Lucy now.

Nevertheless, when Lucy snuck out of her room, she took the utmost care not to make a sound.

Even with the servants acting standoffish around her, it didn't take much time or prodding for Lucy to discover that the two French spies had, in fact, fled. She flirted with a footman, this time successfully wheedling information from him. Armed with the location of the spies' respective rooms, Lucy traipsed through the corridor toward the woman's old lodgings. As she laid her hand on the latch, she heard movement within.

Her breath caught. Was it the spy, returned to retrieve something pivotal that she'd left in her quarters? Lucy slowly eased the door open by a crack, hoping to see inside.

A man stood with his back to her. Not the woman, but maybe her cohort or even Monsieur V. As the man turned away from the small writing desk to hold a blank sheet of paper up to the daylight streaming through the window, Lucy caught a glimpse of his profile.

Not a French spy—Alex.

Releasing her breath in a huff, she slipped into the room and shut the door. He jumped and turned the moment the latch jangled. As he spotted her, the tension melted out of his shoulders, though his mouth remained set in a thin, disapproving line.

"How did you get here before me?" she demanded. "I thought Lord Leighton called for a ride."

Alex raised his eyebrow. He set down a sheaf of blank papers that he'd been thumbing through and turned toward her. "Lord Leighton is getting on in years. It didn't take much convincing to coax him to lie down for a spell while the rest of us went on the ride."

Except, apparently, Alex. Seeing as he was there, in the spy's room, rifling through her belongings before Lucy had the chance. He might have taken anything and she'd never know it.

She crossed the small room to stand toe to toe with him so she could lower her voice. There hadn't been any servants along the corridor when she'd arrived, but that didn't mean that someone wouldn't return to fetch something from their room. If they heard Lucy speak, they might come to investigate.

Like she would be doing now, if Alex hadn't already claimed that honor.

"You shouldn't be here."

He smirked. "And you should?"

She scowled. "These are the women's quarters. At least I don't stick out here as much as you do."

"I'm a renowned rake. I'm expected to be found in women's quarters."

She glared at him and crossed her arms. "Why don't you search the footman's room instead?"

"I already have. I found nothing there."

Had he? Or did he just want her to think he found nothing so that she would give up the search? Lucy narrowed her eyes as she studied him.

"Nothing at all?"

"He left in a hurry, like she seems to have, and there were a few personal affects left behind, but nothing that would give a clue as to his or his employer's whereabouts."

Drat. Lucy nibbled on a thumbnail. "Very well. I suppose I have no choice but to take you at your word."

He ran a hand through his hair. "Of course you can take me at my word. I wouldn't lie to you, certainly not about this. We're on the same side, with the same goal, are we not?"

"Are we?" She tilted her chin a notch higher. "You're the reason I haven't been able to meet with Monsieur V in the first place!"

"That's absurd!"

"Is it? Twice now, he's set a meeting with me. Twice now, I haven't so much as seen his shadow because *you've* interrupted that meeting!"

Alex's gaze turned stony. "Perhaps it was fortuitous that I pulled you away from your meeting that first time. You have no proof to suggest that Monsieur V had been there at all! It was just as likely that you would have ended up in that shed, alone, without anyone to help break the door because he sent his two spies to deal with you instead."

Dropping her arms, she balled her fists at her sides. "Don't let your imagination carry you away. From the very start, Monsieur V has been interested in speaking with *me* and me alone. Every time you shadow me, you frighten him away."

"Yes, I'm certain I do," he said, his voice dry. "Those two spies he set on us seemed very frightened, indeed."

"Perhaps if I'd been alone, he wouldn't have sent them!"

Alex crossed his arms. His muscular forearms bulged beneath his sleeves. "Perhaps if you'd been alone, they might have killed you."

"They did a very poor job of it when they found us both." Lucy shook her head. "Monsieur V wants me alive. He wants to speak to me for some reason. That is precisely why you need to mind your own business and stop interfering."

His expression darkened. "Monsieur V is my business. In fact, he's more my business than yours. You aren't a part of the British spy network. Does your brother even know you've gotten yourself into such dangerous affairs?"

Lucy bristled. "It's none of your business what my brother knows."

"I'll take that as a no."

"And how do you know I'm not a Crown spy?"

A muscle twitched in the corner of his jaw. "Because I am. I know the protocol. If you were assigned to pursue Monsieur V at all, you would be here with a partner."

"Then what's your excuse?"

Alex said nothing. A curtain descended across his gaze, veiling his emotions behind. She might as well have been arguing with a statue.

She tapped her foot. "Were you able to find anything useful here?" If not, she might as well give the room a cursory search herself. Then she could be rid of his company again.

Ignoring her question, he said, "I knowingly put my life on the line. Do you? This isn't a stroll in Hyde Park. There is real danger here, as I would have thought you'd discovered last night."

Lucy gritted her teeth. She wasn't some weak-willed watering pot. She was cleverer than he gave her credit for. "I know how dangerous it is to meet with a traitor. I'm not daft. That's why I'm taking precautions. But meet with him, I will, so you'd best stay away next time."

"No."

She raised her eyebrows. "No?"

"You heard me." His expression looked as hard as granite. "I won't leave you alone with an enemy spymaster."

"He wants to meet with *me*—"

"Yes." Alex bit off the word as he dropped his arms from the hostile stance. "I can't fathom why you and no one else, but he must have a reason. You can't meet with him alone."

"I can and I will." If she had to slip Alex's watchful eye along with Lady Leighton's and Mrs. Vale's, she would do it. She relished the challenge. No one told her what she could or couldn't do. Especially someone not related to her. He sounded like her brothers.

"He's a master manipulator. He's always one step ahead. You can't fathom what he has planned."

She bit the inside of her cheek hard to curb some of her anger. "Maybe you can't. Did you ever stop to think that maybe I am more intelligent?"

Alex's gaze was intense as he held eye contact. She couldn't look away.

"He's outwitted our best spies. He's outwitted your brother, for Heaven's sake! This man has practice on manipulating people into doing what he wants. No matter on what side their allegiances lie, no matter how intelligent they are. He's smarter."

Lucy's fingernails dug crescents into her palms. She still couldn't look away. "You're wrong. I can do this. I know I can." She had to. After all, she was the only person who could. She took that responsibility seriously.

"This is more dangerous than you seem to think—"

"Don't try to dictate my life. You aren't one of my brothers. You have no right!"

Simmering with anger, she turned away, intending to leave him to whatever fruitless search he cared to make. Before she took a step, he caught her by the arm and turned her back. When she stumbled into his frame, he pulled her flush against him and kissed her senseless.

* * *

ALEX KISSED Lucy with all the pent-up frustration and passion that he possessed. He surrendered to the feel of her body against his. The sweet taste of her, from seedcake she must have had at lunch, went to his head like a stiff drink. And her response... She kissed him back, every bit as voracious as he was. She twined her arms around his neck and met the bold strokes of his tongue.

Lucy...

When he feared he might take the kiss too far, he lifted his head. She tightened her arms around him as if trying to urge him to continue. He ached to oblige, but now that common sense had intruded, he couldn't rid himself of it. He straightened and licked his lips. Once she met his gaze, her thick eyelashes fluttering in front of her coffee-dark eyes, he swallowed hard.

"I'm not trying to get in your way, but I do intend to protect you. I care for you, Lucy."

The words resonated in the air between them like the peal of a bell. Lucy's lips parted.

Alex did care for her. He hadn't realized how much until she'd slipped into the room with him, once again bent on pursuing a French spymaster without a partner or a plan. This was dangerous work and if she insisted on doing it, he wanted to be there to ensure that she didn't kill herself in so doing. He worried for her. He wanted to keep her safe. He didn't see anything wrong in that desire, despite the way Lucy reacted with aggravation.

Her brother might disapprove of him, but it was too late for him to worry about that. He desired Lucy. He esteemed her for her intelligence, her charm, her determination and even her wild imagination. He didn't expect to find himself so drawn to her, but how could he resist her? She was a singular woman. Never would he meet another woman who was quite like her.

Slowly, she unhooked her arms from around his neck and dropped them to her sides. She opened her mouth, but didn't speak. Instead, she gnawed on her lower lip.

She didn't feel the same for him. Why had he expected her to reciprocate? Perhaps hope was a better word. A chasm of tension opened between them. Ignoring the ache beneath his breastbone, he took a step back.

Monsieur V. They both had a similar goal, to find the heinous spymaster. They should focus on that instead.

"Shall we continue the search? I'd only just begun when you entered."

Whatever emotions Lucy felt, they didn't show on her face. She nodded, her features composed. "Very well. Which side of the room would you like?"

"I've already started here. You can take the bedside."

Alex's heart beat fast as they split apart. He turned away from her, trying to rein in his wild emotions. She was the first woman he'd ever confessed to having any feelings for. Especially now, when he was so focused on finding Monsieur V, he hadn't expected this attachment to surface. He didn't know what to do with the fact that it had—let alone the fact that she didn't seem to return his feelings.

Work. They had to focus on work.

He returned to the task he'd set himself when she'd walked in. Unlike with the footman, the maid had left behind a sheaf of seemingly blank papers. They might truly be blank, or perhaps they only seemed so. Why else would she have left them, if not to alert any lingering cohorts that her identity had been compromised? He knew better than to hope that something in this room would lead him to Monsieur V, but perhaps if he searched hard enough, he could find a clue that would root out the whereabouts of the two spies who had tried to kill him. With the truth serum that Morgan had commissioned his brother to make, those spies would sing like songbirds. It was a start, at the very least.

One by one, he held the pages up to the window so the light shone through them. The papers themselves weren't overly thick and he could see through them easily when lifted against a light source. Blank, blank, blank. He was ready to give up and admit that his instincts might be wrong in this case when he found one paper with faint symbols on it. These symbols became visible when he pressed the page against the windowpane. Where something had been written, there was a darker shadow than the page itself. He needed to copy that out so he could decipher it.

"Lucy, can I borrow your pencil?"

"Why? Did you find something?" Her heels clicked as she approached.

He felt her presence acutely, an awareness against his right side as she offered him the pencil. "Thank you." Perhaps he could have found some ink, but tracing out the symbols against the window would have been impossible. The ink would have dripped down and ruined his efforts, not to mention the note.

Lucy leaned closer. So close, that her body nearly pressed against his. She didn't appear to notice. He swallowed hard and feigned composure.

"What's that?" she asked, pointing to one whorl on the page.

"A code, no doubt." His voice was a bit tight, but he was proud of its evenness nonetheless. "She must have written in vinegar or perhaps lemon juice. When it dries, it is invisible except when the page is held up against a light."

"Fascinating." Lucy sounded enthralled. Her comment was more than a polite response to his explanation.

Accepting the pencil from her, he used the tip to lightly trace out the symbols on the page. When he finished, he turned to find Lucy standing entirely too close.

Unfortunately, she wasn't paying any attention at all, but was flipping through her notebook. "Can I see that?" She held her book up next to the page, then shook her head and continued flipping.

From the glimpses he saw of the book, it might as well have been written in code, too.

"What are you searching for?"

"I copied some ciphers off Morgan's desk. I might be able to decode the message if I can find the right one..."

That would be handy, carrying around a sheaf of ciphers at all times. Alex had volumes of ciphers at his home. Well hidden, of course. Too many to bring with him. He'd had to memorize the most likely ones, which unfortunately this message didn't qualify as.

"How do you fit an entire cipher into that little book?" Not even using the entire book. It was ingenious, if it worked.

Lucy shrugged. "I don't write down the entire word, only enough of it for me to know what it is that I'm trying to say. See this word?"

She stopped on her current page and pointed to three letters. *CNG*. He wouldn't precisely call that a word.

"That means 'change.' If I want to use 'changed,' I

add a D to the end; if I want to use 'changing,' I add a G. It's really quite a simple shorthand."

To her, perhaps. It seemed ingenuity and quickness of mind ran in the family. Her brother Gideon was a renowned and respected scientist, whereas Morgan was known in the spy world to be especially quick with codes. Lucy seemed the same.

"Does this look like the same thing?" She found a new page and held it up next to the paper. Her eyebrows knitted together, a small furrow forming between them. She held her lower lip between her teeth as she examined the two pages.

She looked beautiful as she thought.

"Alex?"

When she turned those brown eyes up to him, he realized that she'd asked him a question. "Oh. Forgive me. Yes, they might be the same. It's worth a try."

"Is there a blank page for me to use to decode it?"

He pulled out the chair at the writing desk, gesturing for her to sit. She arranged her skirts gracefully as she did, then picked up her pencil again. She paused before putting it to paper.

"These are all blank?"

"Yes. You can write on any of them without fear."

Nodding, she did so. For a moment, he watched her, his gaze lingering on a strand of hair caressing her cheek. He mentally shook himself. They had work to do. He couldn't afford to be distracted, not with Monsieur V. While she decoded the message, he searched the room, leaving no proverbial stone unturned.

"I think I have it."

He stopped running his hands along the underside of the mattress and stood. "What does it say?"

She turned in the chair, her face set. "It's another message to me from Monsieur V."

His chest constricted. How could she say such a thing so calmly? At first, the fact that Monsieur V seemed to have plans for her had seemed a blessing. Follow Lucy, find Monsieur V. But that had been before he'd spent time with her. Now he was afraid that they weren't smart enough to outwit the spymaster, after all. If Monsieur V killed Lucy as well...

Alex swallowed around the lump in his throat. He wouldn't. That, Alex vowed. He would protect Lucy, whether she wanted his protection or not.

When he thought he would be able to keep the worry from his voice, he asked, "What does it say?"

"It sets another meeting and instructs me to come alone."

She met his gaze, her eyes unreadable. He couldn't breathe.

Don't do it. He would follow her, one way or another.

After a moment, he rasped, "And will you meet with him alone."

Her mouth hardened. "This might be our last chance to catch him. If he sees you, he could flee for good."

Given the obsessive way he'd been trying to make contact with her of late, Alex doubted as much. But he didn't say so out loud. Instead, he stepped closer. He perched on the foot of the bed. With the limited space in the room, his knees brushed hers as he did so. He tried to ignore the contact.

"Please don't go alone. I can remain hidden, but you need someone there in case the situation gets out of hand."

He said nothing more. He feared that if he pushed, she would refuse him. She would try to sneak past him and do it on her own and it would be as much of a cock-up as the last supposed meeting.

After a moment, she hesitantly nodded. "Very well. We can work together, but I intend to apprehend him. And you must stay out of sight unless it seems as though he will escape or harm me."

Relief gushed through Alex. "Yes, of course."

With Lucy's help, he was finally going to have that slippery spymaster in his grasp.

18

_W_hy had Alex believed for even a moment that he could watch Lucy deliberately put herself in danger and do nothing? From his concealed position behind the wide trunk of an oak, Alex aimed his pistol twenty paces and slightly to the right of Lucy's slim form. She made targeting easier by setting the lantern at her feet. If he could aim and be reasonably certain of hitting his target from this distance, so too could any French spies hidden nearby.

This time, Monsieur V had dictated a different meeting location. The pearly-gray light of dawn sifted down from the sky along with an intermittent drizzle. Lucy stood, exposed, on the crest of a small rise. No trees grew on that grassy knoll, necessitating for Alex to remain behind where he wouldn't be seen. He'd circled the hill three times, checking the woods for spies and finding none, before he'd admitted defeat and let Lucy await the spymaster.

Now, he wanted to retract that acquiescence. Allowing her to put herself in such an exposed position in order to meet with the traitor seemed like too big of a risk.

Even to catch Monsieur V?

For nearly a year, that had been his single-minded focus. Now, his resolve was shaken, simply because of one imaginative woman with a smile that lit up the room. His instincts warred with the vow he'd made himself to ensure that Monsieur V was one day at Alex's mercy. With Lucy's help, the fiend would finally be in Alex's grasp. But his heartbeat sped at the thought of Lucy being so close to him.

They couldn't underestimate Monsieur V. Last time, the man had had spies lying in wait that he'd sent in his place. If he sent two more, Alex would be hard put to keep Lucy alive. He had one pistol—one bullet. Reloading took time, twenty or thirty seconds during which Lucy's life would be in danger. No matter what, he had to ensure he didn't miss.

He bit the inside of his cheek to try to steady the tremble in his hand. If this meeting went poorly and he took his shot, he didn't want to hit Lucy by accident. He smothered the worry invoked by this dangerous situation. He would feel better if he was standing next to her, or better yet if he was there in her place. It didn't matter that she hadn't reciprocated his feelings. He cared for her and somehow, he would manage to exact his revenge and keep her safe. He had to.

The minutes blurred into one another. His arm ached and he dropped his hand. Did he risk another tour of the woods surrounding the hill? He didn't want to leave Lucy unguarded if Monsieur V arrived, but he didn't want the spymaster to surround them, either. Gun in hand, Alex moved as quickly as he dared while keeping his passage as silent as possible. He kept Lucy in view at all times as he circled the hilltop. He found no trace of any other people, friendly or otherwise.

He'd nearly completed the full circle when movement caught his eye on the tree line. He pressed himself next to the nearest trunk, using it for cover as he aimed his gun in that direction. Shadows swathed the line of the trees and he'd spent so much time looking at the lantern as he passed along his route that it left an imprint on his vision. A figure separated from the trees, but he couldn't tell who.

A man. Definitely a man from the silhouette. Alex guessed him to be about six feet tall with an athletic build. Monsieur V. It had to be.

The blood roared in his ears. His vision narrowed on that figure as he reached the bottom of the hill. Alex had him. He finally had him. He cocked his weapon, took aim, and prepared to fire.

The light wavered as Lucy picked up the lantern. What was she doing? She was supposed to wait at the top of the hill for Monsieur V! She would ruin everything.

He had to get a clear shot. For that, he had to get closer.

Abandoning his cover, he dashed around the side of the hill. The light from Lucy's bobbing lantern as she picked her way through the grass illuminated the man's face. The cut of his jaw, the shape of his hairline —Alex recognized him from the crude sketch Lucy had drawn.

He saw red. The blood rushed through his ears. A memory stabbed at him like a knife. The family solicitor, delivering the news that he was now the Marquess of Brackley.

Stepping into the too-neat study, where his father and brother had been found dead. Their bodies cleared away and everything put back in its place. But the room had a lingering shadow, a dark cloud that tainted the atmosphere.

Poison. The solicitor had informed him it was believed to be accidental, a batch of liquor gone bad, but the servants tiptoed around him, whispering of a different story: suicide. And Alex had uncovered something far more heinous still.

He had him. He finally had the man who had killed his father and brother. Lifting his hand to aim, Alex tightened his finger on the trigger.

"No!" Lucy jumped between them. He nearly shot her instead. At the last minute, he pulled his hand away, aiming the gun toward the trees. It fired, the blast deafening in the too-still air.

The spymaster bolted. The lantern rolled down the hill, guttering out. Alex swore, blinking quickly as he squinted to see where the fiend ran.

He started after him, but Lucy held up her hands, pressing them against his chest, over his rapidly beating heart. "What is wrong with you?"

"What is wrong with you?" he snapped. "He's getting away!"

Stepping around her, he sprinted for the tree line. Her footfalls fell behind him as she struggled to keep up. After stuffing the gun in his pocket, he raised his arms to ward away the tree branches.

Blindly, he followed the noise of the crackling brush ahead of him. The bramble nearly tripped him, but he forced himself to keep moving. Monsieur V couldn't get away. Not this time. The noise ahead warred with the noise behind him as Lucy followed him into the forest. He squinted, but the dawn light didn't penetrate the foliage. Only the barest shadow of the man he chased survived the bleary light. Alex put on a surge of speed, desperation granting him renewed energy. Monsieur V slipped around trees, hopped over bushes, and avoided rabbit holes. Unfamiliar with the terrain, Alex bumbled into all three.

He lost him. Staggering to a stop, his ankle throbbing from one of the rabbit holes, he searched the shadows. His heart galloped. Monsieur V had to be around here somewhere. He had to be. Alex didn't know what he would do if he wasn't. He couldn't spot the traitor.

"Alex?" Lucy's breathless voice emanated from behind him.

A hot, molten feeling bubbled in his chest as he realized that Monsieur V had slipped through his fingers again. Alex punched the nearest tree trunk. Agony ricocheted up his hand, mitigating some of his rage and self-loathing.

Not enough of it. Monsieur V was long gone, and this time, it was Alex's fault.

* * *

Lucy hesitated in mid-step as Alex viciously punched a tree. That thump and his resulting hiss of pain couldn't be good. She took a moment to catch her breath, letting her eyes adjust to the thin light.

Alex's shoulders were hunched as he faced the

tree, as if he warred with himself. And well he should. He had just scared away the spy Monsieur V had sent! If Alex had waited a moment or two longer instead of jumping out like that, Lucy might have been able to wheedle information out of the traitor. Such as why Monsieur V had yet again sent someone else to meet with her in his place. And where the spymaster was now.

As Alex shook out his hand, Lucy asked tentatively, "Did you hurt yourself?"

He released a short breath. "No." His tone was curt.

If he wasn't hurt, then he was going to answer for this cock-up. Striding up to him, Lucy crossed her arms. "What in the blazes were you thinking back there?"

"What were you thinking?" he snapped, rounding on her.

Although his voice was cutting, she pinched the inside of her arm and managed not to jump.

"You were supposed to stay on the top of the hill!"

"And you weren't supposed to shoot him!" She dropped her arms and balled her fists at her side. The heat of his body radiated in front of her, but it gave no indication of his mood. She wished she could see his expression right about then.

"Why not? Monsieur V is a traitor. Lord Strickland will see him hanged."

"*After* they get information from him. Surely you can see that an enemy spymaster is worth more alive than dead?"

Swearing something indecipherable under his breath, he strode away. He took no more than two paces, a branch cracking beneath his foot, before he turned back. "He's a monster. He doesn't deserve to live."

Lucy bit the inside of her cheek to stifle a gasp. His vehement tone told her that he meant it. He not only would have taken that spy's life, but he would have enjoyed it.

"It wasn't even Monsieur V who arrived."

Alex stiffened. "What? Don't be absurd. Of course it was."

She shook her head. "He was a different spy. Or maybe he wasn't working for Monsieur V at all. We can't know that now because you've gone and scared him off!"

Alex stepped closer. His breath teased the hair on the top of her head. "I saw his face. That was Monsieur V. Don't lie to me, Lucy. I saw the sketch in your notebook."

"That?" She threw her hands in the air. "When have I ever claimed to be an artist? It's true, the spy looked similar enough, but you should believe me when I tell you that it *wasn't him*."

He caught her by the shoulders, holding her in place. She still couldn't see his expression, nor even his eyes. It bothered her.

"Swear it. Promise me that you're telling the truth."

Why did he sound a bit desperate? "I swear. I wouldn't lie about this. I want to catch him, too. Catch him—not kill him."

Alex made a disgusted sound and turned away again. This time, when he paced, he stopped several feet away from her, his back turned. He seemed tormented. But why? Did he take his job with the spy network so seriously?

"What's come over you? This entire time, you've been nagging me about having a partner so I'll be safe, and yet you nearly got us both killed today."

He rounded on her. "I wouldn't have if you hadn't jumped into my path! Regardless of whether or not that was Monsieur V, he had to have been a French spy in order to come out to the middle of the forest at this hour of the morning, precisely where you were meant to be waiting. You should have let me kill him."

"Why?" She crossed her arms again. "That's not the way justice is done. Why do you hate Monsieur V so much that you're willing to cross that line?"

"Because he killed my family."

The words rang in the air between them, resonating as they slowly faded. In their place, the mundane sounds of the forest woke. Distant birds chirping, the buzz of insects and rustle of rodents.

Was he...serious? "Your father and brother died from—"

"Poison." Alex's sharp voice cut the air. "It was *not* self-inflicted."

Lucy had heard rumors that said otherwise. Though, come to think of it, she had always thought it odd that the marquess and his heir had decided to commit suicide at the same time in the same manner. No money or family scandals had been unearthed upon Alex taking the title, no explanation for their sudden deaths. So why would they both have taken their lives at the same time? It seemed like the sort of thing one did alone, when one had no hope of solace in another's company.

He stepped closer, his posture relaxing slightly from his hostile stance when she didn't try to argue with him. Softly, he admitted, "Camden—my brother —was a spy. I learned after his death that he was one of the spies tasked by your brother to find Monsieur V in London. I don't know what he found, but it appeared he got too close. Monsieur V killed my father and brother, I'm sure of it."

Lucy didn't know what to say. "I'm sorry. I didn't know."

"No one does. Only Morgan and Strickland."

"And that's why you're so determined to kill Monsieur V." Even without confirmation, Lucy didn't need to phrase it as a question.

"It is."

They fell silent again. Lucy pressed her lips together. Could she trust him? They were supposed to be working together, but today he had deviated from the very plan he had set down.

"He deserves to be killed, for the things he's done. Not only to my family."

"You're wrong."

Alex stiffened. He took a step back.

Lucy grimaced. That hadn't emerged the way she'd meant it. "I mean, of course he's a heinous criminal, but he's worth more alive than dead. Imagine the sort of information he could give to the Crown if only we caught him alive."

"I must see him dead, Lucy."

She stepped forward, laying her hand on his arm in the hopes of giving him some semblance of comfort. "You will. But it can be done both ways. My brother can get the information and then you can have your revenge."

When he made no response, she didn't know

whether to interpret his silence as acquiescence or as an indication that he would go against logic and try another assassination. She still didn't know how she felt about him being so casual about it. He would kill a man without hesitation. He almost had today. A bad man, but Lucy didn't know whether or not that made it right.

What would she do if she discovered that Monsieur V had killed her father? She didn't know. In fact, she barely remembered her father. She'd been young when he died, and his ducal responsibilities had meant that he hadn't spent as much time with her as she would have liked. She hoped Morgan wouldn't be like that with his son.

What had Alex's relationship been like with his father? He obviously mourned him, but she doubted they'd been close. Not many peers had as tight-knit families as Lucy's. Perhaps by avenging his father, Alex hoped to make up for the sins of the past.

He pulled away. "Why don't we worry about it if we're able to find Monsieur V again?"

Again? They hadn't found him once. Even though this time, there had been a meeting. Had that spy only been a frontrunner in case Alex laid in wait? Or did Monsieur V have no intention of meeting with her to begin with?

"You're right. We have to work on finding him again."

She turned away and they slowly made their way back to where she'd left the lantern.

After a moment, Alex asked, "How do you mean to do that?"

"Simple. We'll wait until he sends me another message."

everal days passed and Monsieur V sent Lucy no letter. She and Alex were vigilant, even though he largely avoided finding himself alone with her. Seeing as Lady Leighton and Mrs. Vale appeared to be keeping a sharp eye on them both, it was for the best. The only thing that mattered was finding the next note from Monsieur V. As a man, Alex had more freedom of movement than she did, so she left him to search the manor and grounds for clues and took what opportunities she could find to do the same. Neither of them found any trace of the French or their schemes.

Had that been her last chance? Since she didn't know why Monsieur V had contacted her specifically, she couldn't be certain that he *would* leave her another message. With each passing day, she grew more and more frustrated.

Alex appeared to feel the same. But, as they found little time together unchaperoned, only enough to pass along their lack of progress, she couldn't be certain that his apparent frustration didn't stem from something entirely different. Even during the brief moments they found alone together, nothing in Alex's demeanor indicated that he still thought of her romantically. Then why had he kissed her with such passion? Why had he made a confession of his feelings? She hadn't known what to say, given the lack of warning. It had been such a shock; his kiss had muddled her thoughts, too. The fact that his feelings seemed to have waned left her no closer to deciphering hers. Except, perhaps, a twinge of disappointment.

They were spies. Colleagues and allies against the French. Surely they should focus on that mission at such a time? Even if it had been a week since Monsieur V had last attempted to set a meeting.

Today was the last day of Lady Leighton's house party. As of tomorrow, Lucy would be on her way back to London, where she would have to begin her search for Monsieur V anew. The problem was that she didn't know where to look.

He has to have left some clue here. Whatever it was, she would find it. Today was her last chance.

She spent the morning before the guests awoke poking her nose where it didn't belong. The rest of her morning and into the afternoon was spent alongside Charlie and Mrs. Vale. Her dear friend noticed her agitation.

"Is something the matter? You seem restless today. More than usual."

Lucy forced a smile. She was tempted to lie and pretend as though she wasn't fretting herself to pieces, but she didn't see the point. Charlie had become more and more suspicious during their stay at Lady Leighton's manor, even though Lucy barely glanced in Alex's direction.

Lucy stifled a sigh. "I suppose I am restless. The weather is mild today. Perhaps a walk to the village would help, if you don't mind accompanying me?"

Charlie shrugged. "It sounds like a good diversion. I don't think Lady Leighton has any games planned, since it's our last day. Mama?"

"I'll fetch our shawls and bonnets," Mrs. Vale said.

Although she had been amenable to chaperoning the excursion, Mrs. Vale never took her shrewd gaze off Lucy. With her chaperone in such a snit, Lucy knew better than to try slipping away. Instead, she pretended to be engrossed in what the local shops had to offer. Once they had toured them all, Lucy suggested taking lunch at the inn. She excused herself in mid-meal to use the withdrawing room.

The moment she slipped into the corridor, she searched for someone who worked at the inn. She was lucky enough to find the innkeeper himself. Smiling, she planted herself in his path before he could return to the common room.

"Good afternoon, sir. I wonder if I might have a moment of your time."

The man scratched his mustache as he narrowed his eyes. "You're the miss who was in here a week or two ago. The one who came in with the lord?"

Apparently she had a memorable face. She nodded. "Yes, that would be me."

The man shrugged. "The chap you want hasn't come back in. I did find something in his room when it was cleaned, though."

Lucy forced herself to breathe evenly. If this man caught wind of how pivotal the information he kept was, he might not part with it—at least, not for less than a considerable sum. "What is it? Do you still have it?" she asked.

"He left a letter and instructions for it to be franked to London. He left it with more than enough to cover the cost, so I sent the letter."

Drat! What would be so important that Monsieur V couldn't attend to the matter himself? He must not have expected the innkeeper to read the letter or remember its destination.

"I don't suppose you recall where in London the letter was being sent? Or happened to glimpse the contents out of curiosity?" Her voice grew weaker as she suggested the latter idea. She pressed her lips together as she waited for a response.

"Didn't look at the letter," the innkeeper denied.

He deflated her hopes along with it.

"But I might have the instructions here somewhere. I could part with them, if you'd be willing to compensate the loss. That's good quality paper, and can still be crosshatched over."

Lucy stifled a sigh and emptied her reticule of her pin money. However, the moment the innkeeper returned with the note, she considered it money well spent. The note listed not only the instructions to send the letter, but also the address where it was to be sent.

Grinning, Lucy jotted down the address at the very end of her notebook, cramming it in shorthand into the last scrap of blank space. Once she returned to London tomorrow, she had someplace to look. Monsieur V couldn't anticipate that the innkeeper would keep something as mundane as instructions. Finally, she would be one step ahead of him.

But she couldn't tell Alex. If he lost his temper again, they might lose Monsieur V for good. The spymaster had already made it clear that he wasn't going to contact her again. Or worse, Alex might put his life in jeopardy this time.

So she had only one choice. When she returned back to London, she would follow this lead on her own.

20

*L*ucy Graylocke was hiding something. By this point, Alex would like to think that he was in tune enough with her to know when something was amiss. Earlier that afternoon, when he'd happened to cross paths with her and her chaperones, he had scarcely paid her any attention at all and even cut her off when she'd tried to speak with him. Mrs. Vale had far too keen an eye and Alex feared that his feelings for Lucy were scrawled across his face the moment she came within eyeshot. Later, when they'd had a scant second in the dining room alone as everyone else filed out, Alex had tried to apologize for his curt behavior, only to be gifted with a sunny smile and the flippant dismissal of her hand.

She was hiding something. Lucy was inquisitive.

She liked to know people's motivations. She was never dismissive. The fact that she was hiding something from him now could mean only one thing. She'd found a clue that might lead to Monsieur V's whereabouts.

And she wasn't going to share it with him.

Alex burned with indignation over the thought. She knew precisely what catching Monsieur V meant to him, and yet she was going to deny him the opportunity to help? She was in this for the glory, after all. He hadn't thought so...but why else wouldn't she accept his help?

He didn't know, but he was determined to confront her and find out.

He waited long after the guests retired to their chambers, keeping the door ajar for sounds of movement. With everyone departing on the morrow, they all retired early tonight. For those with insomnia before midnight, that meant traipsing back and forth to the kitchen or library in some vain attempt to lull themselves to sleep. With every new departure, Alex grew more and more tense.

Finally, silence descended upon the guest wing of the house, penetrated by faint snores. Alex lingered at the door, listening to be sure. His heartbeat nearly overpowered all other sound. Slipping into the hall, he tiptoed swiftly and silently down to Lucy's door. He didn't bother knocking, but let himself in and shut it, pressing his back to the door.

She lounged beneath the sheets, a book balanced on her knees and pillows cradling her back. Her braided hair was pulled over one shoulder, the color a dark contrast to her white nightgown. As he entered, she gasped.

He placed his fingers to his lips, urging her to keep silent. Mrs. Vale was placed nearby and not even the loud snores rumbling through the adjoining wall would muffle an exclamation.

She threw the covers back and jumped out of bed, stuffing the book onto the nightstand next to the candle. Her feet were bare. Her gauzy nightdress flirted with her ankles, the last three or four inches in lace. Her pale skin peeked through the gaps. The gown itself covered her—full length sleeves and a neckline that scooped beneath her collarbone—but the drape of the fabric against her figure made his mouth water. He couldn't help but imagine her naked body, hidden beneath the cloth.

She crossed to him, her eyes a bit wild. A stray strand of her hair clung to the corner of her mouth. "What are you doing in here? If you're found—"

They would need to be married quickly in order to smother the scandal. He didn't find that notion as unappealing as it seemed she did.

"Then you'd do best to keep your voice down," he whispered.

She crossed her arms beneath her chest, plumping up her breasts as she frowned. "You didn't answer my question." This time, her voice was so soft, he had to strain his ears to hear it.

He leaned a bit closer. She smelled faintly floral. Rose water, perhaps?

"You found something today. A clue."

Lucy's eyes widened. Her lips parted a fraction of an inch before she pressed them together again. "Don't you think if I'd found a clue that would lead us to Monsieur V that I would tell you?"

The question itself suggested that she would, and yet she wasn't speaking a word of it. She glanced past him to the writing desk, where her notebook lay next to a paper with scribbled notes on it. Was that paper the clue she had found? When he turned to look at it, she stepped in front of him.

"That doesn't answer my question."

"Does this?" She cupped his cheeks between her hands, stood on her tiptoes, and kissed him.

Her body pressed against his in aching detail. Far too few clothes separated them. As she teased at the seam of his lips with her tongue, he opened his mouth to protest. She deepened the kiss instead.

He was powerless to resist. She hadn't kissed him,

hadn't even looked to him like she'd wanted to, since he'd confessed his feelings for her. Was she only kissing him now as a distraction? He didn't care. For this brief moment, he had her in his arms again and he wasn't about to waste the moment. He kissed her back as if it might be the last time. For all he knew, it might.

When she pulled away, her voice was breathless. "I didn't find a clue."

His heart was thundering so loud in his ears that he almost believed her. But that kiss...it had to be her distraction tactic, didn't it?

"I don't believe you." His voice was hoarse.

She wrinkled her nose as she stepped back. "Well, then, I don't know how to convince you."

Letting me read your notebook would do it...

"Not kissing me for no blasted reason would be a step in the right direction."

A crinkle formed between Lucy's eyebrows. She touched her fingertips to her lips as she wrapped her other arm around her torso. "It wasn't for no reason. I wanted to." Color flushed across her cheekbones as she looked down.

"Why? More research?" It hadn't bothered him at first that she was using him as inspiration for her book. But now... He cared for her deeply. He might even love her. Never before had he met a woman as resourceful, resilient, creative. She'd charmed him before he even realized it.

Her face turned cherry-pink. "No, I..." She bit her lower lip and turned her gaze away. "It doesn't matter. Please leave. You shouldn't be here."

He shouldn't. Doubly so if she didn't want him here. But...did she?

He resisted the urge to look toward her notebook again. "What were you about to say?"

"It doesn't signify."

"I think it does." He raised his voice marginally.

Alarmed, Lucy lifted her chin to meet his gaze again. They held eye contact as the silence stretched between them again.

Eventually, in a voice so small it barely carried to his ears, Lucy murmured, "You said you cared for me."

"I do."

She frowned. "You haven't..."

He took a step closer. "I haven't done what?"

"You haven't shown it. Not since we found that last message."

He balled his fists to keep from throwing his hands in the air in exasperation. "You didn't reciprocate. I didn't think you wanted the reminder."

"Oh." She looked down. "I was taken aback."

That was always the response one hoped to get from a woman upon confessing one's feelings. Not that

Alex would know firsthand, having only done it once, but he had to admit to some disappointment upon hearing her say as much.

She still didn't appear to know what to say. He would make it easy on her and leave. She wouldn't allow him access to her notebook, in any case, and it was laid out in the open—he couldn't take it without her noticing the theft promptly. It had been madness for him to come here, in any case.

He took a step back, toward the door.

"I do," she said, her voice small.

He halted. "You do?" What was she talking about?

She lifted her gaze, her jaw set in determination. "I care for you, too."

Was this just another tactic to distract him from the clue she was keeping from him? If so...he was afraid it might work. Over the past week, he'd fallen asleep imagining how it might be to hear these words. For a moment, he wondered if he was dreaming.

Lucy lifted her chin. "I kissed you because I wanted to. In fact, I'd like you to do it again."

She didn't need to ask twice. He crossed to her, cupping her cheeks as he melded his mouth to hers. The way she felt and tasted...it couldn't be a dream. It felt too real. Which meant she truly did care about him.

Suddenly, he understood why she hadn't been able

to answer him. The notion that she felt the same stole his voice. He couldn't find the words to express himself so he funneled his emotions into his kiss.

Lucy surrendered to him. She wrapped her arms around his neck and pressed her body against his. Her kiss was a bit wild, yet decisive. Like her. He held her close, drinking in the sensation and trying not to take the moment too far. They weren't married and she was of a very different caliber than the sort of women with whom he had dallied in the past. She deserved to be respected and cherished and—

Bloody hell, was she trying to undo the laces on his shirt?

Upon reaching his room tonight, he'd made himself more comfortable by divesting himself of his jacket, waistcoat, and cravat. Until this moment, he hadn't recalled that he was only half-dressed. And she was no better. She was temptation incarnate, and he didn't know whether he would be able to resist her for long.

He caught her hands, holding them between their bodies as he broke the kiss. "Lucy, please. This isn't something you can treat as research. Not this."

He wanted to surrender to the passion between them. He wanted to give her the kind of pleasure no one ever had. But he had to control himself, for both their sakes. She was an innocent. She couldn't know how close to the edge of reason she could bring him with nothing more than her kiss.

If he bided his time, he would be able to indulge in the future with a clear conscience, after she was married to him. But he had to earn her brother's trust first, and that would take time. Still, with Monsieur V so near that he could practically taste his revenge, Alex found himself free to consider a future.

And he wanted that future to include Lucy.

She licked her lips, but didn't try to draw her hands away. "I'm not going to put this in a book. This is between you and me." She slipped out of his grasp and tugged his shirt from the waist of his breeches. When she was done, she looked up at him, hesitant.

"We shouldn't. We should wait." This wasn't why he had come to her room.

Lucy pursed her lips. "Why? You're here now. Take advantage of the moment before it slips away. There's no time like right now."

She stood on tiptoe, capturing his lips as she slid her hand around to his back and beneath his shirt. Her hands on his bare skin proved his undoing. He kissed her back, voracious, as he ran his hands over her, learning her shape. She had the body of a Greek goddess and tasted of ambrosia, too.

He'd been without a woman for too long, but if it had been any other woman, he would have been able to resist. Not Lucy. He craved her touch too much. Before he knew it, he was pressing her into the mattress. He gathered the skirts of her nightgown around her knees, slipping his hand beneath to caress her leg. He kissed her as though she were air and he'd been underwater too long. When she drew his shirt up to his shoulder blades, he reluctantly released her long enough to remove it.

He worked her nightgown up her hips and abdomen, kissing the flesh he exposed. Lucy bit her lip to muffle her whimper. He smiled against her skin, enjoying her response. By the time he reached her mouth and tossed her nightgown to the floor, he ached for her. He took her mouth in a long, hard kiss.

They worked the buttons on his breeches free in tandem. He groaned at the feather-light feel of the backs of her knuckles caressing his pelvis. When the last button was free, he left her only long enough to remove his clothes. He left them in a heap next to the bed.

The mattress shifted on its ropes as he rejoined her. He pressed himself against her heat, taking her mouth in a kiss that spoke the words that he couldn't find. That he cherished her and this moment. That he didn't want to be here with anyone else.

His hands wandered, finding her every sensitive spot. He gasped into her mouth when she gave him the same treatment. When they were both trembling, hungrily kissing every inch of skin they could reach, he sheathed himself in her. They moved in tandem, claiming each other and imprinting each other on their bodies and souls. When they reached their pinnacle, they did it together, as he yearned to do everything else in life.

21

*A*lex watched the play of candlelight on the ceiling. Lucy's breathing fanned against his bare shoulder as her body pressed against his side. Her arm was looped across his middle, holding him loosely in place. Given the rhythm of her breathing, he thought she'd fallen asleep. He savored the feel of her for a moment longer, using her warmth as a salve against the pain to come.

This was like a dream. Her heart beat against his arm, a steady beat that lured him toward sleep. He bit the inside of his cheek to keep himself awake. As peaceful as this moment was, it wouldn't last. Come morning, she would loathe him.

That knowledge cut him, but he had no choice except to leave. On that writing desk rested a pivotal piece of evidence. The last thing he needed in order to catch the fiend who had murdered his family. He was certain of it.

Steeling himself to leave her, he gently slipped out from beneath her. He moved slowly to keep from rocking the bed and waking her. Once he attained freedom, he swiftly donned his clothes. He paused to draw the sheets up to her shoulders before he turned away.

Her notebook rested atop the sheet of paper, but he read the paper first. He frowned as he squinted to read it by the flickering light of the candle. At first, he thought he was looking at some kind of unrecognizable code, but then he recognized three key letters. *CNG*. This was written in Lucy's shorthand. Armed with that knowledge, he puzzled out the contents of the page.

It was filled with what appeared to be notes for her book. Wild imaginings involving the redemption of a scoundrel—or was the scoundrel supposed to redeem the heroine and in so doing invoke a change in himself? Alex didn't read far enough to interpret her plans for her book. Given the conflicting ideas on the page, she was cataloguing her ideas as she untangled the path through the plot point.

The faint snores coming from the neighboring chamber covered the small sigh he released. He glanced over his shoulder toward Lucy's peacefully-sleeping form. Had she been telling the truth? Guilt churned his stomach at the fact that he'd been so suspicious of her.

But she *had* been acting strangely. She hadn't wanted him to look through her notes. Perhaps because her ideas were still in the raw form...or perhaps because she was hiding something in her notebook. He had to know for certain which it was. Even though it was another violation of her privacy, he told himself that it was for the good of the nation. A man like Monsieur V destroyed lives. Such a man mesmerized the people around him; how did Lucy hope to get information from him? More likely, he would extract information from his interrogators. Alex had to get to him first. He had to kill Monsieur V, to satisfy his own conscience and to save Britain. But perhaps mostly, now it was to save Lucy. He had no idea what Monsieur V intended for her or why he seemed so keen to meet with her, but if Alex had his way, Monsieur V would never get a chance to harm her.

He flipped to the back of her notebook to find the last thing she'd written. The last handful of pages was jammed with notes. As he deciphered them, he realized that she had written about a kiss in excruciating detail. A kiss with him? If so, it was a heady realization to know exactly how he affected her. It made him want to turn around, rejoin her in bed, and wake her with a kiss every bit as passionate.

At the bottom of the last page, something else was scrawled in the corner. An address. His heartbeat quickened. An address for Monsieur V? How had she found it? She was more ingenious than anyone gave her credit for.

However, he couldn't let her follow it, for her own safety. This was between him and Monsieur V and he wasn't about to let the woman he cared about be drawn into the same dangers as his brother had been. He ripped out the page and stuffed it into his pocket.

"Forgive me," he whispered, barely loud enough to hear his own words. He knew that, when she woke up, their time together would be over. She might never forgive him. In her place, he wouldn't, either.

This was goodbye.

* * *

LUCY WOKE ALONE, well-rested and a bit cold. She stretched in bed and listened to the birds chirping. It was morning.

Perhaps she shouldn't have expected Alex to stay all night, but after the intimacy they'd shared, she would have liked to wake up in his arms. She supposed that's what marriage was for.

Marriage. Babies. A spike of alarm swept through Lucy and she bolted upright. She laid her hand over her abdomen, wondering. Could she be *enceinte?* It wasn't instantaneous, given her brothers' marriages, but there was still a chance. What had she been thinking last night?

She knew perfectly well what she'd been thinking. She'd focused on Alex's arms, his hands, his body surrounding her. She'd lost herself in the passion he awoke in her and soaked in his nearness. She'd never been so close with another person. Never. It had been magical. Although it had started as a tactic to distract him from the fact that she'd hidden a clue from him had turned into something she wanted to experience for herself. Not as a distraction, not even for research. She'd wanted to be that close to him. Even if it resulted in the pain of childbirth, she still couldn't regret it.

She supposed she now knew why her sisters-in-law submitted to their husbands' attentions. And why Phil had seemed so happy, holding her newborn baby in her arms, despite the fact that he had caused her such agony during the birth. They loved their husbands and wanted to share whatever closeness with them that they could.

With a sigh, Lucy slipped out from beneath the sheets. Consumed by thoughts, she found and donned her nightgown again. She didn't know what last night had meant to Alex. In her dreams, she'd half-hoped for a hopelessly romantic proposal, wherein he would confess that he could never live without her in his life and ask her to end the suffering of being apart. In the light of day, if Alex had tried such a melodramatic proposal, she might have laughed at him. Instead, she'd gotten none and he'd snuck away during the night. It was far from romantic...but he was a renowned rake.

Maybe it hadn't meant anything to him, after all. She'd believed him when he'd told her that he cared for her, but...what if she was wrong?

She would just have to find Alex and ask him. That was all there was to it. However, judging by the light slanting in through the window, he probably wasn't yet awake. Did she mean something to him? The question burned at her, demanding an answer. She flipped through her notebook to the back, determined to read through her description of their first kiss while trying to detect any sign that she meant more to him than another woman. That had happened only days ago, before he confessed his feelings, but she hadn't described any of their other kisses, so it was the only material she had to resource.

As she skipped to the end, her heart skipped a beat. The very last page was ripped out. The last page, where she had written Monsieur V's address.

Alex had taken it.

She stared at the ragged edges of the page. It blurred as tears gathered. She hadn't meant anything to him after all. Just like she'd started kissing him as a distraction, he had used passion to distract her. Except he had taken it much farther than kissing. He'd torn out the page so she wouldn't be able to follow him.

She had memorized the address, but that wasn't the point. The point was that he was going to do this without her. He might get himself killed. At the very least, he would deprive Britain of the opportunity to interrogate and learn the secrets of a French spymaster. She had to stop him somehow.

She turned, but couldn't see clearly through the haze of her tears. Her shin knocked against the chair. It teetered. Although she lunged for it, it toppled from her grasp and crashed against the ground. She righted it quickly and dashed the tears from her eyes. She tried to tell herself that it didn't matter that Alex had tricked her—the only thing that mattered was that she stopped him from confronting Monsieur V alone.

As she turned toward the wardrobe to find the sole dress that hadn't yet been packed for travel, a knock rapped at the door. She froze with her hand on the wardrobe door. "Who is it?" Her voice was even, if a bit higher than usual.

"Charlie. I heard a crash. Are you all right?"

Some of the tension melted from Lucy's shoulders,

along with a flood of disappointment. For a moment, she'd hoped that Alex had had a change of heart and returned.

"May I come in? I'm out here in my wrapper."

"Yes, of course." Lucy wiped her eyes one more time, hoping that her friend wouldn't be able to tell that she'd been crying.

The young woman slipped into the room and shut the door, leaning back against it. Strands of her hair escaped her braid and clung to the sides of her mouth. She narrowed her eyes. "Are you certain you're all right?"

Blast! She'd noticed anyway. Lucy forced a smile and attempted to distract her. "Just a bit clumsy this morning. Forgive me, I didn't mean to wake you."

"You didn't. Mama had just come back from fetching a cup of tea for us both. She warned me not to go down. It seems the hostess is in a tiff."

"Oh?" Lucy perched on the edge of the bed. She didn't recall that she was still holding her notebook until she squeezed so tight that the edges dug into her palm. "Did she say why?"

"It seems Lord Brackley left in the middle of the night with nary a word except to the servants. Lady Leighton is spitting mad, trying to convince everyone she comes across to give him the cut direct and rescind their invitations."

Lucy felt the blood drain from her face. He was already gone? If he'd left in the middle of the night, he might be halfway to London by now. She'd never catch him.

Charlie frowned. "Lucy? Did I say something to upset you?"

"Brackley left?" Lucy didn't know why she needed the confirmation. She'd just heard her friend say those very words. She wanted Charlie to tell her that it was a rumor, that it hadn't yet been confirmed. That he might still be in his room.

"Mama confirmed it with the servants. Good riddance, I say. He should have left sooner."

Tears pricked Lucy's eyes and she looked down quickly.

Unfortunately, she wasn't quick enough. "Lucy?" Charlie stepped forward. She tentatively sat next to Lucy on the bed. "Are you okay? That devil Brackley got to you, didn't he?"

In the end, she supposed that he had. Sniffling, Lucy squeezed her eyes closed and leaned into Charlie's embrace. "I think I was starting to fall for him," she confessed in a teary voice.

Clearly, Alex hadn't felt the same. He'd made his priorities perfectly clear. He'd chosen his revenge over her.

Lucy hadn't thought it would hurt this much.

---

22

*A*lex pulled his collar closer to his neck. The intermittent rain had long since soaked his hair and trickled down his spine. If he maintained his position, in the shadows of a ramshackle house with eaves that seemed riddled with holes, he would likely catch a chill.

Across from him stood a non-descript house. If he'd strolled down the street, he never would have paid any more attention to it than any of the others on this street. It was in slight disrepair, not enough to draw undue attention and yet not in as pristine a state as houses in a richer quarter of London. The men and women who strode along this street did so with their heads bowed, pinched expressions on their faces. They kept their hands in their pockets, likely on weapons in case something untoward should happen. They kept their gazes trained on their paths and didn't meet his eye nor anyone else's. They didn't so much as glance at the house he watched.

He glanced again at the address on the page. He was in the right place. Rage seethed inside him at the thought of Monsieur V lazing inside. He should break down the door and wring the fiend's neck. The hot, potent need for revenge threatened to choke out all reason. He clenched his fists. The muscles in his arms, back, and shoulders hardened like rocks.

The last time he had rushed in without thinking, he had aimed for the wrong man. This time, he had to be certain the man he shot was Monsieur V. He had to be certain that he was in there. Somehow, Alex wrestled down his thirst for revenge and bided his time.

Eventually, just as the sun was starting to sink below the horizon and painted the gray clouds with shades of gold, a figure slouched through the street. It paused in front of the door to the non-descript house. The figure, a man judging by the greatcoat he appeared to be swimming in, glanced over his shoulder. Alex froze.

This street didn't afford many places to remain unseen. Alex had chosen a place where no one wanted to look, but the fact that the residents seemed determined to mind their own business had worked in his favor thus far. It was dark, the shadows having length-ened steadily, and he hoped they concealed his posi-tion. He held his breath and remained utterly still.

The figure entered the building and shut the door. Alex released his breath. Relief gushed through him as he inhaled again. He hadn't been seen.

Someone is inside. That someone had been, at his estimate, a man of roughly six feet tall with a build that might have been athletic or lean. At the very least, he hadn't appeared to carry much extra weight.

Monsieur V. It must be. The haze of rage overcame Alex once more and he gritted his teeth. He unwrapped a biscuit from a handkerchief and bit into it. Although he'd scarcely eaten all day, not wanting to leave his post, he found he had no appetite.

The sun disappeared beneath the horizon and what little daylight had peeked between the clouds faded away into shadow. A light winked to life in the house. Alex followed it with his eyes, training his focus on the shadowy figure it produced.

He didn't have backup. One of the first things Morgan had drummed into him during training was always to let someone else—a superior—know where he would be, and always to bring a second pair of eyes in case something went wrong. This time, Alex didn't even have Lucy to act as that second pair of eyes. She would only try to stop him, in any case.

If he had no one to rely on but himself, he had to do this right. He had two pistols with him, both loaded and ready. Nonetheless, he wanted to be certain that there was only one person in the house. He didn't know where Lucy had come by her clue; this might very well be an ambush. If so, Alex hoped that his vigilance would help him to slip around it. He'd been gnashing his teeth most of the day while conducting his surveillance. Despite his impatience and frustration, he forced himself to wait.

He watched the house, the light disappearing in one room to reappear in another. An hour passed, maybe more. Eventually, when the chill of evening started to bite into Alex's bones, he decided that Monsieur V was alone in the house.

Earlier in the day, he had examined the house from all angles, noting all possible entrances and exits. He didn't use the door, but slipped around to the back. He inserted a thin knife between the shutters and used the leverage to unhook them. Quietly, he pulled inside the darkened room and closed the shutters again.

He stepped slowly and silently, his heart thundering louder than his footsteps. A slight shuffle and the occasional squeak of a board indicated movement upstairs. Alex waited with bated breath for the movement to settle. Only then did he slip into the corridor.

For all his surveillance of the outside of the house,

he hadn't had any means of mapping the interior. His ears strained for further sounds of movement and his heart in his throat, he searched for the staircase. When he found it, he pulled one of the pistols from his pocket and held it ready as he carefully mounted the stairs, testing each one to avoid any squeaks before he ascended. Near halfway up the staircase, he feared that his head might be seen if he continued at that slow pace. Not wanting to make himself a target, he abandoned the pretense, hugged the wall, and bolted up the last few steps on his tiptoes. On the landing, he slowly aimed his weapon at each of the doors along the corridor, waiting for a figure to enter one. None did.

The light spilled from the door on the far left. Keeping his back to the wall, he snuck down its length to the door, left ajar. The light flickered within, a candle no doubt. He took a deep breath to steady himself and aimed his weapon in front of him.

He burst into the room, pivoting to find the figure. The room contained an old bed, a round table with the candle set upon it, and a tattered, stuffed armchair. It was...empty?

He stared a second too long. A man jumped out from the shadows behind the door. Alex spun, but the man knocked the gun from his hand. It clattered somewhere near the bed. He tensed, waiting for a misfire from the sensitive weapon. It didn't go off, a relief.

He had little time to process the stroke of luck because the man was upon him. Alex fought back, using the dirty tricks he'd been taught in training. *Your gun...get your other gun.* His hands were too busy fending off a series of blows. The man, a steely-eyed villain of about Alex's height and build, must be Monsieur V. Alex was looking into the eyes of the man who had killed his family.

Rage overtook him. He fought, wild and panicked, trying to end the monster's life however he could. His hand slipped from around the man's neck as Monsieur V jabbed his elbow into Alex's sternum. Sputtering for breath, he stumbled back.

His gun. He started to reach for it just as the traitor pulled a pistol of his own. If Alex dipped his hand into his pocket, he would be dead. He almost did it anyway.

Instead, he thought of Lucy and raised his hands in surrender. If he died, he would never see her again. If he died, Monsieur V would walk free.

Both those things were unforgivable.

With a smile to match his cold eyes, Monsieur V lowered himself into the chair next to the candle. Alex was caught.

$\mathcal{D}$espite leaving Lady Leighton's manor the morning after Alex departed, Lucy found herself unable to slip away from her chaperone's watchful eye until the day after they arrived in London. Mrs. Vale watched Lucy as though she were a criminal, and Lucy's pet parrot seemed to have taken up the cause. Every time Lucy tried to sneak out of a room where Antonia resided, her pet bird shrieked, insulted her, and flapped across the room to join her. She couldn't even hope to approach the front door without someone in the townhouse being alerted to the fact that she intended to go out. Mrs. Vale let her go nowhere alone, not even on a walk around the block.

Lucy chafed beneath the constant supervision. Charlie must have confessed to her mother of Lucy's feelings for Alex. Neither of the Vales approved the match...not that Lucy could consider it a match, precisely. After all, he had chosen his revenge over her. Her only hope was that he had decided to take his time to properly assess the situation, or even reach out to her brother for backup as he had pestered her to do so many times. It was a faint hope, but she clung to it.

The sun peeked out from a sky dotted with grayish clouds when she finally managed to slip away from her testy bird and Mrs. Vale. Wearing her plainest coat, Lucy walked from the Tenwick townhouse to a busier street and hired a hack to take her to the address she had memorized. When the driver clattered away, Lucy shaded her eyes and studied the building.

She would never live there voluntarily. The roof seemed patched, the paint peeled from the doors and shutters, and the only form of greenery were the thin scrubs of weeds clumping around the foundation. Like the rest of the street, the house seemed almost ghostly in its silence.

Cautious but curious, Lucy circled the house. She pressed her face against the shutters, trying to squint through the cracks into the room beyond in order to discern whether anyone was inside. She found no signs of movement, but she was only marginally successful in her spying. By the time she returned to the front, the street was deserted. If Alex laid in wait nearby, he was well hidden. She raised her fist as if to knock on the door, baiting him. Since he'd been so adamant over her safety, he would stop her.

He didn't. Perhaps he called her bluff. She dropped her hand. What would she say, in any case? *Bonjour, Monsieur V. You seem adamant to speak with me, so here I am.* The notion was ludicrous.

Besides, as far as she could tell, no one was inside. Out of curiosity, she tried the latch. To her surprise, it was unlocked. She glanced over her shoulder, checking once more that the street was clear. Then she slipped inside.

The house seemed empty. To be safe, she tiptoed through the lower floor first, then the upper floor, peeking into every room and closet to assure herself that no one was lying in wait. It was as dead within as it seemed from outside. Hoping that the occupant wouldn't return soon, she searched the lower floor thoroughly. If Monsieur V had sent a package here, then the resident must be important to him. Perhaps they knew each other personally, or the resident was a part of the French spy network as well. Lucy found nothing that might identify the occupant of the house—in fact, she didn't find a single personal article below stairs that might indicate whether the resident was male or female. She moved upstairs, searching every room on the second floor until she came to the last on the left.

Here she found the only personal article in the house. On a round table in the bedroom rested a signet ring. When Lucy picked it up to examine the crest, her heart skipped a beat. That was the Brackley seal.

Her head spun. She dropped into the chair and lowered her head between her knees as she forced herself to think. Her ears rang. Tears pricked her eyes as she realized what must have happened. Alex had been here, after all. He'd been captured—or killed.

Worry made her heartbeat flutter and her stomach tie itself in knots. She had to know for certain. Perhaps he'd been here, but left his signet ring in haste. She had to find him, one way or another.

Lucy squared her shoulders and rapped on the front door to the Brackley townhouse. *When you're seen, this will reflect poorly on your reputation.* She was without chaperone, trying to gain entrance to a bachelor's house. However, at the moment, she didn't give a whit for her reputation. If Alex was in there, she was going to slap him for making her worry.

If Alex was inside.

The door opened to reveal an aged butler who had likely been in service as long as the family had been alive. He stared down his long nose at her. "And who might you be?"

He must be blind as a bat not to recognize her for a Graylocke. She fished her calling card out of her reticule and handed it to him, for all the good it would do. "Lady Lucy Graylocke. I'm here to see Lord Brackley. Is he in?" She clasped her hands in front of her to hide the tremor that plagued her while she awaited the answer.

The butler took the card with a raised eyebrow. He tucked it away without looking at it. "I'm afraid Lord Brackley is not at home."

Her lungs seized. She couldn't breathe.

Be calm. He might only be at the club.

She forced a deep breath and kept her tone even as she asked, "And when do you expect him to be back?"

"You mistake me, my lady. I don't expect him back. Lord Brackley is not in London."

Her stomach sank. "You're certain?"

"Quite. He's at a house party in the country."

Lucy shook her head. "Lady Leighton's house party, you mean? That ended two days ago."

The butler frowned. "Perhaps he's on his way to his country estate then, and will arrive when he gets there. He never came here."

Alex's signet ring felt heavy in her pocket. Alex

had ventured to London but never made it to his town-house? Now she was even more worried.

"If he returns home, please have him call on me. Thank you."

Without another word, Lucy turned on her heel and stumbled blindly to the street. She blinked away the tears that stung her eyes as she searched for another hackney to hire to bring her home. By the time she reached the corner of the street, she decided that the exercise would do her good. She didn't care a whit who saw her walking home. The exercise helped to burn away some of the helplessness that plagued her.

By the time she arrived back at the Tenwick town-house, she had come to an important decision. Perhaps one that she should have arrived at a long time ago. She had postponed the inevitable too long.

As she opened the door, Antonia squawked from inside the house and both Vale women trotted into the corridor.

"Lucy," Mrs. Vale chided. "We've been looking for you all over. Where have to been?"

"Are you all right?" Charlie added. Her mouth turned mulish. "This is about Brackley, isn't it?"

Lucy steeled her spine. She resisted the urge to pat her eyes to ensure that they weren't puffy from with-held tears. Ignoring both their questions, she said,

"Pack your bags, ladies. I think it's past time we returned to Tenwick Abbey."

It was time to tell her brothers the truth.

* * *

"This isn't the road to Tenwick Abbey," Charlie said as the carriage turned away from the main road. In order to reach Lucy's ancestral estate, they would have to drive another six hours before taking a different road.

Lucy stroked Antonia as her pet fluffed up her feathers. That bird had an uncanny ability to sense when Lucy was uneasy. She took a deep voice before she answered calmly.

"No, it is not, but I don't think it will put us much out of our way. A half a day, at most. I want to check on something."

"Check on what? Where are we going?"

Mrs. Vale pursed her lips but didn't say a word. She merely observed. Her disapproval hung heavy in the air, as if she knew what Lucy was going to say.

"We're going to Lord Brackley's estate. It won't take long, I promise."

A bit over two hours later, the carriage pulled onto a thin ribbon of a drive. It wove between copses of trees, ringing the bottom of a range of hills, until finally the lofty manor could be seen. It was atop one such hill, a magnificent residence that looked as though it had been built onto the remnants of a medieval fortress. The afternoon sun set an orange glow over the scenery.

As the carriage pulled to a stop, Lucy bid her companions, "Wait here. This won't take a moment." She shoved her parrot into Charlie's arms and hopped from the carriage before the women protested. Straightening her shoulders, Lucy approached the mahogany double doors of the manor.

They opened at her approach. Clearly, someone in the manor had noticed her arrival.

The housekeeper, a curvaceous middle-aged woman with thin lips and narrowed eyes, met her at the door. "May we help you, my lady?"

At least they recognized her for a peer. That was likely due to the fact that she rode in the official Tenwick carriage today, with the ducal seal on the door. Her posture regal, Lucy said, "I'm here to see Lord Brackley. You may tell him Lady Lucy Graylocke has arrived."

The housekeeper's frown deepened. "I'm afraid you were given poor information, my lady. Lord Brackley is not in residence. Last we were told, he wasn't planning to come to the country until August."

Somehow, Lucy managed to keep her ducal mien

in place long enough to thank the woman and turn around. As she neared the carriage, the reality set in and she nearly tripped. Alex was not in the country. He was not in Town. He was gone.

And she didn't know if he would be in one piece when she found him again.

24

By the time Lucy found Morgan in the nursery, cradling his son, she was out of breath. She had sprinted the length of Tenwick Abbey, checking all the parlors, the library, his office, and finally being directed here. She leaned against the door frame to catch her breath.

Morgan looked up, a frown on his face. "Lucy, you're home. I thought you meant to stay in London for the Season."

That had merely been a ruse in order for her to find Monsieur V, which she hadn't done. She gulped for air, her head spinning a bit and her knees weak from the run. It was a very big estate, and the nursery was on the fourth floor.

"Something terrible has happened."

Morgan gently set the baby in his cradle. With a frown, he wordlessly shooed Lucy out of the room. When she backed into the corridor, he followed and shut the door.

His gray eyes pierced her. "What's happened? Where are Mrs. Vale and Charlie?"

Lucy batted her hand as she panted. "They're somewhere on the estate. I ran ahead." She offered him the signet ring clutched in her fist.

He strode closer to the window at the end of the corridor. Daylight spilled in, the scene beyond showing Tenwick Abbey's wide lawn up to the tree line. The moment her brother examined the ring, he looked at her sharply.

"What has that fiend done to you?"

"Nothing." Nothing aside from break her heart when he'd chosen his revenge over her. That didn't mean she was going to let him die. She didn't give up on people that easily, certainly not the ones she cared about. "He's missing. Monsieur V—"

The moment the name left her lips, Morgan's expression turned stony. He advanced on her. She pressed her back against the wall. She'd never seen him look so forbidding.

"Not here. My office. Now."

He granted her little reprieve to catch her breath. She trotted to keep up with his long-legged stride as he led the way. Mr. Keeling, Morgan's assistant, seemed to recognize her brother's agitation, but Morgan waved him away. He shut the door to his study forcibly.

The painting on the wall, of a centuries-old fox hunt, seemed to glare at her. The dogs snarled as if they cornered her instead of the fox.

Morgan rounded on her. "He told you?" His eyes snapped with fury.

"Who told me what?"

A muscle in her brother's jaw twitched. He hadn't shaved yet today, judging by the dark shadow along his jaw line. "Brackley. He told you about the spy network."

She snorted and crossed her arms. "Please. I'm no imbecile. I've known for months."

Morgan looked surprised. Did he think she was that daft?

"Does Mother—"

He cut himself off and fingered the white streak at his temple.

Lucy shrugged. "How am I to know? I've never told her, if that's what you're asking."

He pointed to the chair in front of his desk. "I think you need to explain what's happened."

Her stomach shrank to the size of a pin as she obeyed. She perched on the edge of the chair. He remained standing, arms crossed, looming over her. His silver-gray eyes didn't help matters.

She took a deep breath. She'd rehearsed this. When she felt calm again, she met his gaze.

It was a mistake. Her courage shriveled like a prune.

"I know what Monsieur V looks like. I think I'm the only one."

The bands of Morgan's arms bunched, the only indication of his emotions. "And what led you to believe that? Where did you hear the name Monsieur V?"

Lucy rolled her eyes. "Can you pretend for a minute that I'm not a child? I didn't know who he was when I met with him, but I put it together later. When Lord Strickland sent you a message."

Morgan bristled. "Strickland sent a message? Here?"

Lucy winced. She'd kept that from him. Seeing as Morgan must not have received another message, Lord Strickland must have taken her presence in London to be an indication that Morgan had received the message and assigned her to the task. Apparently Strickland didn't know her brother very well.

"During Phil's labor," Lucy mumbled under her breath. "You were busy so I intercepted it. The code wasn't terribly complex. I figured, since I was the only one to know his face, I would find him for you."

"Find him?" Morgan bit off the words.

She didn't still have the missive or she would have shown it to him. She frowned, rubbing her forehead as she tried to recall exactly what the message had said. "Monsieur V returned to London. Lord Strickland didn't know where he was and wanted your best people on it. Since I know what he looks like and no one else does, I figured that was me. So I went to look for him."

"Alone?" Unlike most men, when Morgan got angry, he got cold. His eyes turned to ice and his expression might as well have been one of the carved busts down in the ancestor's hall. "Or did you have help?"

She looked down, unable to meet his gaze without shaking. "Alone, at first. But Alex—"

"*Alex?*" Morgan bit off the name as if it was poison.

She glared at him. "Lord Brackley, then, if you prefer. He puzzled out what I was about and told me I ought not to go after a French spymaster without help."

"You ought not to have gone after a French spymaster at all!"

Lucy gritted her teeth. "Will you let me tell you what happened or won't you?"

When Morgan said nothing, she took that to be an indication for her to continue.

She straightened her shoulders and spoke the words she'd rehearsed. "I tracked Monsieur V from the costume he'd worn to Lady Belhaven's ball. That led me to a costumer near Bond Street, who had a message to me from Monsieur V."

"A message to you?" The words were delivered with such frost that it was a wonder his breath didn't fog in front of his face.

"Yes. To me. He left a dress and an invitation to meet at Lady Leighton's house party."

"Which you foolishly accepted." It was a statement, not a question.

Lucy took a deep breath and tried not to lose her temper. It wouldn't help either of them. It wouldn't help Alex.

"Lord Brackley was there as well," she said, emphasizing the formal title. "We joined forces in order to bring the traitor to justice."

"But he slipped away." Again, not a question. Morgan must have heard too much of the same story.

Lucy pressed her lips together, struggling to get her emotions under control. "He wouldn't have, if Alex had listened to his own advice and taken me with him. We found a clue, an address where Monsieur V had sent a package. Alex left in the middle of the night and went alone. By the time I got there the only thing left to find was his ring."

Emotion choked her. She breathed evenly through her nose, tasting tears at the back of her throat. She struggled not to cry, fearing that her brother might find it weak. She wanted him to think of her as an equal, not a baby, even if there was thirteen years between them.

"What address?"

Lucy ignored his clipped tone and told him, watching as he scribbled it down. He ripped off the corner of the page and shoved it into his pocket.

"I've already searched the house," she informed him. "The only thing to find was that ring."

Morgan tucked the ring in his pocket along with the address. For some reason, that made the ache in Lucy's chest burn even more. That was Alex's ring. If anyone should have it, it should be her.

"And you think because you found his ring that Brackley is in danger."

Lucy fisted her hands in her skirts. "I know it." She met Morgan's gaze and held it. "I went to his townhouse and his country estate. He's at neither one. He went to that address without me. Monsieur V must have—" Her voice cracked. She shut her eyes to hide the unshed tears that threatened to fall. Once she took a deep breath, she added, "He must have taken him. I didn't find any blood. He might still be alive."

"We'll have to go to London to be certain. I'll say goodbye to Phil and tell Tristan to pack a trunk. We'll leave as soon as may be."

Relief swept through her. Although her knees wobbled, she forced herself to her feet. She reached out to clasp her brother's hand. It was much warmer than hers.

"Thank you, Morgan. My trunk is already packed. Just let me know when we leave."

He pulled away. "By *we*, I meant Tristan and I. You've played at being a spy long enough. Too long, in fact. This is dangerous work, Lucy. You're staying here."

He strode away before she could argue. If he thought that would settle the matter, he was wrong. She wasn't going to give up on Alex. Her brother was only one more obstacle.

* * *

"Shouldn't we be going to the Tenwick townhouse?" Charlie asked as the carriage rolled to a stop.

"You go," Lucy answered absently. "I need to talk to my brothers first."

Charlie sighed. "It feels like we've been traveling forever. I suppose I'll nap after we visit your brothers."

"No." Lucy shook her head. "You go on without me. I don't know how long this will take. In fact..." She thrust Antonia into her friend's arms. "Would you mind taking her? She'll only cause a ruckus if she comes in with me."

Charlie blinked owlishly. "What's this about? We saw your brothers at the inn last night. Why are you so desperate to speak with them again?"

Lucy craned out the window as a second Tenwick carriage pulled up to the curb. *At last.* "There they are! I'll be back at the townhouse before you know it. Thank you, Charlie!" She knew that the flurry of words wouldn't postpone her friend's questions for long, but she didn't have time to explain what was happening. Since they had stopped at Alex's country estate on the way to Tenwick Abbey, Charlie had probably already started to piece together some of what had happened. Even if she couldn't possibly guess all of it. Lucy hadn't shared knowledge of her brothers' involvement in the spy network. That had seemed like something best left a secret.

She flung herself out of the carriage and into Morgan's path. His expression turned stony. "We don't have time for this, Lucy. We have work to be about." He stepped around her and loped up the steps to the door of the St. Gobain townhouse, where Morgan had lived ever since his marriage.

Tristan fell into step behind him. Lucy took up the rear. She didn't say a word as the butler, Mr. O'Neill, opened the door. Instead, she followed as Morgan led the way to his office. As they breached the threshold, she said, "I'm helping. Monsieur V has been trying to make contact with me for the past couple weeks. He might do so again. I can draw him out."

"You can stay out of this," Morgan said, his voice like ice. When he turned, he looked as warm and welcoming as a blizzard. For once, Tristan matched his expression rather than taking the opposite side simply for the fun of it. They presented a united front.

"I will not. Lord Brackley is missing and I will help find him."

When Morgan advanced on her, she instinctively took a step back. He'd never raised his voice to her, never so much as threatened to lift a hand, but it seemed wise not to provoke him nonetheless.

"You will do no such thing. This is a matter for seasoned spies, which you are not. We will handle this. I will send word to you once it is resolved."

He shut the door in her face. A click echoed, indicating that he'd locked it. He'd locked the door! As if closing it wasn't statement enough. She stared at the keyhole, debating whether to try eavesdropping.

He wanted her to stay at home and wring handker-chiefs, hoping that the man she cared for would somehow come home safe? Not bloody likely. If Morgan wouldn't let her help him, then she would find Alex on her own.

She turned and stormed from the St. Gobain house, a woman on a mission.

25

*I*f her brothers wouldn't let her help, then Lucy needed a different ally to aid her search. She couldn't do this alone. She knew of only one woman that she could trust with any secret. One woman who would be very upset that she hadn't shared such titillating information with her earlier.

Lucy found her closest friend in her room at the Tenwick townhouse. It seemed that Charlie had sought out her nap, after all. Lucy felt almost guilty for waking her.

"Charlie?" Lucy opened the door a bit further as she slipped inside. The drapes were drawn, but daylight seeped into the room through the crack. It took only a moment for her eyes to adjust. She found her friend's form on the bed, a shawl thrown over her shoulders as she slept above the covers.

Charlie made nary a sound, which made it difficult to tell whether she was awake or asleep. When at home, she never snored unless she was sick. Lucy tiptoed to her side.

"Charlie?"

The blonde groaned groggily and rolled over. "Is it supper?"

"No. It's mid-afternoon."

"Then why are you rousing me?" Her voice was thick with reluctance and sleep.

Lucy perched on the edge of the bed, next to her friend. "I need your help."

Charlie turned her head with a raised eyebrow. "Are you going to tell me the truth this time?"

"I promise."

The blonde sighed. She sat up and pulled the loose strands of her hair over one shoulder. "Very well, then. I'll listen." She plumped up a few pillows and leaned against them.

Lucy took a deep breath, wondering where to start. It had been easy to confess her knowledge of the spy operation to Morgan—he was involved in it. But Charlie would have questions. Questions that Lucy, since she had only gleaned information because of her own curiosity, would not be able to answer.

She started with, "There is a spy ring in Britain and my brothers are involved in it."

"I know."

Lucy gaped. "You know?"

Charlie shrugged. "My mother is a part of it...or she was, before Harker died."

Lucy had never liked that man, who had acted as guardian to Charlie and her sister after their father had passed away. The fact that he had died at Tenwick Abbey a year ago gave her no sadness. Nor, judging by Charlie's expression, did it bother her overmuch.

Lucy leaned her palm against the bedspread. "You knew about the spy network for over a year and you never told me?"

Charlie shrugged. "Mama swore me to secrecy. It's just as well, since you knew and you never told me."

Touché.

Lucy took a deep breath. "Well, Brackley's a part of it, too. We were working together for the good of Britain and now he's gone missing. I need your help finding him."

"Me?" Charlie's eyes widened. "Why not ask your broth... Oh." She cleared her throat. "You just did."

Lucy nodded confirmation.

"They wouldn't help?"

She made a face. "If by help, you mean conduct the search on their own, then yes."

"Why not let them? They are experienced in this sort of thing."

Lucy clenched her teeth. She was letting them help...why couldn't they give her the same consideration? "I can't sit by and do nothing. You know I'm not that type, Charlie."

Her friend narrowed her blue eyes as she studied Lucy. Whatever her thoughts, she kept them to herself. After a moment, she swung her legs off the bed and offered her hand to Lucy. "Well, I wouldn't mind some excitement, but let's go find Mama. Maybe she can help. She knows that world, too."

Lucy sighed, her shoulders slumping a bit in relief when her friend didn't argue. She knew that Charlie didn't like Alex. She thought him a rake and a reprobate. But she was helping Lucy without question, anyway. Lucy squeezed her friend's hand, as close as she could come to saying *thank you* around the lump in her throat.

They found Mrs. Vale in one of the downstairs parlors, working on correspondence. When the pair stopped in the doorway, Mrs. Vale looked up from the writing desk. "Girls? Is something amiss."

"Yes." Lucy squeezed her friend's hand, needing her support. "I need your help."

Explaining the situation took but a moment. Mrs. Vale listened with an impassive expression. Lucy couldn't decide whether the older woman was proud of her or disapproving.

Once she'd laid out the situation, Lucy bit her lip. "I know you aren't a part of the spy network anymore—"

"What makes you say that?"

Lucy blinked rapidly as she processed the question. She frowned. "Charlie said..." She glanced at her friend.

Mrs. Vale pursed her lips and raised her eyebrows. "Simply because I'm no longer out in the field does not mean that I discontinued my service to the Crown. I serve in another capacity. For the moment, that is keeping an eye on you—"

She gave Lucy a pointed look, one that made the younger woman's cheeks warm.

"—and ensuring that Monsieur V does not try to harm you in any way. You make that task very difficult when you continually slip away from my supervision."

Lucy bit her lip. "If I'd known you were a part of the spy network, I would have asked you to come with me." Then Alex would never have had any complaints about her nosing around alone.

Would she have? The first message the spymaster had sent her had indicated that he had a spy on their side who would alert him if she had help. Could Mrs. Vale be that spy? Lucy didn't want to conceive it. In fact, it didn't matter. Monsieur V still wanted to talk to her, didn't he? Perhaps Mrs. Vale would be able to bring her to him. She could negotiate for Alex's release herself.

If he was still alive.

She pinched the inside of her wrist. He was still alive. He must be. She refused to consider any other eventuality.

Mrs. Vale drew herself up. "I will help you on one condition."

"Anything," Lucy said quickly. She was that desperate.

The older woman raised her index finger. "You are not to go out into the field yourself. I will make inquiries of my contacts. We'll have a slew of information to pore over and clues to follow up on. But you must be patient. You cannot slip away again and deliberately put yourself in harm's way."

That made it sound as though Lucy was doing this for fun. No, she had done it to catch a dangerous criminal, to prove her worth to her brothers, and now she was doing it to save an innocent life.

Mrs. Vale must have read the reluctance on her face. She added, "When you slip away, you put me in a bad situation. I don't like to have to choose between my duty and my daughter."

It seemed, in the past, Lucy had been lucky that

Mrs. Vale had chosen her daughter. She might not have gotten away nearly so many times had she not.

"Very well," she acceded. "We'll try your contacts. I'll do anything it takes to find him."

Mrs. Vale turned. She fetched several sheaves of blank paper and handed one to each of the younger women. "In that case, I'll need your help writing the instructions to each of my contacts. It'll go quicker if the two of you help."

At last, something Lucy could do to help further the search. It was something small, but even that helped to mitigate the feeling of helplessness.

DAYS PASSED. Lucy wrote letters, read the responses, sent further instructions at Mrs. Vale's behest. No one had seen a man meeting Alex's description in any of the meaner parts of London. He hadn't waltzed into any of the usual haunts of the men of his stature, or Lucy would have heard of it. Her brothers offered no updates on their end of the investigation. If they knew that Mrs. Vale was also looking into the matter, they ignored her prying. Or perhaps they saw it as a boon. Whenever Tristan came home periodically, he spoke to Mrs. Vale in private. The older woman offered no explanation for what information they shared.

One by one, their clues and contacts dried up. At last, there was only one left, one last hope. When the letter arrived for Mrs. Vale, Lucy trembled. Could it be from the contact? She took it to the older woman and waited with bated breath in the library as Mrs. Vale read it.

Her expression turned grim. She pressed her lips together and folded the letter once more. When she met Lucy's gaze, her look was almost pitying.

"I'm sorry. That's everyone I can think to ask. If Lord Brackley is in London, I can't find him."

Lucy's knees went weak. "You're giving up?" She sank into the nearest chair. Charlie perched on the edge, rubbing Lucy's shoulders with a worried expression.

"We're not giving up," Mrs. Vale said gently. She sat on the ottoman in front of Lucy and took the younger woman's hand. "There's no one else for us to ask, but that doesn't mean we must give up. We will keep our eyes open, bide our time. Perhaps your brothers will uncover some clue yet."

Lucy blinked hard to banish the tears stinging her eyes. "I can't do it. I can't just sit here and do nothing. I have to find him."

Mrs. Vale clutched Lucy's hand harder. She returned the squeeze. Although she shut her eyes, tears leaked from the corners.

"I can't do it," she whispered. "I feel so helpless."

"I know. I feel the same way about Charlie's father."

Lucy's eyes opened. Her lips parted. "Are you saying that Alex is dead?"

"No. That isn't what I'm saying at all. Didn't Charlie tell you?"

Lucy looked from Charlie to her mother. The younger Vale shook her head in response to her mother's question.

Mrs. Vale explained. "My husband is still alive. His death was faked in order for me to get close to Lord Harker and keep an eye on him. My husband was assigned a position in France, in the thick of the war. I worry about him every day, but there's nothing I can do except to wait for his assignment to be over in order for us to be reunited again."

Lucy didn't know what to say. That was horrible. They would make that sacrifice in order to serve their country? Lucy didn't know whether she would voluntarily separate from the man she loved for years, even if it would save lives. Perhaps she was too selfish. All she wanted was to get Alex back, no matter the cost.

Lucy swallowed hard. "You know where your husband is, even if he's in the thick of danger. We can't find Alex. What if we never can?" She pulled away and wiped the hot tears from her cheeks. "I think I love him. I have to find him." If she didn't, they would have no hope of a future.

He had chosen revenge over her, but that hadn't stopped her from trying to find him. Simply because he had been a brash idiot didn't mean that she didn't love him. They meant something to each other. They had to. And if she didn't find him, she would never know what that something would become.

Charlie said nothing, but hugged Lucy's shoulders. Considering her disdain for Alex, the gesture meant a lot. Mrs. Vale, who also hadn't seemed fond of him, looked sympathetic as she patted Lucy's knee.

"Your brothers will find him. Have faith."

If they couldn't find Alex soon, Lucy didn't know how long her faith would last. She could do nothing except wait.

26

It couldn't be true. Mrs. Vale's contact had to have been mistaken. Why would Alex have disappeared for two weeks only to turn up unannounced in her brother's townhouse? Lucy's heart thundered as she brushed past Mr. O'Neill onto the premises. She raced upstairs to Morgan's office. Alex couldn't be here... He just couldn't. If he was all right, why hadn't he come to her first?

The door to the office was closed. When she tried the latch, she found that it wasn't locked. She stormed in and froze on the threshold.

"Where have you been?" Morgan said, standing from behind his desk, his gaze like sharp stones.

Alex stood in front of him. Despite Morgan's

cutting tone and expression, Alex's stance was casual. He held his arms loose at his sides. He wore a dark gray coat and tan breeches, both of which showed no signs of wear. His shoulders were relaxed. His hair was a bit wind-tossed, but from behind there was no sign that he had ever been accosted by the enemy.

"Alex."

The moment she spoke his name, he turned. He looked hale and whole. A bit weary, perhaps. There was a shadow in his eyes. She'd expected him to light up when he saw her, to be as relieved at their reunion as she was. He must be terribly fatigued. Perhaps that was why he'd presented himself to Morgan instead of her.

At the moment, it didn't matter. Her knees felt like hot water. She launched herself at him, throwing her arms around his neck and hugging him tight. He made no move to hug her back, though he didn't stiffen. Perhaps he was afraid of Morgan's reaction. Morgan tended to have that effect on men who considered courting her. She'd bring him around.

She took comfort in Alex's warm, solid body. He was here. He was home. That was all that mattered. She sank back on her heels, cupping his cheeks in her hands as she looked at him. He'd shaved recently, his cheeks only the slightest bit rough. "What happened?"

Instead of looking her in the eye, he looked over one shoulder. "I needed time to think."

What? She frowned, dropping her hands. "Time to think about what? What happened with Monsieur V?"

"He wasn't at the house."

Lucy could readily believe that, considering that it had been a house where he had sent a package, not someplace she had presumed him to stay. However, Alex delivered the information flatly. Had he been disappointed?

"Why did you leave your ring?"

"I needed time to think."

Yes. He'd said that. It still didn't clear anything up. And why wouldn't he look her in the eye? She balled her fists at her sides, trying not to show her frustration.

"You needed time to think about what?"

"Us."

Her breath hitched. She hadn't known that their relationship had required thought. Was he going to propose to her? She glanced at Morgan, hoping he wouldn't be a prat about it, even if he didn't approve of Alex. She approved. She loved him. She knew he was a good man.

Turning back to Alex, she said, "You should have left a note. I was worried for you. I feared the worst."

"I left you the ring."

That had only made her worry more. She'd thought he was dead! How could he do that to her? Her knees were weak, but she bit her tongue. She didn't want to drive him away, not when he'd finally come home.

He held out his hand, palm up. "Can I have it back, please?"

She glanced at Morgan. Her brother opened his top desk drawer and pulled out the ring. He handed it to Alex, who slipped it onto his index finger.

Look at me, Lucy begged. She pressed her lips together to keep from saying a word. Was he shy because Morgan was in the room with him?

She shot her brother a pleading glance. "Could you give us a moment?"

"No need," Alex said, his voice wooden.

She clenched her teeth as she turned to him. "There is every need! You were gone for two weeks. I thought you were dead."

"I had to think—"

"About us," she bit off. "Yes. You've said." He didn't seem like a man who was about to get down on bended knee. If anything, he seemed more like a man who was on the verge of collapse. He held himself upright in a relaxed pose, but his voice and eyes belied that stance. What had happened to him?

She reached for him, but he took a step back.

"Please, don't touch me."

She glanced to her brother, who wore an impassive expression. He didn't interrupt, but he eyed the exchange with a shrewd gaze.

"It's fine. Alex, please—"

"You should call me Lord Brackley."

The correction was like a slap in the face. Call him by his title after all they'd been through? He cared for her.

"Why?"

"What happened between us...it won't happen again."

Lucy's mouth gaped. She couldn't speak. She swallowed hard and licked her lips. "What are you talking about?"

"Our association is over, my lady."

No. It couldn't be. She loved him. He cared for her too, she knew he did.

She took a step closer. This time, he didn't move away, but he turned his face away from her. He looked at her brother instead, as if requesting that Morgan remove her.

"Our association is *not* over," she bit off. "You said you cared for me."

"I lied."

She couldn't breathe, let alone speak. Her knees threatened to buckle. She didn't know how she remained standing.

No. He couldn't have lied. It must not be true.

Then, finally, he looked at her. The shadow was still in his eyes. Or was it merely a cold, dark expression?

"I only told you that so that you would share your information and leads about Monsieur V. I don't need you anymore."

She reeled. She looked to her brother for help, only to be met with a hard expression. It went without his saying that he considered this to be for the best. But it wasn't for the best. Alex couldn't have lied the entire time, could he? He had been warm, passionate even. A man couldn't fake that.

For her fragile heart, she wanted one of the men to tell her that it couldn't be faked. Neither did. Her eyes welled with tears.

Morgan met her gaze plainly but didn't say a word. Had he done this? Had he scared Alex off, convinced him not to pursue Lucy any longer? It was unforgivable.

But even if he had tried, Alex didn't have to have acceded so easily. Lucy wouldn't have, in his place. She would have fought for the good thing that they'd had.

Apparently, he hadn't cared for her as much as

she'd hoped. His revenge had been an easy choice over her.

Unable to stay a moment longer, she tore from the room, slamming the door behind her. Neither man followed.

27

*W*hen Lucy stepped into the breakfast room, she stopped short. "Mother?" Was she dreaming? She'd left her mother at Tenwick Abbey, coddling her first grandchild.

The stately woman raised her eyebrows. If Lucy looked half as good when she had five grown children, she would be happy. Mother had a bit of gray woven in with her dark brown hair, but otherwise didn't look a day over forty. Her gray eyes weren't as piercing as Morgan's; Lucy had always imagined them more stormy, clouding over the emotions she kept from her face.

"You seem surprised to see me. This is my house."

On paper, it belonged to Morgan, the Duke. But he had moved into his wife's townhouse upon marrying her, so in essence, the Tenwick townhouse was Mother's.

Mustering a thin sort of smile, Lucy took a seat at the table. The family had always preferred an informal dining arrangement, keeping no more chairs than needed to fit the family. There wasn't much space between Lucy and her mother. She'd risen early to avoid the rest of the household, hoping to shut herself away in her room again today.

Three days had passed since Alex had cast her off. Every time she thought about facing anyone, even friends and family, she felt exhausted. She didn't know how he could have fooled her so well. She'd been certain, so certain that he cared for her as much as she did him. Wadding her handkerchief in her hand as a footman set her breakfast in front of her, Lucy tried to muster the raw anger she'd felt toward him at first. She couldn't. She was too tired.

Mother changed chairs to sit next to Lucy. She laid her hand atop her daughter's.

Lucy fought to smile and squeeze Mother's hand, but it felt like a thin veneer. Mother had always been astute in guessing the hearts of her children. "I thought you were at Tenwick Abbey. When did you arrive?"

"Not long ago. I drove throughout the night. Phil has matters well in hand for a few days. She has a mother's instincts. Freddie and Felicia are there as well to lend their support."

Perhaps. Lucy had thought nothing could pry mother away from the company of her first grandchild, though.

Mother patted Lucy's hand. "I thought Morgan had things well in hand when it came to searching for Lord Brackley. I tried my contacts as well, of course, but that is something that could be done from Tenwick Abbey. Now, however, it is clear that you need me here."

I don't. Lucy swallowed the lie. Tears welled in her throat and she tried not to cry. She felt watery inside. She'd never felt this way, so weak and vulnerable. Perhaps having Mother nearby wasn't the worst idea.

"You tried your contacts? Why?" How had mother even known they were looking for Alex? She seemed to have eyes and ears everywhere, Lucy supposed that was a mother's instincts.

Mother gave Lucy an arch look. "I have different contacts than your brother, I'll have you know, a much wider net. You must know I'd go to any lengths necessary to help when you're in need."

Well, yes. Lucy had never doubted that. But Mother's contacts were old women from *le bon ton*, weren't they? The only people with whom Mother ever associated were peers. No wonder she hadn't found him. What Lucy had needed was the reach of spies.

It hadn't helped, in any case. Alex hadn't returned and when he'd come back...he had been different. Perhaps he'd simply discarded the mask he'd used to woo her.

"You're in pain," Mother said.

I'm heartbroken. Lucy didn't speak the words out loud. Instead, she retracted her hand and pretended to be interested in her breakfast.

"He wasn't the man I thought he was. He only left to...to avoid me."

"That may not be true."

Lucy swallowed around the lump in her throat. She blinked hard to dispel the threat of tears. "I know Morgan could force him to marry me, but I don't want that. If he doesn't want me, then I don't want him, either."

If only it were so simple. She didn't want a man who treated her as coldly and distantly as Alex had upon their last meeting. But her fickle heart insisted that that man wasn't him. He was the passionate, driven man who she had fallen in love with. If she was reading this in a book, she would be screaming at the heroine to look at the facts and face reality. It was much easier said than done. She couldn't help the way she felt.

"Don't give up."

Lucy met her mother's gaze, confused. Alex had cast her aside as if she was rubbish and Mother was taking his side? "On Alex—Lord Brackley?"

Crinkles formed in the corner of Mother's eyes. "Or on love. It's worth fighting for. All might not be as it seems. Perhaps your Lord Brackley isn't acting as himself."

Or perhaps he finally was. Lucy pushed her capers around her plate with her fork. "He made himself perfectly clear."

"I'm certain he said terrible things, but you don't yet know why he did. Don't give up on him—but do be careful, dear. Renewing your association might be dangerous."

She raised her gaze once more. "Dangerous how?" She'd already had her heart trampled. "How do you know this isn't how he usually acts and the way he's been with me has only been an act?"

"Call it a mother's intuition. No one is that skilled an actor, not even Lord Brackley." She reached out, stopping Lucy from playing with her food. "Have I ever told you that I once doubted your father? If I hadn't sought him out and learned the truth of his feelings, I would never have had you or your brothers. Love is worth fighting for. Just be careful."

Lucy opened her mouth to answer, but Mrs. Vale

entered the breakfast room. Not wanting to discuss her battered heart in front of the other woman, Lucy shut her mouth.

However, as she applied herself to eating her breakfast, she couldn't help but wonder. This was the second time Mother had cautioned her. What did she think would happen if Lucy chased after Alex? He had torn apart her heart but he would never hurt her physically. If he did, then he truly *wouldn't* be acting as himself.

She shook her head. It didn't matter, anyway, because she didn't intend to chase after him. He'd made himself more than clear in the callous way he'd treated her.

Lucy meant nothing to him.

28

*M*organ Graylocke didn't trust him. Of that, Alex was absolutely certain. He didn't know whether it was due to his abrupt end to the courtship with Lucy or due to his unannounced absence, but Morgan assigned him only the smallest of tasks. The sort accomplished by spies still in training. At first, he performed them without complaint. But as weeks passed and his requests for bigger assignments were met with cold refusals and the kind of glare that froze a man from his insides out, he became increasingly frustrated.

He wasn't the only one.

"That's all?" The man standing in front of Alex spat on the ground.

They stood in a shadowed alcove outside a gaming hell, where Alex had resumed his outward mask of carousing in order to attend to the tasks Morgan had set him. The door to the establishment opened, releasing a torrent of noise. Loud voices, taunts, laughter, laments. All tinged with the slur that indicated those responsible were well into their cups.

The noise bathed over Alex and away from him, leaving him untouched. Numbly, he stared at the man in front of him—swathed in shadow, but Alex knew his identity. He knew the man's identity and somewhere far below the surface he believed that he should care. He didn't.

"Tenwick refuses to assign me to more sensitive pursuits. He doesn't trust me, likely over the fallout with his sister."

Though it was clear that Lucy hadn't spoken of their night together. If she had, Morgan would have sought revenge against Alex in some form. He didn't know whether to be grateful or disappointed. He felt neither emotion.

"Then make amends with her." The man bit off his words.

Dimly, Alex considered them. Make amends? "She would know." What would she know? His thoughts were thick, cloudy. That he cared?

No, she would know that he didn't care. He had cared. Somewhere, perhaps he still did, but he couldn't find that place. All that was left in its place was smoke that curled through his mental fingers.

"It won't matter." The man sliced his hand through the air. The action brought Alex back to equilibrium. Less confused. All he had to do was listen and obey. "If you can't get me the information that I require, then you're of no use to me."

Alex stood still, waiting for the man to come to a decision. Nothing in his last statement had given Alex a command to obey.

Something sparked in the back of his mind. A flame, deep and cloudy as if behind a thick wall of glass. Anger. Outrage. It flared, but couldn't break through. Alex felt a thin sort of warmth as he stared at the man in front of him. It dissipated quickly, leaving him dark.

Why was he angry with this man? Why did he hate him? The questions, along with the confusion that it raised, dissolved just as quickly as the man reached out to tap Alex on the shoulder.

Tap, tap, tap. He relaxed. He didn't know why, but he felt as though he could trust this man.

"Can you read Tenwick's correspondence?"

"No." Alex frowned. Hadn't he just said that?

"Tenwick distrusts me. He doesn't leave me unsupervised in his townhouse."

The man seemed agitated. Not much light stretched into the alcove, but enough to illuminate the curl of the man's dark hair over his forehead, at the same level as Alex's. The other man's eyebrows pulled together in annoyance.

"Can you arrange a distraction and read it, then?"

"Yes..." Alex drew out the word. "But I wouldn't have long, and if Tenwick happened to leave me alone, he might suspect. He might even catch me in the act. You said—"

"For no one to discover what you were about." The other man sounded disgusted. "Yes, I recall." He turned and paced. His obvious distress over Alex's performance made Alex tense.

He had done as the man had requested—or tried. He had listened, and obeyed.

The tension in his body uncovered a new question, like sand blowing away from a treasure beneath.

Why? Why did he listen? Why obey?

As the man opposite him turned and paced back, he laid a hand on Alex's shoulder. The question melted away. The man fiddled with a coin, a nervous habit. Nervous for the man, but soothing for Alex. The play of light on the silver coin reminded him of sunlight on a pond. He'd used to play in a pond near his family's ancestral estate. He and his brother as boys, splashing through the water, laughing.

The memory slowly faded as the man stopped playing with the coin, but the feeling of peace remained. He listened. He waited to obey.

The man squeezed Alex's shoulder. "You're going to do something else for me. You're going to renew your association with Lucy Graylocke."

"But she will—"

What? What would she do? He had the words, there on the tip of his tongue, but he couldn't remember them. Couldn't form them.

"She will trust you," the man said. His voice was low and soothing. "You will make her trust you. You've done it once before. And when you're certain that she'll do what you ask, I want you to bring her to meet me. She is the only one who has not succumbed to my mind manipulations. The only one to truly be able to identify me... and I can't let that go on unchecked. I must make sure she is silenced. Do you understand?"

He understood. In the back of his mind, there was an ugly shadow of doubt, but it was twisted into a knot and he couldn't read why he ought to be concerned over this command. But somewhere in his heart, a sharp pain was growing along with the doubt. As the man tapped Alex on the shoulder, the pain and the doubt tumbled away. Out of sight, out of mind.

Alex nodded and stepped back. "Yes, Monsieur. I will bring Lady Lucy to meet you."

"Good. Then go inside and finish your assignment."

Alex obeyed without question.

29

*L*ucy had never felt more exhausted in her life. She dragged her feet as she climbed the stairs to the third floor of the Tenwick townhouse, where her bedroom resided. Why did her brother have to insist that she attend every soiree for which she received an invitation? It was tiresome. The same faces, the same conversation, the same bland expression covering a vulture's instincts beneath.

The gossips circled her, trying to wring some tidbit of information about Alex from her. They poked at her, informing her of such a scandalous activity he'd been at last week or with which mistress. Maintaining her composure drained her.

As she reached the top of the stairs, Charlie caught her elbow. "Are you all right?"

No. Lucy couldn't even form a smile. She rubbed at her eyes. "I'm tired," she answered truthfully. "I'm going to work on my book."

"Really? You haven't been yourself lately. I know these soirees are tedious but we used to have so much fun. What's going on?"

Lucy felt a pang of guilt. In the past couple weeks, since Alex had spurned her, the only thing she'd been able to think about, the only thing she could think about, was her book. She'd rewritten it, added in a scoundrel who was the epitome of temptation.

Dealing with such a man had added depth to the heroine. She'd changed, seen the world less in terms of black and white, learned about redemption and forgiveness. Now, Lucy was at an impasse. The ending she had for the book didn't feel right. It suited the old heroine better. The new one couldn't carry on as if she hadn't changed. She had.

But Lucy didn't know what to do about it. Nothing fit, unless she gave the heroine a happy ending with the scoundrel. After the way he betrayed the heroine during the book, Lucy didn't see how any reader would find that to be a satisfying ending. He couldn't be forgiven. Not even if he crawled back to the heroine and begged for forgiveness on his hands and knees.

Not that the character would do that. He *was* a scoundrel, after all. He didn't care about anything but his own goals and motivations. If he crawled back into the heroine's life, she would be suspicious and wonder what he could possibly want from her this time. But would she still succumb to temptation?

It didn't matter. Lucy wasn't going to write that. She didn't see how it could possibly work its way to a satisfying ending.

Wearily, she asked Charlie, "I'm sorry, it's just that I'm having trouble with a part of my book."

Charlie dropped her hand from Lucy's arm and said gently, "Well, don't spend all night at it. You need your rest. And you've been spending every waking hour on that book. I miss spending time with you. So does Antonia."

"Antonia would rather fly around the house."

Charlie sighed. "Get some rest?" she pleaded. "You're making yourself sick over this book. Maybe the answer will become clear if you just take a moment to step away from it."

Lucy didn't want to do that. If she stopped thinking about her book, then she would have to start thinking about her life. How Alex had fooled her. How she'd been so blind as to his true feelings of indifference toward her.

He said he cared...

She was heartbroken, and she didn't want to be. She wouldn't let any man do that to her again. But she needed to focus on something, and that something was her book. She was so close to finishing it. All she needed was a little more time—and to solve this one last problem.

Somehow, she found the energy to force a smile. "I won't work on my book tonight," she lied. "I'll go straight to bed and get some rest. You're right, I am tired, and making myself sick won't help me."

Charlie looked dubious, but she nodded and stepped away. "Goodnight. I'll see you in the morning at breakfast?"

"Of course." Where else did she expect Lucy to eat? "Sleep well."

"You, too."

They parted ways. Lucy entered her bedchamber to find that someone had already lit a candle. That somebody was likely the man sitting at her writing desk, sifting through the pile of papers that was the wreck of her story. For a moment, she wondered if the scoundrel had stepped right out of her story.

He looked as handsome as she'd remembered. She'd seen Alex, once or twice from afar, but hadn't spoken with him since he'd cast her off. The candle-light burnished his reddish hair with strands of gold. The shadows it cast caressed the seductive curve of his mouth. He leaned back against the chair as she entered.

"Shut the door, love."

She shouldn't. She should call out. The Vales or the servants would be here within seconds to remove him. Instead, her hand trembling, she obeyed. He wouldn't hurt her. Not physically, at least.

He looked good. Too good. She felt like a mess without him—pouring all her time and energy into writing her book so she wouldn't have to think about how she missed him. How he'd broken her heart with what he'd done. He'd fooled her. She felt like a gullible child.

She probably looked like a shipwreck. The cosmetics she'd applied before the soiree would likely have worn off, leaving the rings around her eyes and the other telltale signs of her exhaustion. Charlie was right; she was pushing herself so hard to complete her book that she was making herself sick. Even knowing it couldn't prevent her from doing it. It was the only way she knew of to distract herself from thoughts about Alex.

And now he was back, without warning. What did he want from her this time?

She rubbed her eyes, surprised when they weren't wet. Apparently, she was too fatigued to cry.

"What information do you want this time?"

He stared at her for a moment, his expression impassive. Whether a trick of the light or a willful act of concealment, she couldn't read the emotion in his eyes. It was as though he'd drawn a mask of composure across his face. He made no move to rise.

"I've been an idiot."

She couldn't argue with that. She clenched her hands in front of her and pressed her lips together.

"When I thought of the future, what you meant to me, I got frightened. I said what I needed to in order to drive you away."

He didn't sound frightened. He sounded...matter-of-fact. Distant, perhaps even a little cold, as if he recited a speech he'd rehearsed a hundred times. It lacked all emotion. It intrigued her. Just what was he up to?

She crossed her arms, hugging herself as she leaned back against the door. "Congratulations, your brilliant plan worked."

"No, it didn't."

When he stood, she couldn't help but find her gaze drawn to his muscular legs, encased in black breeches. The cut of his jacket accentuated his form. Especially his arms. She recalled too well what his arms had felt like surrounding her. She bit her lower lip and counted the stitches on the toe of her shoe.

Alex stepped closer, until his black boots came into view an inch away from her toes. The heat and solid presence of his body awakened her senses. Her breathing quickened and she hated herself for it.

"I didn't realize then how much I needed you in my life. I do. I need you, Lucy."

He spoke the words she wanted to hear. These, too, sounded rehearsed, almost deadened. Did she trust him?

She wanted to. Oh, how she wanted to. She lifted her gaze to meet his. Did he mean it? Could he mean it? If he didn't... It would only hurt her again.

She tried to find the truth in his eyes, but she didn't see anything in them. It was as if the door to his heart was closed. Was this some sort of trick? But to what end?

"I'm angry with you," she admitted. "You broke my heart."

"Forgive me."

His voice was so soft, she scarcely heard.

"It wasn't my intention."

Yes, it was. He'd just admitted that he was trying to drive her away. And why—because he was scared? She didn't know if she could forgive him for that... unless there was another reason.

"What are you so frightened of? Me? My brothers?"

When she tilted her face up to meet his gaze, he turned away and paced the length of the room. He stopped across from it with his back to her. "All of it, I suppose." His voice was leaden. "I've never had a woman in my life the way you were. Nevertheless, I shouldn't have acted that way. I want you back in my life, Lucy. It isn't the same without you."

Another wooden delivery. Had he rehearsed saying that as well? Part of her desperately wanted to believe him, but the other part would not be played for a fool again.

She studied him in the dim light. This was not the Alex she had come to know. In fact, he'd changed ever since he'd gone missing. Since she'd found his ring at the address linked to Monsieur V. Was Monsieur V at the root of his odd behavior?

Her mother's words came back to her. Was there a deeper reason that Alex had tossed her aside? Something that had nothing to do with what she knew they'd felt for each other. Something that might be dangerous, but also might shed light on the truth that she knew was buried somewhere under the surface. Was it worth finding out more?

Maybe it would be smart for her to play along, to see what he was up to. And maybe if she did, she'd find a clue to what her fictional heroine would do and finally be able to finish the book.

Making her decision, she crossed to him and laid her hand on his back. His muscles were as stiff as she expected. He held himself relaxed, casual. How did he manage that? She felt as though the tension would snap her in half.

Turning, he caught her hand and lifted it to his lips. "Let me make it up to you, please." His gaze was downcast. He still didn't release her hand.

"Very well. What did you have in mind?"

Nothing less than loving you for the rest of your days. Those romantic words, and others, flitted through her mind as possibilities. Perhaps that was what the scoundrel in her book had to say in order to convince the heroine to forgive him.

Alex, on the other hand, said something different. "Come with me. I've parked my phaeton in the livery down the street. I'll fetch it. I have something I want to show you, to make up for my absence."

It wasn't terribly late. She and Charlie had left the soiree early, just after midnight. Lucy nibbled on her lip as she fought to make a decision. It would ruin her reputation to be seen out alone with him at night, but the request was so odd and the way he was acting so strange, her curiosity got the better of her. Warning thoughts of Monsieur V flashed in her head.

Was Monsieur V still after her? Was there still a chance to capture him? If Morgan was telling the truth, no one in the spy network had discovered any messages meant for her. No one had been able to find his location, either. He'd slipped away into the wind, as he had months ago.

He'd been so close. If she and Alex had only worked together...

She stifled a sigh. He'd said Monsieur V hadn't been at that location, nor had the person intended to receive the package. Morgan and his spies had searched the house as well. She didn't think they would have found any clues that she'd missed, given the depth of her search, but knowing him he would have attempted it in any case.

To be truthful, she didn't want to help anymore. She only wanted to be left in peace to write her book. If she left with Alex, maybe the inspiration would come. She sensed there was more to his invitation. At the very least, she might gain a new experience for her book.

"Where are we going?" she asked.

He kissed her fingertips, ducking his head over them. "It's a surprise. You'll like it, I promise. Will you come with me?"

He still sounded wooden, his words rehearsed. How long had it taken him to work up the courage to come here?

Curiosity won out and she nodded. "Very well, I'll come. Bring 'round the phaeton and I'll meet you downstairs."

* * *

AT THIS HOUR, the streets of London were all but devoid of traffic. Alex gave the ribbons an idle flick, turning the matched bays down a different street. Lucy sat beside him, silent. She was wrapped in her pelisse and nibbling on her lip.

Convincing her to leave with him had been easier than he'd expected. All it had taken was a kiss and a profession of his desire for her. Dimly, he questioned whether she truly had forgiven him for his transgression or if she was only playing along out of curiosity. It didn't much matter. Soon, she would be in Monsieur V's care. That *had* been what she'd wanted all along, after all—to meet with Monsieur V. He could arrange that.

Something beat inside him like a bird flapping its wings against the bars of its cage. Why was he unsettled? It was what she wanted; it was what Monsieur V wanted. Everyone was happy.

Except Alex didn't feel happy. He turned the horses down another street, slowing to take the curve. As he did, he glanced over his shoulder, searching for signs of pursuit. Monsieur V wanted to visit with Lucy alone. Alex must ensure that her pesky chaperone hadn't followed them. It would take longer, but thus far, Lucy hadn't complained.

She glanced at him. "Are you all right? You don't seem yourself."

He flicked the ribbons. "I'm focused on driving. It's dark. It needs my full attention."

She touched his shoulder. "Are you certain? You've been...quiet."

That touch rippled through him. Warm, like the press of her body. For a moment, he forgot why he was bringing her to Monsieur V. He didn't want to. Then the itch to obey had returned and he'd removed himself before her presence had caused him to forget his task. Monsieur V wanted an introduction, a visit. He must do that.

Satisfied that no one had followed them from her townhouse, he turned toward their true destination. If Lucy noticed the winding path, she didn't comment on it.

They passed a street lamp. It lit up the contours of her face and her glimmering eyes, fixed upon him.

"I've been busy," he repeated. "I need focus."

Another woman might have obeyed the warning in his tone to remain silent while he navigated the darkened streets. Lucy, on the other hand, transferred her hand to his leg. There wasn't as much fabric between them, there. Only his breeches.

"Alex, talk to me. Why are you acting so strange?"

"I'm not."

His mind was like a pool of water. Or perhaps more like ice, the surface frozen over to present a pristine reflective sheet. Thoughts slid away from that surface, none finding a grasp.

"Alex, please." She sounded annoyed. "If you're going to shut me out, I don't see the point in this. You said you wanted to make up for the way you've treated me."

"And I shall. I'm giving you what you wanted."

"And what is that?"

"You'll see."

She didn't accept that answer. She turned in the seat to face him. "Where are we going?"

"It's a surprise." He turned down another street. Only one more and they would nearly be there.

His heart beat quick. Too quick, to be honest. Something irked him, a buzz in the back of his mind like an itch that could not be ignored. The closer he got to his destination, the louder it roared.

Lucy laid her hand on his. Her thumb landed in the exposed strip between his glove and sleeve. The touch of her bare skin against his felt as though he was struck by lightning. It ignited something in him, something long buried and all but forgotten.

He loved her. He would never put her in harm's way. He was doing just that. Monsieur V could hold nothing but ill will toward her.

Swearing, Alex yanked the horses to a stop. He lurched from the phaeton, storming toward the nearest building. He rested the palm of his hand on the brick façade. What had he almost done? What had *happened* to him?

Frustration, anger, and self-loathing mounted like an inevitable tide. He punched the wall. As pain splintered through his hand, he hissed and drew back.

"What is wrong with you?" Lucy sounded appalled.

Yes, what *was* wrong with him?

"Go. Get back in that phaeton and turn around. Can you drive?" She was curious and capable; it seemed like the sort of thing she might have learned.

But he'd taken such a winding path to reach this neglected part of London that she might have been turned around.

"I'm not leaving you. There's something you're not telling me."

Shaking out his hand, he kept his back turned to her. How? How could he possibly tell her what he had been about to do? How had Monsieur V dug so far beneath his skin? Alex's hatred for the man was soul-deep. It ate at him. Never, for a second, should he have considered doing anything but killing the traitor.

Morgan had been right not to trust him. Hell and damnation, Alex didn't even trust himself!

Lucy feathered her fingers over his back. Her touch was light, at first. After a moment, when he didn't pull away, she grew bolder.

"You haven't been yourself tonight."

"I haven't been myself in weeks."

The sound of his breath was overly loud in his ears. He shut his eyes as he wrestled with the implications of what he'd done, what he was ready to do. He didn't know if he could ever forgive himself for that. The silence was shattered by the stamp of the horse's hoof. The carriage creaked as if one of the bays had a mind to continue walking. Alex turned away and caught the reins, preventing them from leaving.

They stood in the middle of a darkened street. The nearest street lamp was at least twenty feet back, the foggy circle of its light not quite stretching far enough to illuminate the street in more than dismal blacks and grays. Lucy's eyes were bright, reflecting that light. Was she crying?

If he'd made her cry, it was only one more sin to add to a long list. He gritted his teeth and stared at the sky. How had he let this happen?

"I'm worried about you."

"You should have been more worried about yourself. You shouldn't be in this area of London, certainly not at this hour." And no one knew of their departure; he'd made certain of that.

"I know I'm safe with you."

But she wasn't. She wouldn't have been.

Fisting the reins in one hand, he rubbed at the throb in his temple with the other. "No, you aren't. You need to get back home. Immediately."

Lucy had never been particularly obedient when it came to keeping herself out of harm's way. His warning didn't change that attitude in the least. She drew herself up and crossed her arms.

"It's your carriage."

"I give you leave to take it." He held out the reins.

She made no move to accept them. "And where do you intend to go?"

"I have business to which I must attend." He spoke the words through gritted teeth. It was the same business he'd meant to take care of weeks ago. This time, Monsieur V would not gain the upper hand.

"Then I'm coming with you."

No. His heart pinched. He couldn't let her do that. Monsieur V was expecting her; he had plans for her. Whatever those plans were, Alex could not let them come to fruition.

"I can't let you do that."

"Then you'll have to leave me here, in the middle of an unlit street in a dangerous neighborhood."

The neighborhood wasn't nearly as dangerous as some of the places Alex had been, though it was a far cry from Lucy's townhouse in Mayfair. Alex clenched his teeth and looked down. He knew where Monsieur V was...he could kill him now and the danger would be over.

But he couldn't leave Lucy to her own devices. He was the reason she was here to begin with.

She stepped closer, cupping his cheek in her hand. Her touch was warm. He turned his face into it.

"What's going on, Alex?"

He flinched and pulled away. "Monsieur V is waiting less than a block away."

"You were taking me to meet him?" Her voice was heavy with a frown.

"I was." It cost him to admit that much. His stomach tied itself into intricate knots.

"Why?"

He didn't know the answer to that. He couldn't fathom how, for a second, he might ever have considered deliberately bringing her into a dangerous man's clutches.

Defeated, he muttered, "Because he told me to."

Lucy dropped her hand. He half-expected her to slap him, but she didn't. He would deserve it.

That, and so much more.

The silence rang until she filled it. "You hate Monsieur V."

"I do." He'd forgotten that for a time.

"I don't understand."

He sighed. "Neither do I."

Her form swayed in front of him, as if she was shifting on the balls of her feet as she thought. "No one knows where Monsieur V resides."

"I do." Or, at the very least, he knew where to meet the man. It amounted to the same thing.

"You told me otherwise. My brother—"

"Doesn't know, either." He ran his hand through his hair. "I lied. You have to go back home, Lucy."

"Not until I understand. What happened to you?"

He wondered that, himself. Hanging his head, he admitted, "Monsieur V was at that address you found, but he got the upper hand. He captured me. I don't remember... I don't rightly know what happened after that. It's all such a fog. By the time he released me back, I was willing to do anything he said."

How was that even possible? The man had killed his father and brother. There was no way Alex would have cooperated with such a man.

And yet...he had.

For an impossibly long moment, Lucy was silent. Alex's lungs ached from holding his breath. He forced himself to exhale.

"If you brought me to him, would he have killed me?"

He matched the softness of her voice. "I don't know."

"Would you have let him?"

"I don't know."

"When you said—"

He raised his voice. "I don't *know* what I said, Lucy. I don't remember."

"It was memorable to me."

It must have been. He was supposed to have driven her away. He rubbed at his head. "It's all such a fog. I don't recall much of anything anymore."

"You told me that you didn't care about me. That you'd only pretended in order to get information from me."

"You know that's a lie."

Did she? He must have been convincing in order for her to give up on him. She wasn't the type to give up—on anything.

"And tonight? When you said that you'd changed your mind?"

He rubbed his throbbing forehead. "Forget everything I've said in the past few weeks. I wasn't myself."

"And are you back to being yourself?"

She sounded accusing. Perhaps she should. He gritted his teeth and nodded.

"I am."

Not that she could take him for his word, not after

the lie upon lie he must have heaped upon her. When he tried to pull up the memory, his head throbbed. It was like trying to see in the pitch black. Whereas there had been some dim recollection earlier, now there was nothing there.

Perhaps it was better that he didn't know exactly what he'd done. It would only make him feel guiltier.

She stepped closer, granting him no quarter. "Then how *do* you feel about me?"

"I love you."

He'd meant to tell her that he cared for her. Perhaps that he admired and esteemed her. The profession of the true depth of his feelings slipped from between his lips unbidden. Now that the words had tasted the air, he couldn't hide them any longer. Nor take them back.

He held his breath. When he'd taken that page from her notebook weeks ago, he'd been certain she would loathe him for it. Now he'd managed to hurt her so much worse in the interim. He had no hope of hearing her confess to the same tender feeling for him, and yet...

"I love you, too."

Her voice was thick with emotion. Maybe even tears. He hooked the reins around a decorative flourish in the phaeton design, hoping that the bays wouldn't think to escape again. He had to touch her.

He reached out to cup her cheeks. "Are you crying?"

She was. He gently wiped away the moisture beneath her eyes, then gently kissed each cheek. His eyes stung as well at the reminder of how he'd hurt her. "I never meant to hurt you. If you'll believe nothing else, please believe that."

"This was Monsieur V's doing."

Was it? If he loved her so much, he should have been able to break the spymaster's hold on him sooner. But at least he'd been able to break it in time. That counted for something, didn't it?

He still didn't know how he'd done it—or why Monsieur V had succeeded so well with him before. If it was torture, he would have endured it had he known that he would make Lucy cry.

He'd known from the beginning that he didn't deserve a woman like her, but this seemed to make it worse.

The mention of the spymaster's name reminded him where they were. He kissed her forehead, then stepped back. "We can't stay here. I'll drop you off at your townhouse again."

She captured his wrist. "And then what will you do?"

He gritted his teeth. "I'll do what I should have

done the first time. I'll kill him. I know where he is now."

Her hand tightened. "Don't."

The word coiled through him. She wouldn't ask him to give up his revenge. She couldn't. If he had to choose between her or avenging his family...

"I have to, Lucy. He's a monster. Look what he made me do—" He cut off, afraid that he couldn't hide behind Monsieur V as an excuse. Why hadn't he stopped himself? He would probably agonize over that for the rest of his life. "He deserves to die."

"He deserves to be caught. My brother can use him and the information he provides. Catching or killing him could make the difference in the lives of other spies. We *need* him alive, Alex."

"And I need him dead." His voice brooked no argument. For too long he'd fantasized about this. He'd made it his solitary mission in life. He couldn't let that go.

"Be smart about this," Lucy begged. "We can eradicate this evil if we work together. We can both get what we want."

Could they? Or would Monsieur V talk his way out of Crown custody with his strange mind manipulations. He wouldn't put it past him. After all, he'd made Alex do something he'd never thought he would be capable of. His mind persuasion—yes, that must be exactly what it was—was very powerful.

"If you care for me at all, you won't do this alone. You'll talk to my brothers."

She was asking him to choose between her and his revenge, after all. He stared at her, his heart aching, before he pronounced, "I do care for you. More deeply than I've ever cared for someone else." He shut his eyes to stave off the pain of his decision. "Let's go talk to your brother, then."

He chose her.

$\mathcal{B}$y the time Alex finished explaining himself, his throat was sore from talking. He didn't know if any of the information was relevant, but he'd dug as deep into his memory as possible and tried to unearth every small detail. The fact that the past few weeks, ever since Monsieur V had captured him, were a blur did not make it easier.

Nevertheless, for Lucy, he tried.

His voice rang into the silence as he finished. Although the night was mild, a fire had been lit in the hearth in Tenwick's office to shed light. Morgan stood at one corner of his desk, his eyes like ice as if he tried to freeze Alex where he sat. On the other corner of the wide oak desk, Tristan leaned his hip and crossed his arms. Neither seemed particularly welcoming or trusting. Alex fought not to fidget. It would be an admission of guilt.

He sat in one of the two chairs in front of the desk. Lucy sat next to him, tapping her heel or rearranging her skirts as he'd spoken. Now that he'd stopped, she reached out to squeeze his hand.

His heart skipped a beat. *Don't draw attention to yourself, love.* She was fearless. Perhaps she had reason to be; her brothers would never harm her. Alex, on the other hand...

He didn't have the heart to pull away, so he squeezed her back. Morgan noticed the touch, his eyes narrowing and that eerie stare sharpening. Aside from that indication of his displeasure, the duke showed no outward sign of his emotions. Alex might as well have delivered his story to a portrait.

His heartbeat thundered in the silence. A crackle of wood nearly made him jump before he covered himself. He released Lucy's hand to wipe his sweaty palm on his breeches.

Morgan turned his attention to his sister. Although it should have been a welcome reprieve, Alex bristled. *She's blameless in this.*

"Leave us, Lucy." Tenwick's voice was clipped.

She clenched her fists on her lap. "No."

"This has nothing to do with you."

"The devil it doesn't!" She jumped to her feet, her expression fierce. "We started this together. That's how we'll finish it, too."

Tristan Graylocke straightened. He resembled his brother in build and hair color, but didn't share the eerily light eyes. Despite that, he managed to appear just as formidable.

"Lucy, trust me. You're not going to want to be here for this next part."

Alex stiffened. They were going to interrogate him as if he was an enemy spy. Alex would do the same in their position, but it didn't make the notion sound any more appealing. Tristan was right; Lucy shouldn't be in the room for that. He didn't know how far the two men were willing to take the interrogation, but if there was any chance it would cause him pain, he'd rather not subject Lucy to viewing it.

Give me the truth serum. Unfortunately, the serum that Gideon Graylocke had created with his wife was far from limitless. It took time and rare ingredients to make; he didn't know if Tenwick had any on hand in his townhouse to give, or if Lord Strickland took command of the supply.

Lucy rounded on the duke. "I'm not leaving. I love him and I'm staying right here!"

I love him. Three words Alex had never thought to hear in reference to himself. He ached to kiss her, but restrained himself. He didn't know how she could be so adamant on the subject. He'd treated her abysmally, and he hadn't been a heroic sort of man before then, either. Not the kind of man women fell in love with. But she had, and Heaven help him because he returned those feelings tenfold.

He reached out to catch her hand, squeezing it. "Lucy, I'll be all right. Your brothers just have a few more questions to ask, is all."

She frowned at him. "I'm staying. I don't care if we're here all night."

He swallowed around the lump in his throat. "They're sensitive questions, love. Things that you don't yet know about the spy network. It won't take long, I'm sure."

She narrowed her thickly-lashed eyes, as if she didn't quite believe him. Just as well, since he was lying through his teeth. Trying to keep his expression calm and composed, he added gently, "Do you trust your brothers?"

"Of course." She answered without hesitation.

"Then so do I." He lifted her hand to his lips and kissed her knuckles. "We'll be done in a moment."

Morgan added, "If you'll wait in the corridor or in one of the parlors, I'll let you know the moment we finish."

Lucy held Alex's gaze for a moment, her expression conflicted. Then, her face stony, she turned to her brothers and looked each one in the eye. "I'm waiting in the corridor." She turned her gaze back to Alex. "If you need me..."

"I'll be fine. I love you." A flush crept up his neck at uttering those words in front of her brothers, but she looked as though she needed to hear them. She relaxed a bit, her shoulders lowering from their hostile stance. With a curt nod, she turned on her heel, strode from the room, and shut the door behind her. Tristan followed, locking it before he turned back.

Alex curled his fist over his knees. His hand felt empty without Lucy's in it. He tried not to show the weakness.

As he lifted his gaze to the Graylocke brothers, he said, "You're going to get the same answers out of me. This will go a lot quicker and easier if you give me a bit of truth serum."

Tenwick exchanged a glance with his brother. "We can call for some, but it will take a while to arrive."

Blast, it had been more than Alex should have hoped for.

He gritted his teeth. "We don't have that kind of time. Monsieur V is expecting me to bring Lucy to him tonight. At the very least, I'll have to show up in person to offer an excuse." Perhaps it was best that he didn't take the serum, after all. He didn't know how long it took to wear off and it would be disastrous to still suffer the effects while engaging with the French spymaster.

He stifled a sigh and squared his shoulders. "Very well, let's get on with it. But try not to leave any marks. I'd rather not upset Lucy."

DID LUCY HEAR SOMETHING? The men had been in that office alone for an hour now. The wood was thick and she barely caught their muffled voices, let alone any other sound. Her feet ached from pacing back and forth as she waited. She was worried. What were they doing in there? Morgan and Tristan hadn't seemed in the friendliest of moods when she'd left.

The door cracked open. She turned, holding her breath as Morgan slipped through the opening and swiftly shut the door behind him. She caught only the barest glimpse of Tristan, hovering over Alex's seated body while Alex grimaced and rubbed his hand. What was happening? Were they finished?

Morgan touched her elbow. "Come with me a moment. I'd like to talk."

He led her down the dark corridor to a parlor overlooking the street. The curtains were open, letting in the glimmer of light from a nearby streetlamp. It was just enough for Lucy to discern her brother's silhouette as he found a tinderbox and lit a candle. He set the candle on a small table between two chairs.

"Sit, please."

Her heart pounding and her palms clammy, Lucy sat. Morgan claimed the seat next to her, turning to face her. He leaned his forearms against his knees.

"I'd like your opinion." His voice was as calm and composed as his expression, but there were lines around his eyes and mouth that belied his efforts. He seemed worried.

It was the first time he'd consulted her on professional matters. If he'd only come to her months ago, they might have already had Monsieur V in their grasp and this would never have happened with Alex.

She would never have fallen in love with him, either.

She straightened her shoulders. "What would you like to know?"

"Do you believe him?"

Lucy bristled. "Of course I do! You don't? He's telling the truth, Morgan."

Her brother fingered the white streak in his hair. "I believe that Monsieur V mesmerized him and had him under his complete control. But what caused him to break that control?"

Lucy opened her mouth, but realized that she

didn't have an answer. "I don't know." She'd known that something was different about Alex, but she hadn't realized how completely he had fallen under another man's spell. If she had, she would have found a way to snap him out of it. Instead, he'd somehow managed to do that on his own. She frowned. How *had* he done it? Why then?

Morgan dropped his hand. He caught her gaze, studying her as he said, "He claims that it was you."

"I didn't do anything." Much as she would rather say something different. "I only pressed him for answers because he seemed distant to me."

"He says that the notion of putting you in danger, something he would never knowingly do, was what gave him the will to break free of Monsieur V's hold."

Lucy's chest warmed. Alex did love her, after all. She blinked back tears.

Morgan didn't seem as impressed by Alex's statement. "Do you think he has truly shaken free of Monsieur V's control?"

Lucy opened her mouth, then shut it again. After swallowing around the lump in her throat, she asked, "You think he's still under the spymaster's control, that this is a trick?"

Why? It made no sense. He could have delivered her to Monsieur V, if that were the case.

"That's what I'm afraid of," Morgan answered, his

words measured carefully. He reached out to clasp Lucy's hand. "I can sense no deception in him, but you know him better than I. If there is even a sliver of a doubt in your mind that he is fully on our side once more, we can't risk using him to take down the spymaster. There is too much at stake. Please, take a moment and think before you answer me this: is he the man you knew before Monsieur V took control of him?"

Yes. Lucy buried that instantaneous answer and bit her lip. She shut her eyes, recalling every moment she'd had with him tonight, from the time when he entered her bedroom to the time when she'd left him with her brothers. *Was* he the same man?

She opened her eyes. "He's not under Monsieur V's control anymore. I'm sure of it."

"Are you?" The crinkles at the corner of Morgan's eyes deepened. "You might very well be risking your life to vouch that he is loyal."

"I'm certain," she said, stressing those words. "You wanted my opinion, and there it is. Now you have to trust that I'm not acting like a lovesick schoolgirl. I'm a grown woman, Morgan. It's about time you realized that."

He stared at her a moment more before nodding. "I know you are. Very well. Let's go back into the office and see what trap we can set for Monsieur V."

The moment the door opened to the office, Alex

rose and held out his arms to her. When she stepped into them, he wrapped his arms around her and pressed his lips to her forehead. His heart thundered and his hair seemed a bit matted at the temples with sweat. She held him for a moment until his breathing and heartbeat returned to normal.

Still embracing her, he lifted his head to look over her shoulder at Morgan. "Have you come to a decision?" His voice was a bit raspy.

"We can't let this opportunity pass."

Alex's body relaxed and he released Lucy. She stepped back, but didn't move far.

Her brother continued. "I'm still not entirely convinced that Monsieur V doesn't have a hold on you somewhere in your memory, but we don't have time to waste. After this assignment, you'll have to endure the full training again."

Alex nodded. "Very well. And now?"

Morgan motioned to the chairs in front of his desk. He sat behind it and said, "I've asked Lucy to join us in here while we hash out a plan. Her presence here is pivotal because none of this will be possible without her and your complete cooperation." Rubbing at his temple, he looked pained. "If this is going to work, Lucy must play the bait."

Lucy squared her shoulders. She was ready to do this—for the good of Britain, for her family, and most importantly, for Alex. She pulled out her notebook, a new blank volume, and took one of the chairs in front of her brother's desk.

"Let's get to work, then. It sounds as though we haven't a moment to waste."

31

*A*lex should abandon the plan. He should shoot Monsieur V the moment the man stepped out into the open. Hell and damnation, he should have done it two nights ago when he'd informed the spymaster that he hadn't been able to bring Lucy as directed. Burying his rage and loathing for the man had been nigh impossible. Only the thought of Lucy had kept him sane enough to continue the ruse.

It had taken all his strength not to flinch when Monsieur V tapped him on the shoulder. This time, his body had relaxed instantly but his mind had not. He'd remained alert and submitted himself to the Graylockes the moment he'd walked away from the French spymaster. They and Lucy had determined that he was no more beneath Monsieur V's control than he had been upon walking into the meeting.

Monsieur V had set a new date, a new time and place for Alex to bring Lucy. Since Alex's excuse had been that it was too late for him to remove her from her townhouse unescorted, they'd set an earlier time of night. At the moment, the evening soirees were in full swing. Alex and Lucy had both attended, before he'd pretended to whisk her into his phaeton and away from the party unnoticed.

His departure had been noticed, of course. It had even been planned. They might have to abide by the time and place Monsieur V had set, but that didn't mean they arrived unprepared. Alex escorted Lucy into the junction between two streets, too narrow for a carriage to pass. He'd hitched his horses outside an eatery not far away. The further they walked, the more difficult it became to blank his expression and maintain a relaxed pose.

The Graylockes might be hiding in wait, but this was a far from ironclad plan. It hinged upon Lucy being able to draw Monsieur V out of the territory he had chosen and into one that they had prepared instead. In the meantime, the Graylocke brothers and the trusted spies that Morgan had hand-chosen for support had to keep their distance. Essentially, Alex was Lucy's only protection.

Worse yet, no one uninvolved in the plan knew of it. When Lucy had confessed her fears over the first note she'd received, that someone connected to the family was in Monsieur V's employ, everyone had agreed to keep the plan to themselves. They brought in no more help than what they expected to need. Not even Lord Strickland had been alerted to the coup they were about to enact today.

Secrecy was to their benefit if they hoped to pull the wool over Monsieur V's eyes. However, it had its detriments as well; namely that the support they might have had was far limited, especially in the location Monsieur V had set. In order to keep from arousing his suspicions, the only person hidden nearby was Tristan Graylocke. Morgan and the remainder of their support waited at the location where Lucy would lead Monsieur V.

If all went according to plan.

Lucy played her part with enthusiasm. She all but skipped next to him. The wind stirred by her skirts made the light in the lantern dance. "What a terribly daring part of the city for you to take me. Is this for research for my book?"

They reached the junction of the streets and she turned to face him. Her eyes danced, alight with life and fire. She smirked. "Or do you have a private romantic location set up for you to propose?"

Was that a suggestion? Cheeky woman. He wasn't about to get down on bended knee in the middle of a spy mission, and well she knew it. Afterward...

He would think about what came after only once Monsieur V was safely in the Crown's possession.

Struggling to keep his expression and tone neutral, he said, "You'll see."

She planted her hands on her hips. "Will I? You seem bent on dawdling here."

He hoped Monsieur V would arrive before too long, or else she would storm off in a huff while playing impatient. She couldn't do that, or else risk ruining the careful plan laid down, but he wouldn't put it past her. She would tell him that it was what her character would do.

Never mind that she was supposed to be herself tonight, simply a version of herself that allowed her to be caught in Monsieur V's trap. Seemingly.

Fortunately, they didn't have long to wait. A blessing, for Alex found it increasingly hard to answer her teasing in a bland tone when all he wanted to do was laugh and kiss her senseless. There was a time and a place for such things and he would never put her life on the line by giving in to desire and doing it now.

When he spotted a shadow coming from the north street, he met Lucy's gaze and told her in a monotone, "Have patience. Your surprise is here."

"My surprise?"

She turned as the spymaster stepped into the ring of light. From the sudden stiffening of Lucy's shoulders, it was certainly him. Monsieur V. They finally had him.

Lucy gasped as she caught sight of him. She whirled on Alex, her expression pinched with feigned betrayal. She did a convincing job of it, though. Her eyes even welled with tears.

"You brought me to Monsieur V? You've been in league with the French? How could you!"

She slapped him soundly. A bit too soundly, in Alex's opinion. The pain flared along his cheek and he hunched his shoulders as if expecting another blow. His ears rang as he rubbed his jaw.

He couldn't even hear Monsieur V's response, nor Lucy's departure. According to the plan, she would run and Alex would be too preoccupied to follow after her if Monsieur V demanded it. In that, he might not be acting. By the time his ears stopped ringing and he looked up, the spymaster bolted after Lucy.

Alex swallowed hard. He shook off the lingering pain and bent to retrieve the lantern. Lucy had done her job; she'd baited the trap. Now all that was left was for her to lead Monsieur V to where the duke laid in wait.

Once he was certain that the spymaster wouldn't

turn around, Alex sprinted down a different path to head them off. He trusted Lucy to do her part. Now, he had to make it to the trap in time to help her if something went wrong.

* * *

LUCY MEMORIZED the map of haphazard buildings and every gutter between. Morgan had made absolutely certain of that over the past couple days. Even then, he'd seemed tentative about going through with the mission.

Lucy was determined. She knew she could do it, and she would prove it. Her role in this was small, but pivotal. She had to play the bait. She had to bring Monsieur V to the correct location, where her brother would be waiting to take him into Crown custody. So she ran.

The route Morgan had worked out was seemingly random. She was meant to appear as if in a blind panic, taking turns at random as if to blindly escape. The trouble wasn't in recalling which turns to take, but in making sure that she ran exactly as instructed. Too fast and Monsieur V would lose sight of her; too slow and he would catch her. At every turn, she glanced over her shoulder, judging the gap between them and putting on a burst of speed or slowing down accordingly. A stitch bloomed in her side, but she was close. She would make it. The rush of triumph pushed her that last stretch through the open wooden gate into the fenced-in yard. She dashed to the far end and leaned against the wall to catch her breath.

A heartbeat later, Monsieur V bolted in after her. The spies crouched behind the fence leaped forward, disarming and subduing him in a rush. A faint light illuminated the flurry of blows, from the lantern which had been set in the window of the house.

Monsieur V fought dirty. He tried everything in his power to shake the three men attempting to restrain him. For a moment, as he elbowed Morgan in the manhood and bashed another spy's nose with his skull, it looked as though Monsieur V would succeed. Alex, in the shadow of the building, standing near to her, took out his pistol and turned the corner to help.

Her heart flew into her throat. She lunged forward, touching his arm. "Don't!" He could hit her brother.

Tristan entered through the gate and entered the fray. Between the four spies, they wrestled him to the ground with relative ease. One held Monsieur V's arms while the other kneeled on his back.

Alex still didn't look as though he would stop. He strode forward with a sinister look in his face, the pistol held as if an extension of his arm.

"We need him!" Lucy raced to stand abreast of

Alex. Given the look on his face, she thought better of running in front of him. He looked consumed by rage. She raised her hand to touch him, but didn't want to throw off his aim in case he accidentally pulled the trigger. "Alex, we have him now. It's over. Soon we'll know everything he does."

Monsieur V spat on the ground in front of him. "You're too late. It doesn't matter whether I have her or not. The rest has been set into motion."

"The rest of what?"

Morgan was much more brazen than his sister. Despite the gun Alex held, Morgan stepped between them and fisted the spymaster's hair. When he yanked the man's head back, instead of getting an answer, he got spat at. He shoved the fiend away from him.

Alex hastily pointed his pistol at the ground. His arm trembled as he warred with himself.

Oblivious to the conflict going on behind him, Morgan stood and ordered, "Tristan, take him back to Strickland. We'll feed him the serum and he'll sing like a songbird before morning. Whatever he has planned, we'll stop it."

Alex looked down. He stuffed the gun into his pocket once more. Lucy laid her hand on his arm, which was as stiff as rock.

As Tristan supervised the spies as they hauled

Monsieur V to his feet, he asked, "What will you be doing?"

"I'm seeing Lucy safely home."

Her role in this was done.

"Very well. I'll meet you there and let you know what Strickland says."

Lucy barely heard Tristan's answer. She turned her face up to meet Alex's gaze, but she didn't like what she saw there. He looked miles away from her, a deep sadness and defeat clinging to him like a cloak.

"Alex?"

He didn't look her directly in the eye. "Let's get you home."

hroughout the carriage ride to the Tenwick townhouse, Alex kept reliving the look in Monsieur V's eye as the spies were holding him down. It wasn't one of defeat. It was one of triumph. *Did* he have a convoluted plot laid down or had he only claimed as much in order to stall Alex from taking his life? Although Morgan insisted they had the spymaster well in hand, Alex wasn't so certain. What if Monsieur V managed to get a hold on someone the same way he had with Alex? They could set him free to wreak more havoc. Alex couldn't allow that.

Logically, he knew the Graylockes would never knowingly allow that to happen, either. Alex had explained to the best of his ability what had happened to him. If he could be turned to serve Monsieur V, then anyone could. Perhaps even Lucy.

He squeezed her hand as they approached her townhouse. She was safe. That was the most important thing. And that look in Monsieur V's eyes...

Whatever it was that he had planned, it wouldn't harm Lucy. That, Alex vowed. He would keep her safe.

After that mission, they still had to be questioned by the duke, each providing their separate tale and report in case Monsieur V had said or done something in private that might have proven to be a pivotal clue. Morgan conducted those interviews separately in the office in the Tenwick townhouse.

As Alex was concluding his rendition, a door downstairs slammed shut. Alex and Morgan exchanged a glance. Both bolted for the door, meeting Lucy in the corridor outside as someone thundered up the steps. Tristan entered the circle of light spilling from the office, his face twisted with disgust.

"Dead," he spat. He stormed into the office and helped himself to the whiskey decanter. His movements were jerky as he poured himself a couple fingers. He splashed as much on the sideboard as he managed to get in his glass.

Tenwick said nothing. He followed Tristan inside

with a pensive expression, his gaze suddenly sharp. Alex and Lucy followed after.

"Who's dead?" she asked. Her voice shook a bit. Alex groped for her hand and squeezed it. She clutched him back, the only outward sign that she was upset by the pronouncement.

"Monsieur V," Tristan answered, his lip curling with distaste. He downed the contents of his glass in one gulp.

Alex barely heard the explanation that followed— that the spymaster had manipulated one of the spies into killing him en route to the secure facility they would use to hold him. They would never know the secrets Monsieur V kept, nor whether this new plot could be stopped. Only that his new plot involved the head of all the spy-masters, someone even higher than Strickland himself. Alex's ears rang. A numbness settled over him.

The man who had killed his family was dead, and not by Alex's hand. He didn't know how to feel. As Tristan gave a full report, Alex slipped away from Lucy and strode to the window, blankly staring at his reflection in the glass.

Should he be relieved? Triumphant? His father and brother were avenged. They could rest peacefully now.

But what of Alex? Revenge had consumed him for

so long, directing his life. Without it, he felt...adrift. Purposeless.

"Brackley."

Morgan's voice cut through Alex's thoughts.

"Are you still with us?"

Alex frowned. "With the spy network?"

"Well yes, that too. You will have to be retrained. I was serious on that point."

Alex's gaze drifted over the three Graylockes staring at him. He settled on Lucy. She looked concerned, her eyebrows pulled together and her mouth drawn.

Perhaps he did have purpose. Or he could.

He met Morgan's cold stare. "Tenwick, can I speak with you a moment alone?" Even before the duke nodded, Alex strode for the door.

Morgan followed him out into the hall. They didn't move far, still within the circle of light. Distantly, Alex heard the shutting of a door, not as loud as Tristan's slam earlier. He'd best make this quick before they were interrupted.

"What's this about?" the duke asked. "I won't reconsider the training. You've undergone a trauma and I don't want that to emerge on the field, regardless of whether or not the man who caused it is dead."

"Actually, I won't be continuing on as a spy." It was for the better. Neither he nor Morgan could ever truly be certain that all remnants of the mental upset Monsieur V had caused were eradicated. Better he not put others in jeopardy. "I was only ever in this to see my brother avenged."

The duke sighed. He fingered the white streak in his hair. "I could recite your duty to you, you know."

Did he think it would make a difference? Alex was a renowned rakehell. Before the death of his father and brother it had been well known that he eschewed anything resembling honor or duty.

Then again, he wasn't the same man now as he was then.

"I have a different sort of duty I'll need to attend to." He squared his shoulders and met the other man's gaze fearlessly. "I'd like your blessing to marry your sister."

He hadn't expected a favorable response—in fact, if Morgan had viciously denied him and thrown him out of the house, Alex wouldn't have been surprised. However, he hadn't expected the man's drawn silence to be so cutting. He fought not to fidget and show weakness.

"We're in love. I'm not the man I was before my brother died. I want to do right by her."

Morgan's expression turned stony. The only indication of life was in his snapping gaze. "If you ever harm her, it will be the last thing you do."

"I have no intention of harming her." He would sooner harm himself. He already had a violation of her trust to overcome. Even if she had forgiven him for the way he'd treated her while under Monsieur V's influence, he hadn't forgiven himself. Fortunately, he would have a lifetime to prove to Lucy that he loved and cherished her above all else.

Morgan nodded, his jaw tight. "Very well. Then I won't stand in your way—provided she'll have you."

Alex's knees weakened for a moment. He swallowed hard and nodded. If Morgan had granted his grudging blessing, then Alex had only one person left to convince—Lucy.

It wasn't the most romantic time nor place. They were tired from the assignment, the thrill of the moment long gone, and the future uncertain. But he loved her. Surely something good could come of tonight.

Although his insides fluttered with nervousness, he squared his shoulders and strode back into the office. Lucy, standing with Tristan by the mantle, turned as he walked in.

"Is everything all right?"

"It will be." He took a deep breath and sank to one knee in front of her. "Lucy Graylocke, I love you more than I thought possible. Will you do me the very great honor of becoming my wife?"

Lucy's eyes shone with unshed tears. She pressed her hand against her mouth as she nodded, unable to speak for the moment. It would likely be the only time in their marriage that he rendered her thus.

As she dropped her hand to give her answer, a woman's voice rang from the doorway. "Another marriage? It's a plague!"

Alex, still on one knee, paused to give only the briefest glance to Charlie, still dressed for the evening's soiree. She must have just arrived home.

Shaking her head, she cut her hand through the air. "Don't look at me next. There is no way I'll be married soon."

Lucy laughed. "You might be surprised. I didn't expect to fall in love, either." She turned her attention to Alex and reached out to clasp his hand. "Of course I'll marry you. Stand up and kiss me! And take your time, I want to write this down later."

He laughed and made it a kiss worth writing about.

EPILOGUE

*L*ucy whooped. "I did it!"

The summer sun beamed through the window of Brackley Lodge, which contrary to the name was nearly as sprawling as Tenwick Abbey. The light frosted a mound of papers, most with crossed-out words or notes crosshatched in the margins. In front of her, at the end of a neatly-scribed page, were two words.

The End.

With a grin splitting her face, she straightened the stack of neatly-written pages and arranged it front and center on the writing desk Alex had bought her as a wedding present. The rest of her notes, she pushed to the side.

Looking harried, Alex entered the room. "Are you all right? I heard a shriek."

She jumped up, unable to contain her excitement any longer. Running to her husband, she threw her arms around his neck and stood on tiptoe to kiss him soundly. He chuckled as she dropped back onto her heels again.

"If I'd known this was to be my reception, I would come to your rescue more often."

Lucy bit her lip to contain her excitement. It bubbled inside her like a pot about to overflow. "I did it! I finished my book!"

"You did?" He picked her up and twirled her. "That's marvelous! Does that mean I get my wife back?"

She giggled. "You always had me."

"I did, but I had to share you with a book. Will I now get to read the book that has stolen you away from me for so many hours?"

He wanted to read it? Her heart warmed, rivaling the sun. "Of course you can. I told you, it's finished. I can move on to the next chapter in my life." And the next book.

He lifted her hand and kissed her knuckles. "That sounds like a cause for celebration."

She snaked her arms around his neck again and smiled. "I have a lot in my life worth celebrating."

****

HAVE you read the rest of the Scandals and Spies series?

Kissing the Enemy (Book 1)
Deceiving the Duke (Book 2)
Tempting The Rival (Book 3)
Charming The Spy (Book 4)

Sign up for Leighann's VIP reader list and get her books at the lowest discount price:
http://www.leighanndobbs.com/newsletter-historical-romances

If you want to receive a text message on your cell phone for new releases, text ROMANCE to 88202 (sorry, this only works for US cell phones!)

Join Leighann's private Facebook group and get the inside scoop on all her books:

HTTPS://WWW.FACEBOOK.COM/GROUPS/LDOBBSREADERS

Goldwater Creek Mail Order Brides:

Faith

American Mail Order Brides Series:

Chevonne: Bride of Oklahoma

Contemporary Romance

***

Reluctant Romance

***

Sweetrock Sweet and Spicy Cowboy Romance

Some Like It Hot

Too Close For Comfort

Magical Romance with a Touch of Mystery

***

Something Magical

Cozy Mysteries

Silver Hollow

Paranormal Cozy Mystery

* * *

A Spell Of Trouble

Mystic Notch

Cat Cozy Mystery Series

* * *

Ghostly Paws

A Spirited Tail

A Mew To A Kill

Paws and Effect

Probable Paws

Blackmoore Sisters

Cozy Mystery Series

* * *

Dead Wrong

Dead & Buried

Dead Tide

Buried Secrets

Deadly Intentions

A Grave Mistake

Spell Found

Mooseamuck Island Cozy Mystery Series

* * *

A Zen For Murder

A Crabby Killer

A Treacherous Treasure

Lexy Baker Cozy Mystery Series

* * *

Lexy Baker Cozy Mystery Series Boxed Set Vol 1 (Books 1-4)

Or buy the books separately:

Killer Cupcakes

Dying For Danish

Murder, Money and Marzipan

3 Bodies and a Biscotti

Brownies, Bodies & Bad Guys

Bake, Battle & Roll

Wedded Blintz

Scones, Skulls & Scams

Ice Cream Murder

Mummified Meringues

Brutal Brulee (Novella)

No Scone Unturned

Contemporary Romance

***

Reluctant Romance

***

Sweetrock Sweet and Spicy Cowboy Romance

Some Like It Hot

Too Close For Comfort

ROMANTIC SUSPENSE
WRITING AS LEE ANNE JONES:

***

The Rockford Security Series:

Deadly Betrayal (Book 1)

Fatal Games (Book 2)

Treacherous Seduction (Book 3)

Calculating Desires (Book 4)

ABOUT LEIGHANN DOBBS

USA Today Bestselling author Leighann Dobbs has had a passion for reading since she was old enough to hold a book, but she didn't put pen to paper until much later in life. After a twenty-year career as a software engineer with a few side trips into selling antiques and making jewelry, she realized you can't make a living reading books, so she tried her hand at writing them and discovered she had a passion for that, too! She lives in New Hampshire with her husband, Bruce, their trusty Chihuahua mix, Mojo, and beautiful rescue cat, Kitty.

Find out about her latest books and how to get discounts on them by signing up at:

http://www.leighanndobbs.com/newsletter-historical-romances

If you want to receive a text message alert on your cell phone for new releases, text ROMANCE to 88202 (sorry, this only works for US cell phones!)

Connect with Leighann on Facebook
    https://www.facebook.com/leighanndobbshistoricalromance/

ABOUT HARMONY WILLIAMS

If Harmony Williams ever tried her hand at being a chemist, she would probably wind up blowing something up like Giddy almost did. Instead, she lives an explosion-free life in the middle of the Canadian countryside with her enormous lapdog, Edgar. In her spare time, she likes to sip tea, read too many books (if such a thing is possible) and dream up funny new ways for characters to fall in love in Regency England. Join her newsletter at www.harmonywilliams.com/newsletter and get a free novella!

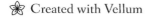

Made in the USA
Columbia, SC
18 January 2024

30629473R00215